THE COUNTRY UNDER HEAVEN

a novel

FREDERIC S. DURBIN

 MELVILLE HOUSE BROOKLYN • LONDON

The Country Under Heaven

First published in 2025 by Melville House
Copyright © 2023 by Frederic S. Durbin
All rights reserved
First Melville House Printing: February 2025

Melville House Publishing
46 John Street
Brooklyn, NY 11201
and
Melville House UK
Suite 2000
16/18 Woodford Road
London E7 0HA

mhpbooks.com
@melvillehouse

An earlier form of the chapter "Someplace Cool and Dark"
was first published in the anthology *Challenge!: Discovery,* edited by Jason M. Waltz
(Spokane, Washington: Rogue Blades Entertainment, 2017).
The chapter "The Fresh Air Above" was first published under the title
"The Fate Machine" in the anthology *Dead Keys: Typewritten
Tales of Terror*, edited by Richard Polt, Frederic S. Durbin, and Andrew
V. McFeaters (Cincinnati, Ohio: Loose Dog Press, 2021).

ISBN: 978-1-68589-169-5
ISBN: 978-1-68589-170-1 (eBook)

Library of Congress Control Number: 2024947577

Designed by Beste Doğan

Printed in the United States of America

1 3 5 7 9 10 8 6 4 2

A catalog record for this book is available from the Library of Congress

The authorized representative in the EU for product safety and
compliance is Easy Access System Europe, Mustamäe tee 50, 10621 Tallinn, Estonia.
gpsr.requests@easproject.com

THE COUNTRY UNDER HEAVEN

Also by Frederic S. Durbin

A Green and Ancient Light

For my mother, who truly did stop a runaway horse;
and for my father, who loved the Old West;
and for Julie, always.

THE COUNTRY UNDER HEAVEN

I went to the grave afore I went to the house. Some intuition told me I ought to do it that way, to pay my respects to the dead afore I saw the faces of the bereaved. It wasn't much of a trail that led to the homestead, but I left it when I knew I was getting close. Jack was a little more than two that summer, and he was a pretty horse, the color of a buttermilk flapjack with a white mane. Called him Flapjack at first, but shortened it—he seemed to like Jack better. He was sure-footed and steady, and he took us right up through the swamp milkweed, its pink brushes rising past the stirrups and tickling Jack's belly.

Up on the ridge, we rode through the cottonwoods, their leaves sighing above us as I looked down at John Clement's farm. It was humble and peaceful. I knew that's what John wanted—open sky, good earth to turn, hills to the west, and a meandering creek making its music like a balm in Gilead.

I was sorry to my core about the darkness that had come to John after all he'd been through. I dismounted and crouched afore the marble stone that John had ordered special, making his firstborn's grave finer than most for a hundred miles around. New grass was growing over it, but it was still just over a year since this hole had been dug.

ANNIE ELLA CLEMENT
1861–1879

John didn't put months and days on the stone. He and Margaret might have wanted to remember the day they brought Annie Ella into the world, but they didn't want to remember the day she left it.

I'd heard about it from a friend of a friend and didn't want to believe it. Annie Ella had been fishing in the creek on a spring evening, dark of the moon when they bite, within hollering distance of the house. Had a Navy pistol with her, case a painter or a coyote got ideas. No one looked for harm in this little plot of Heaven, these twenty acres John had been granted for meritorious service.

Annie Ella didn't holler, didn't come home, and she still had that Navy six, loaded, right beside her when they found her body on a sandbank some hours later, a couple hundred yards downstream. Whatever unholy sonofabitch had done it—had his way with Annie Ella, strangled her, and bashed her head against a rock to make sure she wouldn't tell tales— had left that pistol alone as if he didn't want to add thievery to his crimes.

Posses hunted round the country. There were rumors of

some cattlemen passing through, and someone told of seeing five or six Mexicans over south of Poke, or maybe they were Chinamen, but no one was made to answer for what happened to Annie Ella.

The grave was shaded by a big oak and couched in a purple mist of lavender. A warm breeze up the hill brought the scents of horses and something Margaret must be stewing.

I put my hat on and gave Jack a pat, and we walked down to John Clement's house.

John came out to meet me, along with a yellow hound who nosed me and swished his tail, sensing that John and I went back a ways. Lot of gray in John's hair and whiskers now, and he walked with a limp. But the age was mostly in his eyes— age and winter.

John said, Hell of a thing to see you, Ovid.

Yes, Sir, I replied. Hell of a thing to see you, too, Captain. I'd sent him a letter out of St. Louis to tell him I was coming. I guessed he'd got it.

He embraced me like a father, and I told him how sorry I was for his loss.

At their urging, I hunkered down for about a week with the Clements, making myself as useful as I could. I told them how

I was heading farther west, looking for what, I didn't precisely know. Open space, mostly—a sky to breathe under.

Margaret had got old, too. Still mostly blonde, though she'd browned and hardened in the sun. Seemed she could scarcely remember how a smile worked, though she made the effort for the company in the house. Always seemed to be looking a lot farther off than what she was looking at. She and John worked a big garden, vegetables to sell and trade with their neighbors. Margaret did the greater share of the work in it, while John saw to the fields—corn, beans, and hay.

The only other Clement was their younger daughter, Grace Given, who was twelve that summer. A boy, William, twixt the two girls in age, had died of the same fever that had run through the children when Grace Given was an infant. Grace had never spoken after the fever, didn't seem able to absorb any learning, and wasn't much good with her hands. But she listened to her parents and mostly understood them. She sat quiet, like a cat or dog, and often came to her mama or papa just to smile and wrap her arms around them. It occurred to me that all the expressions Margaret's face had lost were there in abundance with Grace, who stood in sunbeams with open-mouthed awe. The girl laughed at the buttonbushes in the yard, batting at their little pincushion blooms. For no reason anyone could fathom, a shifting white cloud or a stone by the pasture fence might make her burst into tears. At her most active, Grace Given would run with the yellow hound through the pasture, her downy hair flying like her head was on fire.

I put in a fence for John across the end of a field. He had

all the materials—just hadn't scratched up the time to do it himself. He came out to inspect it, and we stood in the clover and watched a storm brewing over the purple hills.

You still have them visions, Ovid? he asked me, leaning his arms on a post. The breeze was full of rain smell.

Yeah, I told him, they're what's telling me to head west.

He was remembering how the battle ended for me that day near Sharpsburg—Antietam Creek, within sight of the lower bridge, which we'd been trying to get across all day— that bridge with its shady elm right at the near end, a good fishing bridge. Thickest fight I ever was in. Never saw our Burnside that day, though I could've sworn I saw General Lee, just for a passing moment through the smoke—way across the creek, far away, his beard gleaming like clean snow as he sat astride his horse.

And I definitely saw my Captain Clement, right there with us, shoulder to shoulder, shooting back at the Rebs who were Hell-bent on holding onto that bridge.

Well, the Rebs lobbed something at us that went off right behind me. The boys told me I flew twenty feet. I don't remember that. All I remember was how quiet the world got. Not a sound—no more cannons, no more hollering, no more of that blood-chilling Reb war cry. Not even wind. Just me on the earth, lying in a patch of cardinal flowers that leaned over me like men with red mustaches, and above us all, the clouds, slowly changing their shapes, the sun trying to come through.

Took four days for sounds to reach me again. And ever since then, I've had the visions now and then—pictures I can't get out of my mind. I can find things, and more importantly, I know when it's time to look. I'll tell you more about that as I go along.

John wasn't done asking me about my visions.

They tell you anything important, Ovid? he asked. They tell you reasons for it all?

I told him regrettably no, they weren't much help at understanding the why of things.

He said he wished he knew why Annie Ella. It always sounded, when he said her name, like he was saying Ann Yella. She was born the year afore Antietam. Back then, Captain Clement talked to us about that beautiful baby girl, how he hoped the storms would get themselves over with and she could grow up in a land where the only thunder came from the sky, just afore a soft or a drenching rain watered the soil, and our bloody grounds would look to her eyes like nothing but green fields where you could plant or you could build or you could just sit with your back against an oak tree and breathe, and no one would make you afraid.

That storm's coming this way, John said.

We got Jack and the other horses into the barn. Jack was enjoying his holiday here. I could see the contentment in his big soft eyes, not having me and my packs of paraphernalia on his back every day.

It crashed and washed that night, great blinding trees of lightning, thunder like all the cannons of the Potomac, and it felt like the Red Sea coming down on Pharaoh's head. Margaret was mending clothes, and John settled by the lamp and read aloud, mostly to Grace Given, from the Bible and from some of the English poets—I couldn't say which, as it's hard for me to assay where one leaves off and the next begins. But Grace Given liked it, and that was the important thing. She had a smile like on those cherubs in the big churches out East. She was tracing with her long fingers all the cracks twixt the stones of the fireplace like she was ciphering out some code that would lead her somewhere, and all the tumult and the gulley washing didn't bother her a quarter ounce.

Two days after that, one of John's neighbors rode up on a big bay mare to tell us there was to be an Attraction that evening down at the Corners. The nearest town to John's place was Buckeye, a smattering of buildings seven miles to the northwest. Halfway there along the same rutted road was a sawmill on the creek, an enterprise run, ironically, by a man name of Cutter. The dirt trail up from Poke joined the road there, and among the trees stood Cutter's house, with three other farmsteads within walking distance. Whoever was putting on the Attraction must have allowed it was worthwhile to do it at Cutter's Corners for one night afore moving on into Buckeye. The neighbor said he reckoned the Attraction was some kind of magical show.

John figured Grace Given would like that sort of show, and it would do the womenfolk good to get out of the house and see the neighbors. So when the sun was casting long shadows, we hitched up John's two pulling horses to the Schuttler wagon. I took notice that John had that Navy six on his belt, and his twelve-gauge in the back of the wagon. Even if he hadn't, I'd have taken along my Schofield pistol and the Winchester lever-action. Being safe was an illusion—I knew that much. Pine boxes were full of men who wished they'd brought a gun along, and full of those who wished they hadn't.

I was going to ride Jack to give him a stretch, but Grace Given took hold of my arm and would have nothing but for me to ride in the back of that Schuttler with her and her mama. John drove us down his lane and onto the main road, where the greenish-yellow sumac crowded close, just ending its bloom time, the little hard fruits beginning to mature. There were doves somewhere in the hedge, making their low, dusky calls. The air was warm and fragrant with alfalfa.

Grace Given pointed out a hawk gliding in lazy circles over the edge of the timber, and she looked like she was telling me a secret, her mouth pressed tight and her eyes aglow with mischief. Margaret leaned against the wagon's side and let out a sigh, her gaze fixed on the fields and on nothing. John was a broad, stiff back in his Stetson and galluses. It was a back I'd marched behind all over Maryland and Pennsylvania and West Virginia. Endless hard roads on sore feet, and shivery nights, and joyless dawns that only meant another march. We learned to watch the trees and the hills and the rocks; you never did know when Johnny Reb would throw down from that bucolic shade, when he'd start waggling his tongue and war-screaming like a legion of devils.

The sun was touching the treetops as we pulled up at the Corners. Across the road from the creek and the mill, there was a swatch of flat ground in front of the thicket that framed a pasture. Ninebark grew thick there, its leaves the color of wine.

A fancy contraption was set up there—a wagon, on account it had wheels, but tall and trimmed with banners and shiny metal gewgaws. Its side opened up to make the whole thing a stage, like a splendid theater, closed off as yet by a red velvet curtain. The four horses that pulled it were grazing in a corral a little up the road.

Out in front of the corners of the stage, two bonfires of deadwood had been set ablaze, casting their flickering light over the whole uncanny thing. It put me in mind of pagan temples like in the old books, like where Samson was chained twixt the pillars. On a part of the wagon that didn't open out, letters in gilt paint read:

DOCTOR BELLEROPHON CINCH

SPIRITUALIST

MYSTIC TRAVELER IN THE UNKNOWN

SAGE OF SAGES THROUGH THE AGES

MASTER OF THE FATE MACHINE

DISCOURSER WITH THE DEAD

Another sign, standing by itself on a pole, announced:

SEE THE SHOW-TEN CENTS
RECEIVE FROM THE FATE MACHINE A
MESSAGE FROM BEYOND.
YOURS TO KEEP AND PONDER-FIFTY CENTS

This Doctor Bellerophon Cinch had been busy, building fires and setting out about twenty little fold-up camp stools. These were spread in a fan shape, across the road from the stage, in the mill's yard.

We unhitched the horses, and I took them to the corral to let them graze. As the twilight deepened, John and Margaret socialized with their neighbors, the women clustering in their utilitarian but presentable dresses, soft voices and laughter like the gentle sounds from a henhouse. The men positioned themselves side by side, looking at things rather than each other, chewing their plugs, spitting amiably into the mud and grass. Fifty cents! someone muttered, reading the sign—He think this is Chicago?

John introduced me around, calling me his friend: This here's Ovid Vesper. We fought together in the Army of the Potomac. I guessed John knew his neighbors well enough. I'd learned not to talk about the War out here, not until you figured out where your listener was born and raised.

Grace Given stared at the curtained stage contraption as if she were beholding the Burning Bush and the Bethlehem Star and El Dorado all at once. She stood afore the front row of seats with her hands pressed together, laughing and wriggling with delight. Margaret and John kept a close eye on her, and Margaret told her not to cross the road or go near the fires.

There were other young ones, some close to Grace's age. I wondered how they'd treat her. What they did was leave her alone; they were neither mocking nor friendly. I expected they all had instructions concerning Grace Given. I could hear it in my head: Don't you go adding to that family's grief. Lord knows, John and Margaret Clement have suffered enough.

This audience was assembled from five, maybe six families, with perhaps a few boarders and farmhands—so if everyone chucked in ten cents, I allowed that Doctor Cinch was right to hold his Attraction here. The twenty stools weren't enough, but plenty of the men were content to find stumps or fence rails or to stand around in the back, arms folded. A tough-looking audience, I thought, like fence posts baked by the sun, polished by the wind, cracked by ice, full of rusty nails; I wouldn't have wanted to say a piece in front of them.

Full dark settled in, and stars lit up like they were another part of the crowd arriving, first the big bright ones, then all the little sparks betwixt them, then the glowing dusty smudges in the sky that my granddad called celestial cobwebs.

One of the ladies spoke kindly to Grace Given and led her to a stool in the front row. Margaret exchanged some pleas-antries with that woman and then sat behind Grace. John and I perched on a big rock to the right of all the stools. We were maybe thirty feet from the stage.

A figure all in black appeared from behind the fancy

wagon and shuffled through the ninebark, someone in a black hood that covered his face and a cape that went all the way to the ground, so you couldn't tell if you were seeing a man or a spirit. This sinister figure stacked more wood on the two fires, poked them, and then picked up a basket from the stage corner and passed it through the audience. Seemed a safe conclusion that we were seeing a man—most likely Doctor Bellerophon Cinch himself.

The basket traveled along the rows and among the stand-ees, and we all put in our ten cents. The hooded figure vanished behind the stage again. A wiry boy from the audience carried the basket across the road, moving cautiously, set it on the stage's front corner, and hightailed it back to the crowd.

With squeaks and rustles, the velvet curtain parted and rolled to the sides, revealing a black cavern. There was no sound from the audience except the creak of the seats as folks moved their heads around and leaned forward, trying to see something.

A magnesium flash went off, drawing gasps and screams. When we'd all blinked the green and blue suns from our eyes, the Doctor had the stage lit with a fiery red glow from a lantern on a hook.

His hood and cape were gone. Doctor Cinch wore a black peacoat and a pair of spectacles. He had wild white hair that went in all directions and the eyes of a madman. A human skull sat on a cloth-draped stand, grinning at us and staring with the black pits of its eyes. A cow skull occupied the floor, and a taxidermy raven clutched a perch with its dead claws.

Something large and ominous hulked under a shiny, gold-fringed cloth on a stout table, right behind the Doctor at the center of his diabolical cavern inside the wagon.

ABANDON HOPE, he roared at us, making people flinch again, YE WHO ENTER HERE! Eat, drink, and play, for after death there is no pleasure!

I couldn't see Grace Given's face, but she sat quite still and straight, and Margaret had her hands on Grace's shoulders.

Somewhere in the timber, an owl hooted.

Doctor Cinch stalked around his stage, glaring at us. Easy the descent by Avernus, he intoned. Night and day, black Death's door is open wide; but to retrace your steps and emerge to the fresh air above, this is an undertaking—this is a labor!

Beside me, John cleared his throat and shifted position.

The Doctor went on to recite a fair amount of poetry, some of it about damned souls and the fires of Hell. His voice rose and fell, and I had to allow that he was a thespian; the rock underneath us was getting hard, but there was an eerie fascination in watching this old goblin Doctor loom in his flickering shadows and hearing what words he wove. The words he found, wherever he found them, were about the closest thing to the visions in my head that I'd encountered. That's nigh impossible to explain, so I won't attempt it.

I remember the Doctor saying: Midway on the journey of our life, I found myself in a dark wood, where the straight road was lost . . . and from the corner of my eye, I saw tears on John's face.

The Doctor seemed to come to the end of his words. He

stood like a statue, gazing up at the bright, nearly full moon in the sky until most of us looked at it as well. The hour grows late! announced the Doctor—The walls of worlds grow thin!

He moved abruptly to the covered shape and whisked off the fringed cloth. The crowd's breath rushed in again. The thing he'd revealed there looked like a tall bread box or some such: sort of a block made of curving black metal, and painted with elegant little designs—it was hard to see from far away, but I thought they were flowers and vines. When he lifted a lid at the front, there were keys, but not quite like a piano's. There was also some kind of wheel or pulley on one side, with a rope running down to a foot treadle. I couldn't tell if he was fixing to play us music or start sewing.

The dead speak to the living through the Fate Machine! said Doctor Cinch. Who among us longed, he wondered, for a word from the dearly departed?

A river of whispers went through the audience.

Grace Given bounced to her feet and did a spinning dance, laughing and waving her arms. John rubbed his hand across his mouth. Margaret got up and gathered Grace in a hug and sat her back down. John put his hands on his knees and stared at the ground. We oughta head home, he mumbled.

A woman marched up to the stage. I reckoned she was in her sixties, her straight hair mostly silver. Doctor Cinch offered her a hand up the steps, accepted her coins, and grandly welcomed her, placing her on a chair cushioned with velvet.

The spell of the poetry was broken now, at least on me, and

I could see the charlatan taking the thespian's place. I knew where this was going; I'd seen plenty of snake-oil salesmen. The Doctor asked the woman her name—it was Tallulah Pole. He asked whom among the dead she was seeking to hear from. Her departed husband Edward, God rest his soul. The questions went on, and the Doctor looked Tallulah Pole up and down, noticing the details of her dress, her eye color, listening to what she said and how she said it—gathering up plenty he could use to bring her a convincing message from Edward. His chief advantage, of course, was that Tallulah wanted that message so badly.

At last, the Doctor cracked his knuckles, sat himself down at the Fate Machine, and began to press its keys with his two pointer fingers. It made clacking noises—a dry sound, and a mite unsettling, like a real slow rattlesnake. He went methodically at first, but then he started going faster. The top part of his machine slid back and forth as it worked, and when it got as far as it could to one side, the Doctor stepped on the foot treadle to pull that top section back across.

Tallulah sat there weeping, wiping her eyes.

Watching the Doctor's face, I took note of something curious. He'd proven he was a masterful actor, but this didn't look like acting to me. His eyes got wide, and sweat gleamed on his brow. His whole body looked rigid. One emotion I knew better than I knew my next of kin was fear. I'd seen men deathly afraid, and terror is what I saw in Doctor Cinch just then. It looked like that Fate Machine had hold of him somehow and wouldn't let go.

John pushed himself up from the rock and paced away into the dark, wrestling with emotions of his own.

The Doctor practically tumbled over with his chair as he tore himself away from those keys. He shook his head as if to clear it, dragged a sleeve across his face, and only when he saw Tallulah Pole looking at him expectantly did he seem to recall where he was. He pounced on the machine and pulled out a page of paper, which he didn't look at but shoved into Tallulah's hands and bustled her off the stage. Even far away as I was, I could see the dark lines of printing on that paper. The Fate Machine had written all over it in inked letters.

The more Tallulah Pole read that page by the light of the bonfire, the harder she wept, and folks gathered around her.

Doctor Cinch stood at center stage, breathing hard, and raised his arms. The Fate Machine has spoken, he told us, and now I bid you good night. He meant to shut down his show, but when he grabbed for the cloth to throw over the machine, he found himself eye to eye with Margaret Clement, who had Grace Given by the hand.

Margaret had climbed right up there on the stage, and she was determined. She slapped her coins into the Doctor's hands and pointed at the Fate Machine.

John was beside me again. He'd returned out of the night, and all the color had left his face as he stared at his wife and daughter up there in the red light.

Doctor Cinch shook his head. He shrank away from Margaret like a coyote backed against a wall. But she pointed at the Fate Machine, and Grace was smiling at him like a cherub, though it was more than a smile, too. When I say cherub, I mean maybe her face was something like the face of that cherub with the fiery sword at the edge of Eden. I felt like an icicle was touching me twixt the shoulder blades.

Some of the crowd was all around Tallulah, reading over her shoulders, jabbering, crossing themselves . . . I could tell she had got a message wondrous and dreadful in its specificity. The rest of the people were mighty invested in what was happening on the stage.

Doctor Cinch gave a kind of groan and sank onto his chair again. He didn't ask Margaret even one question. Grace clapped her hands and turned in a circle.

Don't you need paper in that thing? Margaret asked.

The Doctor clawed another page from a packet, and his hands shook as he raised the machine's lid, curled the paper into place, and closed the top.

As he lifted his fingers to the keys, a hush fell over the crowd. Even those neighbors surrounding Tallulah grew still and paid attention.

But instead of writing, Doctor Cinch lunged to his feet, sending his chair to the floor. He stood gasping, off-balance, risen to his toes—if I hadn't known better, I might have thought he was a man-sized puppet on invisible strings. Eyes wide as dollar coins, he cried out with a voice that in nowise resembled his own: Mama! Papa! he hollered. It was Lyman Smollett who done it! Lyman Smollett come up behind me on the creek bank and done all that!

There was a great inrush of collective breath, and most

of the crowd did an about-face to look back toward the fence beside the mill.

Liar! a man there yelled, jumping down off the fence rail. That's a lie!

I figured out in a twinkling that this was Lyman Smollett protesting. I heard later that he was a hired hand at the farm of William Furniss. Smollett had drifted out this way from Ohio, smallish and skinny, with a low forehead and close-set eyes. He was about twice the age of Annie Ella, whom he savaged and murdered at the creek behind her house.

Beside me, John fell to his knees, and I looked down to see if he was all right. I shouldn't have taken my eyes off Smollett.

The shifty little cuss pulled out his iron and cut loose on Doctor Cinch, three shots splintering the night. I doubted Smollett could do any good aiming at that distance, but he managed to put one wild bullet in the Doctor, who had just delivered his last message from the dead—his last, but it was a crowning achievement.

I don't know if Smollett meant to take shots at Margaret next, but she and Grace were already off the stage, down in the crowd, and folks were running and screaming.

Someone who had a gun—might have been Cutter, the sawmiller—yelled at Smollett to stop, but he vaulted that fence and lit out into the trees by the creek.

John swore an oath and nigh knocked me over as he ran for the wagon. I went after him, urging him for all I was worth to calm down.

We know who he is, I told John. Let the law get him.

Ain't no law in forty miles, John said. Sonofabitch'll be in California afore the first sheriff hears about it. John put my Winchester in my hands and grabbed up his twelve-gauge. Ain't gonna happen, Ovid. He ain't going nowhere.

Getting our heads blown off wouldn't help John's family none, I thought, but there was no telling John that. He was going after Lyman Smollett, and that was that. I wasn't sure yet what to believe; I allowed there was no real proof that Smollett had done that to Annie Ella—just the weird accusation from a charlatan who would have no reason on God's Earth to know Smollett's name. Unless you believed there was something to it . . . unless you believed we'd heard from Annie Ella herself. But it was certain, at least, that Smollett had gunned down Doctor Cinch.

I tried to keep John steered into the trees and shadows so that we weren't obvious targets. Fortunately, Smollett was doing more running than shooting, though he was fool enough to cuss at us and take a wild shot now and then, so that we kept pretty good track of him. I heard some others coming with us a ways behind, hollering at John to come on back, not to do anything crazy, let the law go after Smollett . . . like I said.

The water wasn't far to our left, and the moon lit up a meadow on the right; the road had bent away now, running up toward Buckeye, and we were out in the bottoms. A shot from Smollett whined off a tree trunk just beside us.

Up ahead was a patch of open ground, the grass silver in the moonlight. Beyond it was a stand of witch hazel, bare and ghostly, its fanning limbs like dynamite blasts frozen in the air.

Smollett was back there in the witch hazel, and by the sound, I could tell he had stopped running.

John and I pulled up behind two big oaks just shy of the open stretch.

I can see you! Smollett hollered. You just go on back now.

John yelled at him to come out of there, calling him some names I won't repeat.

Cutter and a few others showed up behind us, and I warned them to take cover.

Smollett figured out that we weren't alone, and he took another shot.

John and I both saw the muzzle flare, and we opened up on him. I levered that Winchester, John emptied that shotgun, and then he went at it with his Navy six.

Then there was a long silence. Smollett stopped talking, and there were no more shots.

We reloaded and held on there, trying to decide if Smollett was being tricky.

Suddenly, Smollett let out one short, agonized scream—sounded more like terror than pain. Then nothing more. The silence really did set in.

You think a copperhead bit him? asked Cutter, coming up beside me.

I just shook my head. No way to know.

We gave it one more long count, and then we all went together—six of us. If he was going to shoot, Smollett might get some of us, but we all figured we couldn't wait all night.

Crossing that moonlit ground took me right back to

Antietam, walking with Captain Clement right up into the cannon barrels, into the bores of Johnny Reb's guns.

Back in the witch hazel, we found Smollett with his eyes wide open, dead in a patch of delicate white yarrow. The brush tangled thick past that, so he couldn't have gone on farther. One of us had got him, or maybe we both had. He was shot to Hell. But when we bent close, we saw two more things that were hard to explain.

Something had scratched his face—not a tree branch, on account that there were four long scratches running side by side, just like a person's fingernails had torn ruts in his skin.

What's on his neck? Cutter asked.

That's when we found the necklace, a fine silvery chain with a little pendant in the shape of a cross. The necklace was dug into the man's flesh and twisted hard, and it went a ways toward explaining the bulge of his eyes.

John shook the necklace loose and looked long and hard at it. When he found his voice, he told us it was Annie Ella's, no mistaking it, that had been around her neck when they put her in her coffin.

Back at the Corners, Margaret hugged John for a long time, and she hugged me, and with tears in her eyes, she said, Look what Grace Given wrote.

When we'd gone off after Smollett, when the others were trying and failing to help Doctor Bellerophon Cinch, Grace

Given had set the Doctor's chair back up, sat herself at the Fate Machine, and pushed its keys down, one after another, humming herself a tune.

Her mama watched her, amazed at how smooth and steady and calm Grace's fingers moved, that couldn't peel a potato or tie up her own boots. When she was done, Margaret figured out how to pull out that last piece of paper the Doctor had put there.

She expected it to be gibberish, a string of letters as meaningless as the choices Grace made when she laughed at wild geese or cried when her mama swept the floor or when Grace stared at the moon like she was seeing it for the first time.

But this was on the paper, written out by a girl who hardly knew her letters:

PAPA. MAMA. GRACE GIVEN. I AM WELL. HERE
WITH WILLIE. IT IS BEAUTIFUL. WAITING FOR
YOU. PLANT MORE LAVENDER. I LIKE IT AND
LOVE YOU. DO NOT WORRY.

John and I talked that over later, how it's mighty comforting when you hear from beyond the grave not to worry. It's easy enough to start worrying in this vale of tears, as they call it.

I didn't think there was anything mystical about the Fate Machine. A year or so later, I learned that E. Remington &

Sons churned lots of them out of a plant in Ilion, New York, and they were called Type Writers.

No, it was little Grace Given who had the eyes to see and the ears to hear. I saw it clearly in my head; I see a lot in there that I can't with my eyes. That girl was like a lightning rod, or like a doorway betwixt those thin walls the Doctor jawed about. Her proximity to the machine made it work in ways that surprised the Doctor more than anyone. And the messages didn't all come with words—Lyman Smollett had gotten a different kind, even half a mile away. Grace Given has a talent like a bright fire in the dark of this world. I hope she keeps watching and listening and taking good care of her mama and papa.

On the day Jack and I rode off, heading west, I told Captain Clement that it was real fine marching with him again. Margaret did a little better at smiling like she meant it. Grace Given didn't want me to go, but she found some consolation in the clover growing by the front fence, and in the fact that the yellow hound was ready for a good run through the field.

INTERLUDE

I first saw the Craither at Antietam. My hearing had come back, and it was determined I could keep on with my regiment and not be invalided home.

I saw it on the very next day after President Lincoln stood right there on the battlefield and delivered his first Emancipation Proclamation. For all kinds of reasons, I was thankful I could hear again—I had not liked the prospect of living in a silent world the rest of my days. Sound returned for me just in time to hear the President speak. I've never forgotten that day, when there was great excitement among the boys, and they let us all turn out to see Mister Lincoln. I wasn't too far away from him, and once, I thought he looked right at me with a gleam in his eyes. It might have been my imagination, but I'd like to believe it wasn't. It was a sight, that tall and lanky Railsplitter who was piloting us through some stormy seas . . . and to hear his voice!—well, that was a gift.

It was a start, anyway: the slaves weren't free yet, but that first Proclamation declared them free in the states that were in rebellion—which wouldn't respect the order, anyway, until they were forced—but it sure reminded Jeff Davis what we were about, and how this was going to end.

But the Craither—now that was another matter.

I saw it at dusk, out among a grove of hawthorns by the creek when I went to fill a water bucket for boiling. I wasn't sure I was seeing anything at first, on account ever since that explosion, my head had been full of ghosts and echoes. I didn't entirely trust myself to see what was actually there.

But I was awake, and it was a moving shape. I took note of the fine details of the trees' bark and roots and leaves to be sure everything else about the scene was consistent. When I got the visions, they were of a particular quality, and this was different—I want to be clear about that. I was actually seeing an entity that was there.

It was like shadows had come together somehow; like the Craither, when it walked, picked up the shadows as if they were thick cobwebs, and they were streaming and trailing off its form. And yet it was also like I wasn't really beholding the thing itself, but the way it bent the world by being there—like a person under a blanket, or coming through a curtain without parting it, so that what you see is a blanket or a curtain shaped like a person, more or less.

It had arms, sort of, and sometimes legs, but otherwise was dim and wavy, like the edges of a fire with little tongues of flame licking upward, loose from the main fire. But the Craither had no color or brightness like a fire, no heat or sound. It was always hard to see, and it hardly ever showed itself in bright light . . . until toward the end.

The eyes were vivid, though—round like two moons, and glowing with a color impossible to define, for sometimes they seemed green, sometimes gold, sometimes blue.

I froze when I saw it and stared.

Somehow, I knew that it didn't belong here. It was not a thing of this world. And I knew that I had brought it with me in those moments when I'd been senseless in the battle. I'd been dead for a little stretch. I knew that, too—floating, out of my body. Then I had come back, waking up among the red cardinal flowers with Richard Decalne and Captain Clement leaning over me.

And when I did, that Craither had come in with me, into this world, like someone ducking through a door behind you while it's open. I didn't know why—my weird certainties never told me as much as I wanted to know.

I knew I'd let in a thing that didn't belong.

Another disturbing part of it, though, was that I also felt a *tug* on me . . . a tightening around me, somehow—at once a crushing and an outward pull, and along with that a sickening, thrumming charge, like when static arcs or lightning strikes close by. The Craither's presence caused it somehow, and I didn't like it.

In another second or two, the Craither had vanished among the trees, and the unpleasant feeling went away.

I carried on with the business of life, and the War got itself over, and I didn't see the Craither again for a long time. In fact, I almost forgot about it.

CHAPTER TWO:

THE HUNGRY HILLS

TEXAS, 1881

Francis Eames had got himself stuck in life like a steer with bob wire round its leg, and the more he pulled and thrashed, the more those bobs tore in. Mister Allingham took him on, being as we were later than he wanted getting off, and hands were scarce. We needed a horse wrangler. Francis was the son of a horse rancher, and a few things about horse work had sunk in to him. If he could have spent all his time wrangling, he would have had it smoother. Horses don't care what nonsense comes out of a man's mouth, long as he doesn't say it in horse.

It started at the end of that first day, when we'd finally got to a creek and the herd was settling for the night. The sun was going down in big piles of cloud like cotton on fire, and the sky stretched out all mottled from gold to lavender to deep amethyst—the kind of night when peace wells up out of the earth, and all you got to do is drink it in. First days are always the hardest on a drive, when there's never enough water and the cattle are spooked about leaving their home range. Francis started it by moving to a rock on the other side of Ike Denton.

He made such a production of it that everybody looked.

That rock softer? Cookie asked him. Cookie had finished dishing out the beans and biscuits for the rest of us, with some salt pork and dried plums, and he was just sitting down with his own.

Francis looked round at us—Cookie and McElroy with their backs against the wagon wheels, me and Ike and Jay Bird Ward on our rocks, and Will Dew squatting with his feet flat, perfectly in balance leaning against nothing. Will was like some kind of acrobat; he could bend his elbows a little bit backward, which gave us the jeebies. Anyway, Francis looked at us with a defiant sort of glare and said he couldn't eat downwind of Ike.

That didn't sit well.

Whoa there, son, Cookie said. You need to rein that in right now.

Just saying a fact, Francis told him.

Ike was broad across the shoulders and could have pulled the arms right off that kid, but he gave Francis some grace. Maybe I don't want to be downwind of you, neither, he said, but he said it amiably.

Francis had the hundred options afore him that we have at every breath of this life, and somehow, he chose the very worst one. Ike had a stutter, and Francis repeated what Ike had said, exaggerating the stutter.

We had trouble wrapping our minds round what we were

hearing. It was like Francis wanted to be smacked flat—like stepping up to a bull and flicking it on the nose.

Hey, hey, hey, said Jay Bird.

Son, Cookie said. You don't bring that here. Cookie was second-in-command after Mister Bowdler. In addition to cooking the chuck, he was the closest thing we had to a doctor. He was doing his best to doctor now, in a preventative way, following a basic principle: instead of sucking out poison after the fact, it's better to keep someone from tromping on the rattlesnake.

McElroy set down his coffee and his plate, slow and deliberate. The kid might have been too green to see it, but you didn't want to get on McElroy's wrong side. He'd come from the War, too, like me—I got out of him once that he'd fought at Gettysburg. McElroy wasn't much for telling stories, though. He was efficient with the cattle. But he spoke little and had a shadow on his face.

Jay Bird Ward, on the other hand, talked more than I ever heard a cowboy talk, whatever came into his head. He found his way into telling a story now, some balderdash about a show he saw, a chicken that could use Gypsy cards and tell fortunes, right every time.

How do you know he was right? asked Will Dew.

I saw him do it, Jay Bird insisted. Told fortunes for fifteen, twenty folks.

But you never seen any of them after that, Will said. How do you know if the fortunes came true?

The perilous moment had passed. Ike chuckled at what

Will said, and Francis sat there shoveling in beans, which was a far wiser use of his mouth.

When Jay Bird's story didn't end with the chicken, Cookie said he'd tell Mister Bowdler to put Jay Bird right at the back of the herd. Won't even need the rest of you, Cookie said. Those steers will run all the way to Kansas just to get away from that relentless oration.

Men poke one another all the time, but there's a gentle sort of poking, and there's another kind. Francis didn't know the difference yet. I figured he was trying to prove something and didn't know how. He was the youngest one out there, and he knew everyone dumped on the wrangler, who wasn't a cowboy but just watched over the remuda. Each of us needed three horses, on account we worked them hard. Mister Allingham took me on, I think, even though I was new to him, as I brought my horse Jack into the mix, and his herd was short.

So we drove on up the Talbot Lucky Trail through the dusty spring days, the sun gathering strength—three thousand head of longhorns, nineteen of us. We averaged about fifteen miles a day; we could have pushed harder, but the trick was not to let the cattle get too lean. By taking our time, resting and grazing them at midday and at night, Mister Bowdler intended to deliver them safe and heavy to the Kansas railheads.

The two hairiest times were both at night, when I was part of the watching shift. Once early on, some yowling thing spooked the cattle, and with some hard and determined riding, we just barely got them stopped afore a full stampede. The other time, just prior to the main thing I'm here to tell you, Mister Bowdler saw a rider silhouetted against the sky on top of a ridge, and we suspected miscreants among the herd. Turned out to be a sheriff's posse out looking for a missing stagecoach. From their camp, they'd seen the glow of our fires and had just come to get a look at us.

Francis Eames was having no success at making any friends, nor did he give it an honest assay. That boy was like a wood splinter in your palm when you've got a handful of salt. Mister Bowdler sent me and Will Dew out to round up some strays, and as we were bringing them in, Will muttered about Francis. That kid, he said: Comes into every sitch'ation mouth first. Gonna get his ass kicked out through the top of his head.

Most of us had tried talking to Francis, extending the hand of camaraderie, asking him about horse ranching and what his aspirations were. Francis wanted to get out of this wretched land and go east and get rich, though he didn't have a particular plan. He said he felt sorry for those of us who couldn't see that we were trapped here in this land of rocks and cow pies, where you couldn't get anywhere.

I can go anywhere, Will Dew said to me. I point my horse left, I go left. I point him right, I go right. If a man can't go in a direction out here, there's something wrong with him.

You got a most affable name, I said to get the subject off Francis. Will Dew—sounds like you're agreeable to just about anything.

Will mock-laughed. No one's ever pointed that out to me afore, he said, not in all my years. Never once.

I'm certainly in no place to talk, I said, with the name
Ovid Vesper.

Sounds like some kind of church service, Will said. But—
this is the honest truth, he went on, I growed up with a kid
named Will Knott. Same age as me. Will Dew and Will Knott.
You wouldn't think it by our names, but we got right along,
peas in a pod.

Mister Bowdler never smiled, but he seemed to approve of the
work I was doing. The trail boss and I sat in our saddles, having a look at the country ahead from the top of a rise. The cattle ranged out behind us, grazing under the hot sun, so many
of them that they faded and blurred in the distance, a long-
horned, ragged-edged blanket thrown over the land. Cookie's
chuckwagon, modified from an Army-surplus Studebaker, was
the only human structure in all the vast panorama.

Surveying the herd, Mister Bowdler said, Sometimes I feel
like I'm leading the children of Israel.

I smiled at that. These longhorns are a wayward folk, to
be sure, I said. But they're not bound for a Promised Land.

Mister Bowdler rewarded me with the only laugh I ever
heard from him, though he managed it without smiling. He
studied the horizon with eyes that had been squinting into
the distance for about six decades. Mister Bowdler rode a big
gray called Chappie, short for Chapultepec. We ambled along
through a sea of blue-eyed grass—the ground was wet enough

for it. The herd had found mostly plentiful grass all the way so
far. The bluebonnets were finished now, but yellow tickseed
was just starting to spring up; if color could be sound, tickseed was like a chorus under the azure sky. There'll come a
day, Mister Bowdler said, and not too far off, when they'll run
enough rails that we won't be doing this.

I reckoned he was right. If you could load cattle into train
cars close to home, there would be no need to drive herds over
all the miles, trying to stave off their bad decisions, keeping them
motivated to put one hoof in front of the other and get along.

Well, Mister Bowdler concluded, I doubt I'll be around to
see it. Wouldn't want to be.

I could understand his point. This wasn't easy; it could
fairly be called a misery at times. But for the men and for the
longhorns, this was just about as good as life got—open country, painted with blazing red firewheel, purple spiderwort like
jewels on a green net . . . and the rocks, sculpted by time and
the great Artist. There was the music of coyotes at night, the
crackle of logs burning, and the aroma of coffee in the morning chill. Even where there were no trees, we had wood from
the canvas sling under the chuckwagon. We had the breath-
taking display of the stars every night, telling us there was no
end to wonder or distances to be crossed, no end to beautiful
things. Men and cattle marched across all this, under it and in
it, bound for the slaughterhouse, bound for their graves; but
what a march it was, an odyssey of breath in your lungs and
the wind on your face, far better than chewing grass in one spot
and seeing nothing but the patch of ground your shadow fell on.

That's what was so jarring about Francis. Out here, acts of ugliness stood out like a fly in the jam.

Mister Bowdler looked serious. That kid's still a problem, ain't he? he asked.

Yes, Sir, I said. He's not making it easy.

I told him I'd bullwhip him if it didn't stop, Mister Bowdler said. Looks like I'll have to carry through.

One morning when we were watching a line of bruised clouds low in the west, hoping they weren't heading our way, Francis ran afoul of a cowboy named Ferris. I didn't hear what was said initially, but I got close enough to hear McElroy, in a soft, calm voice, say to Francis, You just say one more thing. As McElroy spoke, he gave Francis the gentlest of pats on the shoulder, just one pat. I felt the breath sucked in by Jay Bird and Will, who were standing there and saw it. In the context, that gentle pat was the most dangerous way a man could move and speak, the almost invisible spark of the match dropping toward the coal oil.

Francis said one more thing. He was absolutely determined to provoke the wrath, like a steer set on eating a poison buffalo bur right down to the spiny stem. He said he was talking to Ferris, and that both of them could go to Hell.

Ferris knocked the kid down with his fist, sending his hat rolling away. He descended and followed that blow with another and another and another. Francis wailed and spit out teeth, his face a mire of blood.

Mister Bowdler got off his horse, but he didn't put a stop to it until Ferris was through. When Ferris pushed back and walked away, rubbing his bloody knuckles, Mister Bowdler crouched down beside Francis as he writhed and moaned and sobbed.

Son, Mister Bowdler said, is this going to be enough of a lesson for you? Is it? When Francis nodded, the trail boss said he damned well hoped so.

Later, when it was just me in earshot, Will Dew said Mister Bowdler saved that kid's life. I allowed he was right. When he saw it was Ferris beating on Francis, the boss knew it was better to let it happen that way. Maybe now Francis would never make McElroy do it.

Francis made like he didn't want help, cussing us and telling us to leave him be, but his face needed some attention. Jay Bird finally got him to his feet and lent Francis an arm as he hobbled off to the chuckwagon.

Cookie was handing out breakfast, frying bacon that he unwrapped from grease cloth to go with the beans. When he saw Francis wasn't dying, he made the kid sit on a rock till he got all the men served, though Cookie didn't eat himself yet. As we ate, we watched Cookie mop the blood off Francis and examine his lip, which was split in a couple places, and his left eye, which was swollen nearly shut, all puffy and purple around it. He straightened the kid's nose a little, and when Francis hollered, Cookie said, Yeah, that's broke. He said Francis would just have to mend on his own—his lip wasn't bad enough to stitch, and there was nothing a dentist could do about the missing teeth. I can pull them, Cookie said, but I can't put them back in. He fixed some bandages and pasted

them on, and he gave Francis some big spoonfuls of painkiller
from a bottle.

I thought Francis would benefit from a day to reflect, alone
with the remuda. We drove the herd on north. The morning
after the altercation, I found Francis down at the creek, per-
forming his necessaries.

He gave me a dubious eye, as if he expected me to light
into him. I gave him plenty of space, splashed water over my
head, and sat a while to dry off in the air. It was plenty warm,
even at that early hour, the sun rising over some pines. There
was daisy fleabane on both sides of the water, growing thick—
white petals around gold centers, like eggs frying. A light mist
rose from the creek, the last ghosts of the night fading away.

I asked Francis how he was feeling.

He didn't give me an answer.

Francis, I said, things don't have to be the way they were.
Every morning there's a chance to start something new.

He dabbled with a stick in the water, listening and pre-
tending not to listen.

Good thing about our theology, I went on. You never have
to be what you've been. I looked up at a big possumhaw tree
on the higher ground, the light shifting as the morning breeze
stirred its branches. I liked the fresh draft along the creek—
water and stones that dried only on little patches of their top
halves. It was good to smell something other than dust.

You a Christian, Ovid? Francis asked. He was talking, and
he used my name—that was something.

Course I am, I answered. How else you going to make

sense of the world? Somebody's got to save my sorry hide, and I can't do it myself.

The world make sense to you? he asked.

Much sense as it needs to, I said. Men don't want to hate each other. Men don't want to hate themselves. You just give them half a chance. Most folks only want you to see and hear them, and not get pissed on. You got to learn to be kind and receive kindness.

Francis said, I don't need nothing from nobody.

For a while, I just watched the light getting stronger through the branches. A mourning dove called near at hand, and another one, farther off, seemed to be answering.

Well, I said, I think life gets a whole lot better if you learn to breathe. Like this herd, moving forward. If a man ties himself in knots and drives too hard, he loses what he hadn't ought to lose. I think one's got to slow down. Man's heart needs to graze.

That is horseshit, Francis said.

Well, I said, settling my hat, you're doing good with the horses, Francis.

Things got quieter after that. Francis kept his mouth shut, and no one gave him a hard time. Jay Bird made space for him on a rock one night and told him to get closer to the fire.

We drove through some rain, which at its worst was a gulleywasher, and we had to stop and get under canvas as best we could, on account we could hardly see. Cookie had some rolls of canvas that we stretched up on frames, though the rain dumped on us so suddenly that we were mostly soaked through afore we got the shelters up. The rain splashing and bouncing made the longhorns look like they had halos of silver radiance. Moods ran foul, but Will Dew said at least the creeks were swelling and the herd would have water. It all made some mud, but that dried soon enough when the sun came back.

Then we got into Indian Territory, and we looked sharp and kept steady. We noticed some plains folk on mustangs keeping an eye on us. Long afore we could see details, I could tell by the way they sat that they were Indians, still and watchful, a part of the land the way white men usually weren't. Will thought they were Choctaw. They seemed to know what we were about and not to care much about us passing through.

About a week later, just as Mister Bowdler was feeling good about our progress, we fetched up against an impediment.

McElroy spied five men ahead, watching us from horseback on a ridge, dark against the afternoon sky—white men wearing Stetsons. They didn't seem like miscreants, since they were in plain sight, clearly waiting for us. Still, we hoped it wasn't an ambush.

Mister Bowdler picked four of us to go with him, and we rode up to see what they would say, though we had a pretty good idea of it. It was not much past noon, the sun beating down. Our hair was plastered, soaking our hatbands.

The man speaking for them said his name was Greenan, and Mister Bowdler introduced himself.

Three miles north, Greenan said, starts the land of Thomas Halperin. You'd see bob wire if you went that far, which you won't. Past the bob wire is all Halperin land. You're in Kansas now.

We're following the Talbot Lucky Trail, Mister Bowdler told him, like we've done since it was marked out.

Trail don't go this way no more, Greenan said. Your longhorns are rife with ticks carrying the Texas Fever. We don't want them up here.

These steers are just fine, Mister Bowdler said.

Texas cattle don't get the Fever, Greenan said. They just carry the ticks. You ever heard about Missouri?

We'll keep our herd away from Mister Halperin's, said Mister Bowdler.

You'll keep it on this side of the bob wire, Greenan said. You turn east and drive them thirty miles. You'll see the picket line where you can come back north.

We're heading for Dodge City, Mister Bowdler said. It's that way. He pointed north.

Not for you it ain't, Greenan said. You take them longhorns east. Mister Halperin ain't alone. We got other ranchers ready to stop you. You come past that bob wire, there'll be trouble of a sort you don't want.

Mister Bowdler looked at him for a long time. Greenan's men sat there, hard-faced. Times change, Mister Bowdler said at last.

Yes they do, Greenan said.

All right, Mister Bowdler said. Down our way, we know

how to be good neighbors on this Earth. You can assure Mister Halperin that we're heading east.

Greenan nodded. We'll be watching, he said.

Mister Bowdler touched his hat brim in parting, a salute that was not returned.

So we drove the herd east for two days, and Mister Bowdler was not happy about all the extra miles taking weight off the steers. Ike found the picket line. Then we turned them back north and went up easy, telling ourselves that there should still be plenty of time to get them on up there.

The one good thing that happened on that drive north, though it was bad for the animal it happened to, was that a steer stepped in a dog hole and broke a leg. There was nothing for it but to put that steer down, and then we had fresh beef, which, with all respect to Cookie's beans, was most welcome. As Ike and Jay Bird were butchering the steer, a few of the prairie dogs popped their heads up and looked like they were laughing at the state of affairs. Will Dew said even the dogs in Kansas were sonsa bitches. I said all male dogs, categorically, were sonsa bitches, and that made him laugh.

That was the night I mentioned earlier, when the sheriff's posse was looking for a lost stagecoach, and at first we thought Halperin's men or some others were out to give us grief. The stage was long overdue in Culvert City. Those boys were courteous enough, so we told them where we'd been and that we hadn't seen lock nor stock of a stagecoach or anyone else except Halperin's crew.

After they went back to their own camp, I noticed Mister Bowdler standing for a long time in the dark, just watching the distance with an attitude of listening. The second night shift was out minding the herd, and I figured I ought to bed down afore the morning arrived with the woes sufficient to itself, but something was buzzing in my head, too, like a mosquito lost in there, or like a storm rolling in, though the sky was perfectly clear and the stars ablaze.

I joined Mister Bowdler, making enough noise so as not to surprise him.

Don't like it, Ovid, he said. Something about this country doesn't seem right.

When I thought about that, not answering right away, Mister Bowdler said, You're a discerning man with good horse sense. How's it strike you?

I hadn't told Mister Bowdler about the things I saw in my head—no reason to. A boss wants a good hand, not some goggle-eyed prophet. I hadn't told him in so many words, but most men with Mister Bowdler's acumen figured out that I heard a different drummer sometimes. I knew he wasn't just saying that the imposed detour stuck in his craw. I said I allowed that something didn't feel quite right, which was true.

Mister Bowdler had a slight limp—not enough to hinder him, but noticeable. I knew he'd fought the Rebs, too. In fact, we'd been together at Antietam, though I didn't know him then, and as far as we knew, our paths hadn't crossed. He'd been in other battles besides. I assumed he'd gotten that limp from the War, but I never had occasion to ask. He could have gotten it any number of ways.

After that night, we hadn't got long to wait afore our disquieted humors proved out. That ominous land began to bring forth blossoms of midnight.

That next day, late in the afternoon, Will Dew and I were out on the right flank, pushing the cattle along. It was like the steers themselves didn't much want to get along northward. I wondered if the prophets among them were having visions of shuddering darkness, walls closed in around them, and a long ride east—a journey that required no more steps from them across dry country, no more hot brands, and from which there was no returning.

In the distance eastward, I saw a tall bur oak off by itself; it got my attention on account trees usually do. Squinting, I saw there was more to it than just a tree. I dropped back and came up alongside Will.

Hey, Will, I said. Is that a person?

That there is a tree, Will said. But when he looked closer, he saw what I saw, down against the trunk in the shade of the bur oak's full crown.

Will swore in disbelief. There was no horse around that we could see. Will kept working the flank while I rode over to figure it out.

I didn't have to get right up close to see I was looking at a corpse. A man without a hat was leaning against the trunk, his legs stretched out, like he was taking a snooze. Except that his clothes hung in shreds. And so did a good amount of his skin. He'd bled copiously some days previous. I didn't want to push Jack too close into the reek, which blistered the air, but I could see horseflies crawling over that dead man. Their droning reminded me of the buzzing I'd heard in my skull.

I waved at Will and headed straight to tell Mister Bowdler.

He decided to pull the herd in for an early night, and while the pokes were settling them down, some of us rode back to the bur oak.

Jay Bird crossed himself, and most hung back, cussing and choking. Mister Bowdler squatted down to look at the dead man in the face, of which there wasn't much left. McElroy had the gumption to take hold of the man's boots and lay him down flat. The man had black whiskers; he wasn't old or particularly young. He wore a holster but there wasn't a gun.

What done that? Jay Bird asked.

We pondered the list of what possible craithers this man might have run against. There weren't obvious claw marks, which seemed to rule out a cat or a bear—nor, of course, was this bear country. It sure didn't look like the work of wolves or coyotes; if they tore up a man this much, it would be after his throat was bitten through and he was dead. There were spatters of blood here and there, leading away to the north. It seemed this man had come a ways in this state and sat himself down under the tree to die.

Bullet in his shoulder, McElroy announced. So this poor cuss had been mauled and shot, and had still done his best to get away.

The coyotes armed out here? asked Will.

Jay Bird tried to get a better look at the bullet wound without leaning in too close. You reckon it could have been Comanches?

Nah, Will said. Colonel Mackenzie rounded them all up. They're all over by the Red River.

Ike added, Ain't even hardly any of them left *there*.

Jay Bird wasn't satisfied. You telling me Comanches don't know how to hide?

Will said, You telling me Comanches would shoot a man and let him run away?

They got no horses, Jay Bird said. The cavalry killed their horses. They're on foot and desperate—starving. Maybe they were fixing to eat him.

McElroy told them to shut the Hell up.

The dead man's eyes were stuck half-open. I wondered what they'd seen. Mister Bowdler told McElroy to close them.

He's been here a week, wouldn't you say? Ike asked. How is it the buzzards ain't found him?

McElroy backed up and sat on a rock. Maybe they got other things to eat, he said.

We looked away north. It was hazy there, and we couldn't see too far.

Mister Bowdler told us to get Cookie's shovel and give this man a Christian burial.

Ike, rather imprudently, muttered that we should make Francis dig the hole, and Mister Bowdler told Ike in no uncertain terms to dig it himself.

It was a subdued evening around the chuckwagon. Someone voiced what we were probably all thinking, the speculation that the dead man might be from that missing stagecoach. One of Mister Allingham's regulars, a poke named Buckles who usually ate by one of the two other fires, was accustomed to playing his Aeolina as the night settled in, but he didn't seem to be in the humor for it. I drank my coffee and tried to see the stars. They were veiled in high, gauzy clouds, making for a dark night. There was a silver glow like a smudge where the moon was supposed to be.

I gave my rock seat to Francis as he came in from the remuda, and I headed out with the first shift. On a night like that, I didn't know how I was going to tell the herd apart from the wells of blackness around them, let alone watch out for varmints. I was glad for my Schofield pistol and the Winchester lever-action I kept athwart the saddle.

Jack needed a rest, so I was on a lanky mare called Banner. She was all black with a white star twixt her eyes. I knew Banner to be a smart and good-natured horse, but we didn't know each other all that well, which made for some uncertainties. I gave her a dried peach that I'd stuck in my pocket, and we agreed to look out for each other as best we could in that Stygian night. We both looked out for the longhorns and tried to lull them away from bad dreams. It is a truth that the right kind of horses do as much as the right kind of cowboys to keep a herd peaceable and in line. I don't know if the horses talk to the steers exactly, but there's some affinity the quadrupeds have; many's the time I could tell a horse was interpreting my intentions to the cattle, or telling me urgently to get in there on account things were about to boil and break.

They were all fitful and restless that night, all those long-horns on that alien ground far from home. They kept lowing and wouldn't settle down, and Banner was on edge, her ears going forward and back, her nose not liking the breeze. I was up by the front of the herd when I came right up on Aaron Frobish afore either of us saw the other.

Don't even know what we're doing out here, he said to me. If this horse don't break a leg, I'll thank the good Lord.

We each moved on.

I found what I hoped were the first few steers up at the north end of the herd. They didn't seem inclined to wander. Ahead loomed the impenetrable dark. A soft wind out of the east made a dry scratching on something it brushed over, some branches or grass. I heard an owl hoot once, and then more silence. Behind me, far back on the herd's right flank, I could see the fires, cheery but remote, as if I were looking at another world.

That's when I heard the sound.

I've spent a good bit of my life outdoors at night, in woods and fields, hills and hollows, in the desert and high up in the rocks, and there are craithers that make some unearthly yowls and scritches. Unsettling as some of them are, still I can usually figure out what is yammering. What I heard, far off in the night, was like no beast or bird I'd heard afore, and Banner hadn't, either. Her ears shot forward and then lay straight back, and that's a bad sign in a horse. I thought she might bolt, but I kept my hand on her neck, and she stood there.

This sound was like screaming, but from many sources at once, screaming together. It wasn't Comanches, and it wasn't coyotes or wolves. I couldn't imagine that it came from human throats. A big cat can sound like a woman, but these weren't cats. It rose up, almost like it was supposed to be some kind of music, and then it stopped. That was all, then. The night's black pit was back to quiet.

The screaming was so far away that most of the steers didn't notice. A few raised their heads inquisitively, but then it was over.

Then a memory came to me that I hadn't thought of in years: *the Craither.* That thing I'd seen out among the hawthorns after Antietam. That shape, like the shadows and dim light were being pulled around something that hid just under the surface of the world, watching with its glittering eyes. Little prickles crawled over my scalp. I'd not been unsettled in quite this same way since that glimpse. That thing had felt *wrong.* And something was *wrong* here, too. I wondered if that Craither were out there again, somewhere in the dark, watching again.

The quiet went on, and ordinary night sounds.

I kept patting and talking to Banner, and when her alarm had subsided, I ventured to turn her and head back along the herd. I met two or three of the other cowboys, but as no one said much, I gathered that they hadn't heard the sound.

Maybe I was only thinking of that Craither because of the strange circumstances, and the darkness.

Maybe I'd never seen a Craither at all: I'd been recovering

then, after being tossed through the air by that explosion.
Maybe Banner and I hadn't heard anything in the night . . .
but now I was only wishing.

When the sun came up, the haze in the north burned away. A
long, high jumble of hills there stood clear across our path. It
was a rankling how-do-you-do; to find an end to the hills east
or west of us would mean more days of driving in the wrong
direction. The men cussed one by one as they laid eyes on that
barrier. None of us could fathom what hills were doing in the
flattest state of the Union, and none of us had the least hankering to drive cattle into the hills. Even if we found a mostly level
way from trough to trough, the herd would be all scattered,
and no way could we keep them all in line. It would have been
like driving them into the Atlantic and telling them, See you
longhorns in merry old England.

Mister Bowdler sat down with some strong coffee to think.
As Cookie was clattering in the chuck box, putting things away
and folding up the shelf, I described to Mister Bowdler the
sounds I'd heard in the night. I reckoned they came from off
in those hills.

That's damn devil land, Mister Bowdler said. I want no
part of it.

Still, not one of us wanted to go anywhere except toward
Dodge, and we were already well behind our schedule. Mister

Bowdler said we'd drive them up that way until the midday graze; that would take us pretty near the hills, and things might look different when we saw them up close. Maybe a marked trail ran through them. And if we did have to turn aside, we could as well do it there as here.

We didn't have good water during the night we'd come through—just a muddy shallow wade where the steers could drink—so Cookie allowed us a little water from the barrel, each man who wanted it, to wash our faces and dump over our heads. I surely was grateful for all the paraphernalia that chuckwagon could haul. It was our bank and our kitchen and larder, apothecary and barbershop and doctor's office and supply ship—a real fine invention, courtesy of Mister Charles Goodnight, who first dreamed it up and built one.

I noticed a couple of strange things on that drive toward the feet of the hills. For one, it was like the land under us was deader and deader the closer we got. The early tickseed thinned out; there was a last carpet of mock vervain still hanging on this late, lavender and pink against the gray mats of serrated leaves underneath, and then that petered out till we were riding over bare, dusty earth. It wasn't like the way a desert stretches into arable land. This was more about a poison barrenness—at least, that's what I sensed. The other thing was like a darkness increasing inside me, a darkness full of whispers and a power like lightning that I couldn't see. Power is the only way to describe it: there was some kind of power in the ground, and it felt like an illness.

Mister Bowdler called a halt well afore midday. The notion of grazing the cattle at the feet of the hills wasn't going to pan out—no water and no grass.

I was riding Jack again, circling and hedging the longhorns to get them stopped. Most of us were thus engaged, but I saw Mister Bowdler across the herd. He sent two of his regulars straight off toward the hills, their horses' hooves kicking up clouds of dust. I couldn't see who it was he sent.

It was easy to cipher what he was doing. He wanted those cowboys to ride up into the hills and scry how far they went. Those were unnatural hills—I'd never seen the like—shaped all wrong. They just began without a rise of the ground leading toward them; the steep sides shone ashy and sick, as if the color had washed out of them. It occurred to me that they looked more like something built later than like hills formed by the Almighty. Maybe they were mounds, I thought, built by the ancients ages ago.

As we worked the herd, I kept sending my gaze out after those two pokes, now little black dots in the distance amidst their long, hanging trails of dust that no wind swept away. Even the air was dead.

The cattle stood still and gave us flummoxed looks, asking us what they were supposed to do on ground like this. They were vocal like they'd been in the night, swishing tails and shifting their hooves, like they didn't want to stand long in one place. The sun beat down hot. I could almost hear its rays ringing on the anvil of the gray earth.

It was when I pulled up beside Cookie's oxen, climbed down from the saddle, and put my feet on the ground that the visions started.

I'd had impressions afore, pictures that came to my head and wouldn't leave, images that nagged at me, sometimes when I was trying to find something—but at other times, too, when the real character of a person or the nature of some place showed itself to me in a flash.

But this hit me like I was at a zoetrope show, flickers and rushing, my head full of motion and sound, so that I had to sit down quick or else fall down. The day around me dimmed away.

In my mind, I was up in the hills, and I could see the herd of longhorns way off in the distance. There were caves in the slopes, caves everywhere, yawning like mouths, and the stone icicles of the caves were like long teeth. In a deep, jagged ravine, I saw a stagecoach, shattered, shoved down there to hide it and be rid of it forever. And there was more beside the stagecoach, rotting piles of stuff—saddles, steamer trunks, bridles, bits, wagons with busted wheels. In another place under the ground, there were bones. Pits full of them, forests of bones all piled and interlocked.

Then I saw rocks out in the sun and in the moonlight, day and night changing back and forth as if I were blinking my eyes. Under the sunlight, I could see the bare rocks arranged in circles, with a big flat one like a table out in the middle of the others, its surface darkly stained; and at night . . .

OVID!

Cookie was hollering, shaking me.

As the day rushed back, filling the well of my mind, and I drew some deep, gasping breaths, what shivered in my ears were the sounds I'd heard in the night, rolling out of the hills— sounds like no other on the Earth.

The hills want blood, I told Cookie, and he looked at me with a lack of comprehension.

I got to see Mister Bowdler, I said.

Cookie said he'd thought I was going to swallow my tongue.

Jay Bird rode off to bring Mister Bowdler, and Cookie made me drink some coffee, bolstered by what he poured into it out of a bottle. I couldn't sit still—not after what I saw.

Mister Bowdler heard from Jay Bird what had happened. Soon as he got there, I told the boss that we had to go after his men fast—if we left them in the hills, they were dead.

He watched me, waiting for me to explain.

Quick as I could, I told him about how I saw things now and again, things that came true or that were true, though nobody else knew it yet. There's something in the hills, I told him. Maybe cannibals. They got the stagecoach and a whole lot of other folks besides. I told him about the saddles and wagons, all dumped down that crack in the ground.

Jay Bird and Cookie didn't know what to make of me, but something in my face or my words convinced Mister Bowdler. He'd called the hills devil country himself, and he smelled the bad air of the place afore I did. He didn't want to send his scouts out there to die. Besides, he could spare a few hands now to go and bring the men back—what else were we going to do while we waited?

Mister Bowdler made to go himself, but I suggested he better stay with the herd. No guarantee we're coming back, I added. Somebody's got to finish the drive, I told him, and get these pokes all home.

He told me not to talk morbid, and that I was damn well going to get my hide back here along with all of his men still breathing and bellyaching. Mister Bowdler sent along Will Dew and Jay Bird, Ike and McElroy, and his regulars Ferris and Buckles. He charged them all to listen to me, since I seemed to know something. He didn't get into particulars. I could see that Ferris wasn't mightily enamored of the arrangement, but he didn't argue.

I made sure everyone was well armed and told them we were probably in for a scrap.

How do you know this, Ovid? Will asked.

Mister Bowdler told him not to waste time with questions.

Cookie took out a scattergun from the wagon and handed it to Ike, with a bag of shells for it. I wondered if there were anything Cookie didn't have in there. I wished he had a bucket of good fortune that he could dump over us.

I gave Jack a pat and told him we had to do this—asked him if he had a hard run in him, and he told me he did. One thing, it was easy to track Mister Bowdler's riders in that barren dust. There was nothing growing to keep the horses' hooves from chewing into the ground.

We set out at a stiff canter that we could maintain until we got to the hills. From the other side of the herd, a rider came along behind us, riding fast to overtake. I knew from the horse afore I could see the man that it was Francis Eames.

What's he doing? Will asked.

We just kept on, and when Francis came aside us, one of the cowboys asked him the same question.

I'm coming with you, Francis said.

Get back to the horses, Ferris said.

I aim to be useful, Francis told him. I'm tired of flicking flies and counting the clouds.

This ain't no job for you, Ferris said.

I looked to see that Francis had his Colt pistol, and then I said, Leave him be. We might need the help.

Ferris muttered something foul, but then he shut up. McElroy just kept his gaze on the hills rising up like some vast wave rolling in from the sea.

That weird power in the ground was getting stronger by the minute. I hoped I wouldn't get swept up in visions again and fall out of the saddle. I had the disquieting sense that lightning was forking upward inside me, its branches crackling down my arms and up into my head.

I thought again what I'd blurted to Cookie, that the hills wanted blood. There was something down under them that called out for it, for death. Death of men, death of horses, death of anything with a throat that could be cut, with life that could be splashed out on the hungry soil. Something wanted slaughter like we wanted the bacon out of Cookie's grease cloth when our bellies clamored.

They're watching us, I said.

Who's watching us? Will asked.

I didn't know, but I felt their eyes.

Then we were right betwixt the feet of the first hills. The horses balked. Jay Bird's started bucking, and the one Buckles was on bolted back out into the open, and it took him a while to calm the horse down and join us again.

We could still see the trail left by the two scouts. With plenteous cajoling, we nudged the horses along it. Though we were still under the sun, it felt like we were riding into a great umbrage, the heat from above not reaching us. There was an uncanny cold below, down in the earth. Someone else was muttering about it, so I knew it wasn't just me as felt it.

The hills, viewed from right among them, were fantastically bizarre. The ground looked like it had been flung up in walls and mounds that snaked away, leaving aisles and canyons running every which way. I'd played with a lodestone afore, watching what it could do when held and moved around underneath a paper on which there were iron shavings. Near as I could reckon, this awful power in the ground had done that to the land itself, buckled and twisted and swirled it, maybe so long ago that there weren't even Indians. It made me curious as to what it would look like from the sky, if you could be a bird and look down on it. I figured it was a good thing that a human being was not a bird, on account I didn't suppose I'd want to see that picture, whatever it was that iniquitous hunger had drawn or written on the earth.

By instinct, none of us wanted to make much sound, but Jay Bird quietly said he felt like his breakfast was coming back up. Ike agreed. The hills had that effect, making us queasy. I kept glancing around fast, having the strong sense of movement here and there where we couldn't see it, shapes darting behind the rocks, always hidden again by the time we looked.

I saw something else in my mind: furtive shapes on open ground in the dark of night. Without really intending to, I said aloud, They hunt at night. They come out of the hills.

No one had time to ask me what I meant, on account just then we saw a patch ahead where the soil was all kicked around, like there'd been a scrambling. The trail left by Mister Bowdler's scouts ended there. It didn't go on any farther. From that point, there were marks leading off to the left—not just hoofprints, but what looked like a crowd had passed that way.

McElroy got down and took a close look.

Barefoot tracks, he said.

Comanches, Ferris said.

They don't go barefoot, Will said.

It seemed pretty clear what we were seeing. The scouts had ridden in this far, not more than a quarter mile into the hills. They'd likely meant to climb the high slope just ahead, which would afford an advantageous view of the land. But they'd been surprised here. We'd heard no shots, and I couldn't see any blood. These barefoot people must have taken them prisoner and led away the horses, too.

I was thinking of the man we'd buried. He'd been shot in addition to everything else that had been done to him.

They hunt at night . . .

Watch the rocks, Ike said. He had the scattergun ready.

McElroy slid the rifle out of his sling, and Ferris had an eight-gauge. Jay Bird got his rifle, too, and the rest of us drew our pistols. Most of the men dismounted then—it was hard to shoot from a horse if it got spooked. McElroy and I stayed in the saddle. I expect he wanted the height for seeing, and I dreaded putting my feet down there.

Cautiously, we followed the new trail. It wound through a narrow gulley for a couple hundred feet, and then ahead of us, there awaited a cave.

We stopped at the last bend to study it. The black maw was twenty feet wide, a rough oval, its arch a dozen feet high. The ground leading up to the entrance was well trampled. Even from the bend, we could smell that cave. The reek of a bat cave is about the evilest odor I know, but this was worse. There was corruption back in the dark; I guessed the bones that my vision had shown me were in there, too.

Far as I go, Ike said, his stutter getting worse.

That's where our boys are, I said. We got to go in.

Will reminded him, You got a scattergun, Little Miss Daisy.

Now McElroy climbed down from his horse.

It was time for me to get down, too. I gritted my teeth and slid to the ground. At once, I could feel that thrumming, that unseen lightning forking through me, even more forceful now. But I kept breathing and didn't pass out.

We moved forward. I laid the reins on my shoulder, and Jack came right along behind me.

At the cave mouth, we tried to see into the gloom. That stench made our eyes stream. There was daylight inside the cave. Way back in there, the ceiling was cracked open, so the place was gloomy but not pitch-black. We lingered there, letting our eyes adjust.

Finally, there was nothing for it but to proceed inward. There was no more soil; now we were walking on limestone, in a hole fizzled out of the rock by water long ago, when this whole country looked a good deal different. I wondered if the cave had been here first, or if it had formed after these preternatural hills had been twisted out like dough.

We ain't coming out of there, Jay Bird said. We got no business going in.

That all you care about those men's lives? Will asked.

You don't all have to come, I said, keeping my voice low. Wait here, anyone who wants to. Matter of fact, we need someone to watch the horses. Just be ready to come in shooting if we holler.

You're gonna have to give orders, Buckles told me. No one wants anyone else to think he's yella.

All right, I said. Jay Bird, you and Francis stay here. Ike, we need that scattergun. If you ain't coming, give it to someone who is.

Aw, Hell, Ike said, and took a step inside.

I knew better than to try telling Mister Bowdler's regulars what to do in this situation, regardless of what he'd said to them.

I ain't staying here, Francis said.

You're the best one with the horses, I told him. What's the point of my giving orders if you're not going to follow them? I handed him Jack's reins and told Jack to be good.

Without waiting for more discussion, I moved into the cave. It was wide enough for us all to go abreast.

It was a huge single room in there, bigger than a dance hall, with a ceiling that soared up thirty, forty feet. Boulders and rubble were heaped everywhere—all kinds of hiding places and shadows. A few lanterns hung from sticks wedged into the rocks. None of them were lit.

At once I saw the scouts' two horses, back against a far wall. They were still saddled, tethered with their reins looped around big stones.

Then I saw the two men, tied down on their backs, their arms and legs stretched wide in four directions, like a big X. Ropes held their wrists and ankles. One man looked unconscious, a gash on his brow oozing blood. The other moaned and tried to raise his head, calling out to ask if anyone was there, if anyone could hear him. Then he started reciting the Twenty-Third Psalm.

We'd found them, and I didn't see anyone else. Everything about it smelled like a trap.

Sometimes it's a trap even when it doesn't smell. This one smelled just like what it was.

As we padded closer, there was a whisper that ended in *thunk*, and Buckles pitched over with a spear in his back.

McElroy fired his rifle afore I'd spun all the way around

to look, and someone behind a rock shrieked and went down.

Then it was like the room exploded. Dark figures sprouted up everywhere, swarming out of hiding. They sprang at us with tomahawks and spears, and they made unholy cries that didn't sound human. I saw ragged teeth and wild, tangled hair.

Ferris let loose with his eight-gauge, and Ike fired the scattergun, which took down two attackers at once.

I opened up with the Schofield, just barely avoiding a spear in the chest.

Ike got off his second barrel, but then a chop from a tomahawk sent him to the ground.

Will Dew was a quick shot, and accurate. He later described those next few seconds as: Will Dew became Will Doing it Fast, trying not to become Will Dead.

I was shooting these shadow things quick as I could. When the Schofield went empty, I had to use the Winchester lever-action, which was slower and built for more distance, but at least it was something.

Ferris dropped the empty eight-gauge and went at it with his six-shooter.

Crazy thing was McElroy, though. He forsook the rifle for a pair of Colts. He made his shots count, spinning and spewing lead, and all our muzzle flares brought lightning into that cave.

The ricochets worked mostly to our advantage, on account there were a lot more of the wild men than there were of us—and anyway, we left most of our bullets in them; not many shots hit the rocks. Still, a ricochet hit Ferris in the leg.

When McElroy came up empty, he gave it out with his knife and a snatched-up tomahawk, cutting a red swath all around him.

The attack slacked off momentarily. I tried to get a better look at who we were fighting. There were bodies piled about us, but the shadows were still full of live ones. They hung back for a long minute, watching us.

They weren't Indians—not Comanches, not any folk of the plains, though they had hair down to their waists. They were pale, as if the sun never hit their skin.

They hunt at night.

Their eyes looked glassy, like the eyes of someone burning with fever. And it wasn't only men. There were women here, and young ones. They wore very little clothing, or none at all.

Strangest thing was, we saw guns everywhere: gun belts looped over rocks, rifles leaned up on boulders. They saved the guns of those they hunted. Why weren't they using them now?

They come out of the hills . . .

Will gagged and covered his mouth with the back of his wrist. I looked where he was looking, and I saw a big silver platter on a flat rock. The platter was tarnished black, covered with an unspeakable residue. But at its center, in a rancid heap of meat, I clearly saw a human hand.

I fumbled to reload the Schofield. There were still way too many of them.

Deep in the earth, something rumbled.

The shadow people listened, their eyes bulging.

Then they came at us again, wilder this time, madder, looking frenzied, looking now like they cared about nothing but tearing us to shreds.

We fired like crazy, and McElroy killed so many it began to appear things could go either way. I guessed now what he must have done to the Rebs when the fighting went hand-to-hand. Ferris was on his feet, blood soaking his leg, but he kept chopping and slashing. Both men knew how to use knives just as effectively as guns.

Jay Bird was right beside me then—he'd come in behind us. I was glad to see him. Will was on the other side. He'd found his way to a pair of pearl-handled Colts that were part of the cave's loot, and if the cannibals weren't going to use them, he was.

The floor shook.

Something stirred then in the earth . . . something that had lain still and silent and vast. I felt its movement in the rock, like when you touch a rail on which a train is coming. I thought it had a *sound* behind the cracking of the land's bones, something reminiscent of a rising wind. It set me ajangle, too, like we were all inside a huge bell that had been hammered on.

Three of the wild men jumped on McElroy and bore him to the ground. We tried to pull them off, but I felt jagged fingernails tearing at my sides, my back, my arms. The breath of the cannibals was vile, and I saw their mouths, glistening, the teeth rotting and snaggled, inches from my neck.

Then there was a splitting noise, followed at once by the *WHOOOMMF* of ignition. Flames roiled and spread in waves, fire that was like a living thing, blinding in the dark space, washing across the littered floor. Fire engulfed the cannibals, turning them into torches. Another detonation to my other side, more searing heat . . . Our attackers shrieked, candles that ran and tumbled. I'd have been right back on the battlefield again, among the cannons and slashing and shooting, but for the overruling impulse to get out of there quick.

We got clear then. The things were off us. Ferris cut a last one down, and the rest were burning and skittering away into black pits and cracks. Will and I pulled McElroy to his feet.

Francis had come in with Jay Bird, and he happened upon a row of kegs filled with kerosene . . . and some blankets that he slashed into fuses. And some sulfur matches. Those cannibals were too adept at scavenging and hoarding for their own good.

I ran for the men tied on the floor. Will and Jay Bird were right beside me. We cut the men loose. One could walk. The other Ike slung over his shoulder like a sack of potatoes. Yes, Ike was alive, though he had a knot on his scalp from a tomahawk blade. Only on Ike's head would the business edge of a tomahawk raise a knot instead of cleaving his skull.

Ferris could limp.

But we'd lost Buckles. The nights after that were a sad and lonely tribute to him with their unbroken silence, on account his Aeolina harp wasn't filling them with music. We laid Buckles across his saddle and brought him back.

We got the men's tethered horses.

I hollered that we had to get out of there fast—out of the cave, out of the hills, for now I understood. My visions—or maybe that power in the ground itself—had told me everything.

Already cracks were shooting through the walls of that cavern chamber. Rocks slid, dust rose, and as we mounted up and charged back the way we'd come, the hills themselves were sliding, rifts opening up to swallow the soil. A prolonged roar came out of the earth.

We hightailed it out of the hills as they crashed down around us, the ground pitching and whomping. It was nothing short of a miracle that the horses kept from falling. We hit the barren plain about three strides ahead of a landslide, broken rocks churning and roiling in a wave right behind us, sweeping us onward.

Halfway back to the herd, we finally felt like we could slow down and take a look back over our shoulders. The horses were all frothy, and we just sat there and stared.

The ground came up then. It was like what you see when dynamite goes off, only bigger than that, the magnitude nigh unto inconceivable. Where the hills had been, it seemed like half the state had been hurled up into the sky. Rocks bigger than houses spun up so high they were black specks, and soil sprayed to the clouds and rained back down. When those boulders crashed to earth, I was seeing the War again, among the canister shot and cannonballs.

It was all caused by something that pushed up through the hills, shrugging them off like a layer of dust. Out in the open country, the sky is vast; there's almost nothing you can't see if it's in front of you or above you. What came up out of the earth was so big we could just barely see to either end of it.

It was a living craither—that much I could tell.

Not what I'd seen at Antietam—this was something else.

It had a color and a texture that I couldn't describe—I'm not even sure my perception could accommodate them. I'll call it a Dragon just to have something to call it. It had wings—beating wings that lifted it, higher and higher. But I don't think they actually were wings, and I don't think it was any sort of Dragon. It's just that our brains needed a way to interpret what we saw. Maybe the other cowboys saw something different than I did, each in his own way. We didn't much want to discuss it afterward.

I didn't know where it came from or where it was headed, except that it was on a long journey, just like we were. It had alighted here for what to it was a little rest, like we bedded down at night. Only its little rest began millions of years ago, and now it was getting on. I think my mind showed me wings to help me understand that it voyaged in the aether, in the infinite darkness among the stars.

When Will asked me at some point why the cannibals didn't use all the guns they had socked away, I told him my theory: They did use them—but they did that out on the plains, when they were waylaying wagons and travelers and passersby. The cannibals knew how to watch over the sleeper, for it told them how. Guns weren't shot off in the caves, where the blasts hammered and echoed in deep places—until we came along and did that, and that's what woke the Dragon up.

This here is what I think I know, though I have no proof of it. When an animal goes down for a long winter sleep, it fattens itself up first. In the same way, the Dragon was fed during its snooze by the spilling of blood. In that sense, it was evil, on account it thrived on violence and destruction. So it called out; so it had led some group of people to become cannibals, to live in the hills and keep it supplied. The clan we encountered was a big, inbred family living there like rats in the dark—but surely they weren't the first. Others afore them must have been feeding the Dragon for a long, long time.

I suspected that, if we were to inquire, we'd learn that this part of the country had a reputation, a hainted land where folks tended to go missing. In fact, I wondered how much that rancher, Halperin, knew . . . and what his intentions had been in sending us up this way.

So much for speculation. Of immediate concern to us was the stampede touched off by that awakening. It was a feat to put what we'd just seen out of our heads and give our attention to the task afore us, but that's what we had to do. Those longhorns ran wild and white-eyed in a heedless panic, and we lost another three days chasing them halfway back to Texas and rounding them up. It was just what we needed at the end of an arduous and unfortuitous drive. We delivered some lean cattle to the railhead. Mister Allingham had gotten many a better price than what they fetched. As we made our crawling, tortuous way around the miles-long crater where the hills used to be, Mister Bowdler said he would not be sorry if they hurried up laying those rails for the iron horses.

It was a long time afore some of us got the medical attention we needed from Cookie. He had to stitch and patch.

Ferris ended up with a limp. But we got out of those hills with the two scouts, who were alive and grateful we hadn't left them there.

We buried George Theodosius Buckles under some tall, whispering cottonwoods. Mister Bowdler knelt on the soil and expressed his apologies to Buckles that he had to lie in Kansas. We tucked the Aeolina into that cowboy's folded hands.

One thing that made me smile: near the end of the drive, when we were bringing in our horses one evening in the purple dusk and handing them over to Francis, McElroy put his callused hand on the kid's shoulder, gave it a shake, and said, Thank you, Francis.

Francis had got himself unstuck. Turned out he just needed one good thump and then the chance to be useful. That's all most of us need. I ran into him some years later in North Texas, and he had a wife and two little towheaded tads and a place of his own. He was all right. He was even going to church.

One night by the fire, as Jay Bird was bellyaching and Will Dew was marveling at how worn out a man could get in a day, we saw three shooting stars, their tails long and brilliant in that magnificent sea of sparkle and velvet. Tiny frogs were singing in the trees, giving us a serenade.

Catching sight of one more meteor, I wondered if those bright flares might all be Dragons, if they might be coming down in this world or on their way to some other. It was not exactly a comforting thought.

Lo and behold, just then Mister Bowdler brought up the subject of the Dragon.

He'd seen it, too. Everyone had seen it, even those clear at the back of the herd. Mister Bowdler said he advised us not to tell stories about the particulars of what we'd run into. We all agreed, but the trail boss went on: Sooner or later, he said, I expect some of you will be drinking whiskey and wax eloquent about it. If any inquiries make it back to me, I ain't going to support any tales of monsters under the hills. I reckon what we come against was a sinkhole that nearly swallowed us.

Earthquake, agreed Ike.

Cyclone, Jay Bird said. Biggest twister I ever seen.

I slept fitfully on those last few nights, my head full of strange dreams. That Dragon had got me thinking . . . about the War, about the dark all around us on our journeys. About how short a mortal life is in the here and now, about what we might see if we looked into the shadows betwixt the trees.

That Craither from the battlefield in Maryland was not gone. It was not far away at all. Somehow, the visions I saw were related to it. I was pretty sure of that.

It was a welcome sight when we pulled up at Dodge City and got those longhorns into the corrals at last. It was quite nice to be paid, too; I hadn't got good pay in a while. We parted ways there; I was going to push on farther west—I wasn't sure where just yet. The others, of course, were riding back south, heading home.

We said our goodbyes to the cattle, watching from the ridge as pokes were loading them up. They were in other hands now, and we had nothing to wrangle but ourselves.

Chappie and Jack both were tossing their heads and prancing, like they felt light. It was a glorious morning.

You want to come round about two years hence, Mister Bowdler told me, we ought to have another herd ready, the good Lord willing and I'm not pushing up grass. Always a place for you, Ovid.

I told him I might just be there, and it would be my honor.

It wasn't an easy thing saying adios to Cookie and McElroy, to Ike Denton and Jay Bird Ward, to Will Dew with his weird bendy elbows, and to Francis Eames. He took good care of Jack when I was riding other horses. Ferris I could take or leave, but he wasn't a bad one. It wasn't easy riding away from Mister Bowdler, who truly was a fine cattleman.

INTERLUDE

In about the spring of 1882—I believe that was the year—I was in Colorado and found shelter one night in the cabin of a prospector named Squally Dan Erath. You don't forget a name like that, and I can see his face plain as day. He had a white beard dyed yellow at the chin from tobacco juice, and he wore a short gray top hat that had somehow lost its flat top, so that he was left with a roofless velvet crown on top of his head. When I remarked on it, he replied, Don't you know? I'm the King of Colorado!

Dan seemed in good spirits. He had offered me the hospitality of the stump water from his still, and we were well into the jug. So I was bold to ask him how the hat got that way.

Put my fist right through it in a fit of anger, he said: In the bottom, out through the top. My favorite hat.

I nodded, passing no judgment.

It's all right, he said. In that way, I kept from hitting my boy. Better to tear up a good hat than to beat on a boy who ain't old enough to know better.

I allowed that it was indeed. He turn out all right? I asked.

Yeah, he said, till he got himself killed down at Dove Creek.

I said I was sorry about that. I'd heard of that battle in Texas.

It probably meant that Dan's son had been Confederate—not at all unusual for Texans.

As if he could see my thoughts, Dan said, He was Texas State Militia under Totten. We hailed out of Coryell County.

I wouldn't have cared which side he was on, I said. Just boys on both sides that hadn't ought to have died. I didn't say what I was thinking: the victims at Dove Creek were the Kickapoo Indians who were just trying to reach Mexico, trying to get themselves away from our War. None of the soldiers bothered to confirm whether or not they were hostile.

Well, Dan said, my boy turned out all right.

A storm had been brewing, and that night it pounded the cabin like we were on the high seas. The rafters groaned and the walls creaked at the joints. Rain dripped around us where it found its way through chinks. Jack occupied an enclosed lean-to added to the cabin's back. I checked on him again and again, making sure he wasn't getting washed away. Sometime in the wildest and wooliest part of the storm, the big ponderosa pine outside broke in half and came down on a corner of the main cabin roof, smashing part of it open.

We just did our best and rode out the night.

In the morning, I figured we were a little bit drier than we'd have been out in the open, but not by too much. Jack was calm and in better shelter than ours.

Dan said we'd have coffee afore we set about getting the tree off of us.

I still had some bacon and eggs with me. I fried the last of those for us. We propped up our feet, watching the rosy gold light slant along the cabin walls, and I remember that as one of the finest cups of coffee I ever did have. Dan looked up into the drippy pine branch just above his head and asked how I liked camping in the woods.

Just about then, a blackbird swooped in through the open roof and got confused, cawing and flapping, circling around the tight space, all noisy wings and shrieks, taking it out on us that the tree it was trying to alight in was suddenly indoors.

Wasn't much for it: we just ducked our heads and waited for that red-wing to find its way back out. When it did and Dan stood up, his old joints popping like the cabin had been doing all night, he let out a surprising laugh.

You have to like a man who makes an excellent pot of coffee and laughs with a tree through his roof.

He pointed into the chimney corner, where the sunlight fell onto the edge of the mantel slab, which stuck out in the recess, forming a shelf. That corner ain't been properly lit up since I built the place! he said. I been looking for my mammy's Bible for two years! Knew it was here somewhere.

The sunbeam shone onto a leather-bound Bible, far enough back that it looked mostly dry.

I stayed with Squally Dan long enough to saw up the tree and fix his roof as best we could.

Many a time after that, I thought of the ponderosa, the red-wing blackbird, and the shaft of sunlight fallen on that lost family treasure. It seemed those things might have brought me closer to understanding the Craither and my visions, at least on some level. At Antietam, I think the world's wall got broken in one little place; maybe I'd been blown right through it. I'd come back in by the same hole, and the Craither had come in behind me. But something else came through, too: some kind of light like the sun, and where it shone, I could see things now.

So the visions and the Craither came with the same falling of a tree, but they were not the same. They'd come, good and bad, together, a curse and a blessing—or so I thought then.

CHAPTER THREE:
THE SOUND OF BELLS

MISSOURI, 1883

Whenever I hear far-off church bells, I think of a September in Missouri when an old friend asked me for help. Richard Decalne wouldn't tell me at first what the nature of said assistance was—said he had to show me.

Two decades previous, Richard's was the first face I saw bending over me that day at Antietam Creek, after the Reb bomb blast had laid me out flat in the cardinal flowers. Scarlet flowers, clouds shifting, the sun through the haze . . . and silence—such a strange, utter quiet after all the cannons and the shots, the shouts and bugles and that infernal Reb war cry. Richard and I had marched and fought together for several months, each giving the other a steady voice to hear when the dark and waiting brought too much thinking. So I wasn't about to refuse when Richard sought me out twenty-one years after Sharpsburg, almost to the day, and asked me for a hand in getting something done.

He'd caught up with me in Trumpet City. A cousin of his worked with me there, loading and unloading at the rail yard—employment for a season or two, afore Jack and I pushed on again. When Richard heard I was close at hand, he could scarcely believe the turn of providence—we'd had no discourse since the War. He'd tried sending a letter to my hometown a couple years previous, but I and my people were gone from there.

When my shift ended one day and I came past the round-house, I spied a man sitting on a corner of the office porch, watching the workers head off in different directions. The cousin greeted him, led him over to me, and I recognized Richard. His hair was thinning out, but I knew that rangy stride. We'd toted our gear up and down many a dusty road in our blue wool coats.

After pleasantries, the cousin left us to it. Richard formed his next words while studying a couple of puffer-bellies getting ready to roll away. You still got the sight? he asked me, and though I didn't know the particulars of what was coming next, I knew he needed help seeing something that ordinary eyes couldn't.

Long and short of it, I settled up with my boss and rode with Richard down the easy road to Woolpit, Missouri, with one night's camp on the way, under the stars. The nights were not uncomfortable yet; it had been a hot summer that was in no hurry to cool down. Finding a patch of good grazing meadow beside a pond where the frogs had a chorus, we made a fire with branches from a mostly dead white pine. Along with the coffee, Richard poured me some whiskey to thank me for coming along.

Watching him in the firelight, I thought he'd aged more than I had, though I reckon we always think that about someone we haven't seen in a long time. He was probably thinking the same thing about me. His gaze flicked up often into the dark, whether there was some sound or whether there wasn't. He had a Schofield pistol like mine, and he kept it handy. I wondered if the War had ever really ended for Richard, especially given that this was Missouri, his native state.

Missouri folk had seen absolute Hell on Earth. Both sides in the War had claimed the state and sewn it onto their flags. Missouri troops had gone to serve both the Union and the Confederacy. In the War's early days, the governor, Claiborne Fox Jackson, did all he could to help the Rebs on the sly, till he was ousted.

Plain folks, who tried to go on with plowing and planting, enjoyed neither haven nor mercy; there was no decency among marauders of both stripes. Some would murder you if they figured you supported the Union; others would do the same if they pegged you as Secesh. Families were slaughtered. It mystified me that the starry campion around us was still blooming, could still spread its frilly petals and be a thing of beauty growing from this anguished soil. Studying the campion—near the end of its season now—I thought of how it stayed open in the dark of night and closed its flowers in the bright sun of midday. Maybe that was how it had got through the War, and maybe that's how Missouri had done it: clenched itself up for the worst of things, then kept watch and held courage until morning came.

Some assignment had gotten Richard transferred east to join us in time for Antietam, but afore long, he was back here where he'd been from the outset. He told me more that night, there by the fire. He'd been a Jayhawker, hunting down the Bushwhackers under Bloody Bill Anderson. I already knew that a year afore Antietam, Richard had been at Wilson's Creek, serving in Lyon's Army of the West.

But it was the fighting against Bloody Bill's men that had rattled him most.

We had 'em pinned down, he told me, in a grove of silver maples, just at the edge of a farm they'd torched. They'd left a little girl dead against the fence, Ovid, and her mama stretched out where she'd been running to her. We found the farmer shot and fallen onto his plow, hung up in it. Mule kept dragging it, past the end of the row, still plowing a furrow and bringing the farmer along—mule just trying to get free.

I shook my head and kept listening.

So we pinned 'em down and kept on shooting into the maple brake. Some of 'em slunk out the other side and got away when night fell. With the morning light, we found a lot of 'em in there.

Richard swallowed more whiskey. One of the bodies, he said, was my brother, Robert. He'd been fighting for Bloody Bill, and I never knew till I saw him there. Shot twixt the eyes, like he'd been executed. I was firing into that brake, Ovid, till there wasn't no one firing back. It might'a been me that got him.

There wasn't much I could say to Richard, save that I was sorry, and it was a Hell of a thing. This was a land of blood and ghosts. Such wasn't Richard's fault, even if he had put a ball of lead in his brother, which was impossible to know. He'd seen what the Bushwhackers did. I hoped Richard and his bunch hadn't done similar things to other homesteaders who only picked up a gun to hunt squirrels or coons and just wanted to be left alone, who just wanted their boys to come home alive.

This part of the country had its share of new woes, too. Wanted posters for the Sunday gang were up in Trumpet City. Ma Sunday and her boys had been on a spree, robbing banks and waylaying stagecoaches, murdering without compunction, and managing to stay two steps ahead of the law.

It was good to be out in the open air and the green space, away from what human craithers did to one another.

Richard and his wife Emma lived in a cabin among the hills northeast of town, under a canopy of pin oaks and ash trees that were just igniting into bright yellow. A weathered barn stood to the north, and a stream meandered in back. Birds warbled near and far. A black-and-white cat eyed us from the barn doorway, tail twitching, as we rode up. We unsaddled the horses in the corral and slung the saddles on the fence rail. I gave Jack a pat; he seemed glad for the cowgrass, which was past blooming now but plenty sweet and thick. We leaned our rifles up against the cabin wall. I remarked that this was a good and peaceful place.

Emma was the schoolteacher in Woolpit. She was off doing that now. Richard did all sorts of things with his hands: he caned chairs, made furniture, sharpened knives, and grew some vegetables.

As Richard brought up the well bucket for a drink, I glimpsed a small figure watching us from the deep shade among the oaks. As soon as I looked, the shape vanished, so that I wasn't sure I'd really seen someone. Was it just shenanigans of the light through the green leaves?

Was that a kid? I asked.

Richard followed my gaze. Yeah, he said, that was one of 'em. Reckon they like you. When they don't take to someone, they throw sweetgum balls. It's a bad habit, but they got their ways.

I gave him a quizzical look and said, I thought you didn't have kids.

He grinned oddly and offered me the water cup. Guess we'd better go find 'em, he said.

Something made my scalp prickle; something I couldn't quite cipher had seemed wrong with the light when I'd glimpsed that diminutive figure back in the oaks. And I wondered why we were going into the woods to find Richard's kids instead of him calling them to come to us.

I know where they'll be, Richard said. They got their favorite spots.

A blue jay shrilled overhead. The shade slipped over us

as we crossed from the yard into the trees, back into a world
of emerald dusk. The cool air was scented of mint and fern.
Ghost pipes clustered in the deep shadows, white trumpets
curving from yellow pods, the petals flecked with black, like
someone had peppered them. The stream got louder as we followed a well-worn trail down to its edge. The last stretch was
steep, almost a slide.

The creek bank was like a cellar in the woods, misty and
damp, aromatic, almost shivery after the noonday heat. Strider
bugs flitted over the water, which sparkled where the sun shot
through. Big boulders emerged from the earth, some with
sharp edges and angles.

Solemnly awaiting us on the near bank, two children stood
side by side.

From the way they stood, quiet and still, my first impression was of Indians. But at once, I knew what had troubled me
about that earlier glimpse. This girl and boy—who looked to
be about twelve or thirteen—were entirely green. Their hair
looked like corn silk, the boy's down to his collar, the girl's almost to her waist, the black-green color of plants underwater.
Their skin was a deep, rich green, their eyes shaped like those
of Chinese folks.

They watched me without expression but looked ready to
spring away like rabbits. Their clothes were ordinary, the one
thing about them that wasn't green.

After the silence had stretched out a while, I closed my
mouth and then said, Well, hello. I was trying to fathom
where they'd come from or what might be ailing them—I'd

known some strange things, but I'd never heard of green people. I had the mad fancy that Richard might have grown them in his garden.

Ovid, Richard said, this here's Abbie and Jim. And this is Mister Ovid Vesper, my old friend. We fought together in the War.

Instinctively, I took off my hat and said it was a pleasure to meet them. I knew it wasn't polite to stare at them, but then, they were staring at me, too. Toward the last, I thought the girl might have almost smiled; there was a little softening in her gaze.

Richard patted my shoulder and suggested we have a sit-down on a couple of big rocks. As we did so, it seemed to release the two children. They turned back to the creek and moved off a little farther, returning their attention to what they'd been building, scooping in the sand and mud of the creek's edge with a trowel and a sharp stone. It looked like a miniature town they were making, with canals and houses of bark, with moss patches for the roofs.

Richard chuckled. I must have looked pretty dazed.

He explained, They been with us about four years. I had some business over in Fort Smith. One night, I saw a kind of traveling show. Some old charlatan making himself out as a Professor or some such had a big, black curtain on a circular frame, like a stockade made of velvet. Easy to put up and take down. He'd let paying customers go inside to view his museum. There was a giant skull of some animal—the Tricornus, he called it. There was a stuffed lizard-bird . . . and another

thing like a fish with a human face . . . some teeth, bones, and
the like. A mummy he'd dug up. A jar with a two-headed rat
floating inside.

Well, Richard went on, at the center of the enclosure,
there was another curtain in a circle, and if you paid more,
you could peek inside at these two: the Green Children. Not
bones or old stuffed hides, but living and breathing. The main
attraction of his show.

He looked toward the pair, and I could tell they were listening, though they kept busy with their construction.

Richard scratched his ear. They looked sad and pathetic,
he said. Half-starved. That old sharper had 'em chained like
animals. I couldn't abide it, Ovid. After things I've seen . . .
and done . . . I can't leave any creature to suffer.

So what'd you do? I asked him.

My business in town was finished, Richard said. So I
loaded up my wagon, and when the crowd had gone home for
the night, I sprung 'em out of there.

You sprung them? I asked. The Professor didn't catch you?

He objected, Richard said, but he didn't argue with my
twelve-gauge.

So you robbed him, I said.

I did not. I informed him that slavery was now against the
law and left him a good saddle horse and a new saddle and a
tin of fancy coffee by way of reimbursement. I gave him the
choice of using my bolt cutters or his keys, and he obliged me
in unlocking the chains. Seems he didn't want to take it up
with the law; I warrant he didn't do too good with sheriffs.

He might have shot you dead, I said.

Now the green girl was watching us, sitting on her heels, though the boy still worked on digging.

I could see the lack of nonsense in Richard's face, the hardness left by the War. I understood why the charlatan Professor hadn't tried anything.

A thought occurred to me, and I asked, Did you get that Professor's name?

Richard shook his head.

But suddenly, the girl spoke up.

Doctor Sintch, she said, and repeated it: He Sintch. Doctor Sintch.

Doctor Bellerophon Cinch? I said.

She nodded.

I think that *was* it, Richard said. It was painted on his signs—I'm seeing it now. Like the cinch on a saddle. Then Richard frowned and asked, You know him?

I saw a show of his, I said. To the girl, Abbie, I asked, Did you like Doctor Cinch?

She shook her head, stuck out her tongue, and struck the ground once with her fist.

Well, then, I said. I'll tell you that he came to no good end. The man is deceased.

The boy and girl exchanged a look. Richard said, Hope he enjoyed that coffee.

What's the diss east? Abbie asked me.

It means he's dead, I told her, and she nodded.

Where are you from? I asked Abbie, keeping my tone cheerful.

She looked down at the ground then.

I'm from Illinois, I offered. But I've been all over.

After a moment, Richard said, They're not big talkers. Tell you two taters what: I'm gonna tell Mister Vesper about you, and if I get anything wrong, you just jump in and set me straight.

Richard spun out a tale that seemed incredible. But I was looking at these green kids with my own eyes. Something had to account for them; they had to have come from somewhere, and I knew of no illness that turned a person so green. Sometimes Abbie called out to correct or clarify something Richard said. The boy, Jim, looked at us now and then, but he didn't say a word.

I noticed, too, that the pair would raise their heads together and peer into the woods sometimes, like they saw or heard something. I would follow their gazes, but I never could tell what had gotten their attention. Once, Abbie pointed through the trees and solemnly announced, Fox. Fox. I could tell she had fun exaggerating the *f* sound, which seemed amusing to her.

That's another thing, Richard explained. They hear all sorts of things long afore we do. I've no doubt there's a fox over there somewhere. These two tell me when someone's coming to see us, and I usually got a good ten minutes to finish whatever I'm doing—then I hear the horse or the wagon coming.

You can tell it's a fox by the *sound*? I asked the kids. Abbie nodded and moved her hands and shoulders up and down as if she were dancing, showing me how a fox padded. I couldn't help but laugh at her antics. I saw now that her and Jim's ears were a tad bigger than most, though I wouldn't have seen it if I hadn't been looking close.

Richard's story went like this:

When the two came to live with him and Emma, they could say no more than yes and no in English. Emma had been teaching them ever since, and now they could say a lot and understand more. It came more easily to Abbie than to Jim; he just didn't seem to need to speak, especially when his sister looked out for him and did most of the communicating with others. Abbie looked a little older than her brother, but the Decalnes weren't sure of their ages. The kids didn't count years in the same way. Abbie said her age was Cloud but not yet . . . some word in her own language.

Richard allowed that Emma had been surprised when he'd come home from Fort Smith with two green children. Everything was bewildering to the pair. They sniffed and poked at most foods, showing no interest. Any sort of meat revolted them, even its smell. The first time they'd seen meat on the table, they glanced toward the cat curled up by the stove and looked at Richard and Emma with apparent horror, as if they thought no living craither was safe from these pink-skinned ogres.

But then, when Emma brought in a pail of raw green beans, the children pounced on it and stuffed the pods into their mouths fast as they could. They liked anything green from the garden, and they could tolerate other vegetables and fruit, even canned or dried, which got them through winters.

After that discovery, they grew less cadaverous, and their hair took on a glossy shine. The next spring, their first with the Decalnes, Richard had planted a second garden just for the children, with all their favorite vegetables, and they promised not to eat everything in the other garden faster than the grownups could pick it.

On account that they never said names that their new caretakers could grasp, Richard and Emma gave them names, which the two accepted, though they said Abbie's name in two parts, Ahb Ee, and they said Jim as Simma. They spoke to each other in a soft, high-pitched, whirring language. When Richard described it, Abbie gave me a demonstration, and Jim joined in with her—the first time I'd heard his voice.

The Decalnes decided not to make the children go with Emma to the schoolhouse. For one thing, Richard didn't want folks coming from far and wide to gawk at the two. For another, the green children would have been miserable in school. And, most importantly, Richard knew the brother and sister wanted to go home. He never supposed they were meant to be here for long. They weren't happy. Often, Richard saw them looking forlornly at the ground, or into the distance, and Abbie said her brother, especially, needed to go home soon.

Where is home? I asked.

Both the children listened now, to see if Richard would get it right—or maybe they just liked hearing about it.

As Abbie had explained it in bits and pieces to Richard and Emma, their home was a place called the Land of St. Martin. It was never very bright there, and never completely dark—which was why the pair preferred the forest shadows here, or being indoors. In St. Martin's Land, the sun traveled low around the horizon, shrouded in mist. It was a green sun in a green sky. Everything there was green. Even their blood—seen once when Jim had stepped on a piece of broken glass—oozed out green. Abbie named this world of ours Blow Land, puffing out her cheeks. When Emma had asked her why she called it that, Abbie blew on a dandelion gone to seed, sending its gray tuft scattering: Like that, she said, and then pointed at things around her that were all different colors.

I'd never heard of a St. Martin's Land. From the part about the sun that never set, it sounded like it might be up near the North Pole—only then it should have been dark some of the year, and very light for some of it.

How did you get here? I asked, looking at the kids.

Richard said they'd been picking fruit one day. Abbie chimed in with its name, I supposed, though it didn't even sound like a word to me. They'd climbed up to the top of a hill, on account that, from high places, they could look across a shining river in the far distance to a country that was much brighter than St. Martin's Land. It seemed impossible to reach it, but the view of that gleaming land on the horizon fascinated them.

Bells, Abbie whispered. Bells.

Richard nodded and said, They remember hearing far-off bells ringing. It happened many times a day when they were little. They never knew what kind of thing was making the sound until they came here and heard church bells. They loved Sundays, when the church bells in Woolpit rang.

In the absence of day and night, Richard said, the sound of bells told the people of St. Martin's Land when it was time to wake or work or sleep. The bell sounds maybe came from that shining realm across the river, where no one had ever been, though they seemed to be ringing much nearer at hand than that place looked. (Abbie nodded that this was right.)

As the two children came down off the hill, they saw a small wild goat springing over the rocks, and they watched it trot into the mouth of a cave. Curious, they followed it a short way inside. Though they reckoned they'd gone no more than a few steps into the dark, somehow, they lost all sense of the entrance behind them. Yet ahead, they could see faint light. So they moved forward, and the passage sloped upward. The light got brighter and brighter, and it wasn't the green light of the sun they knew. They found themselves in a pit, with tree limbs stretching above them, but everything looked different.

Blow Land, Abbie said, making a bursting motion with her fingers.

Richard said that he figured out in due course what Abbie meant by Blow Land: she was expressing what colors looked like to her and Jim. They hadn't had a word even for green afore they came here; it was just the color everything was, so it didn't need a name. Our world looked like some kind of constant explosion to her, a bombardment of variation. When I thought on it, listening to Richard, it surprised me that these children could see colors at all; why were their eyes and brains built for that kind of perception? But they were, and the two kids knew that they weren't outside the cave near their home. Everything was different. There was a forest where hills should have been.

The kids had come up out of the hole where a tree had been standing. Richard reckoned there must have been a storm that uprooted some trees, and underneath one of them was a tunnel. Abbie and Jim were just turning to scramble back down into the comforting dark when they were set upon by hunters—rough, hairy, pink men who wore animal hides. Abbie made sure I understood that the men smelled bad. At the time, she'd thought they must be ghosts, as some of them were toting dead birds around. These men tied the green children up, marched them out of the woods, and Abbie wasn't sure what exactly happened after that. The pounding white sun made her and Jim keep fainting and half blinded them, giving them headaches. At some point, they wound up with Doctor Bellerophon Cinch, who most likely bought them from the hunters. The kids almost died afore Cinch found what they could eat.

Richard told me that the pair had no idea where they'd come up out of the ground, which made it mighty hard to know how they might get home. It could have been anywhere from Georgia to Texas, on account Cinch dragged them all over, raking in coins from folks who wanted to see the Green Children.

I understood better why Richard had felt compelled to get them away from Cinch. Furthermore, I reckoned Cinch had made back plenty more than he'd paid for his green slaves, and had been paid for them over again by Richard. And anyway, Cinch was beyond concerns over mammon now.

By that point, I'd pretty well ciphered out what Richard wanted my help with.

He said, I been trying to help these two find St. Martin's Land. We wriggled into caves all over this state. Last year, we went over to Kentucky, to the Mammoth Cave there. Went late in the fall, so the kids could bundle up, with gloves on and hats pulled low, scarves around their faces. Had to pay the guide a little extra, but he lowered us all on a rope, one by one, into the Bottomless Pit, and he asked no questions.

I said, I guess the Pit had a bottom.

Yep, he said, but it didn't have any tunnels leading into a green country. Every place we been under the earth, we just saw the dark.

I thought that over. It apparently wasn't just a matter of going down into the ground.

We wondered if maybe it had something to do with bells, Richard said. So we tried skulking 'round some churchyards at night—and in the daytime, on Sundays, when the bells were ringing. No luck.

Richard had gotten books and tried to find out about St. Martin. After a lot of searching, he came across the story of a Peruvian holy brother called Martin de Porres—a child of an Indian and a former slave. On account of his parentage, the law forbade him to take holy orders. But he was so compassionate in working with the poor and sick that his local head priest let him in. Many said he was a living saint. When sick folks were shut away to keep their disease from spreading, St. Martin could walk through locked doors to bring them food. It was said he could heal terrible maladies by bringing the afflicted a cup of water. And when his boss upbraided him for bringing sick, dirty people into the monastery, St. Martin apologized and humbly asked to be instructed, saying he hadn't known his vow of obedience was meant to supersede charity. That made his boss give Martin rein to do what the Lord told him to do.

It was all quite interesting, Richard said, but he found no connection to any green land, any place under the ground. Abbie said she didn't know how her land got its name or who St. Martin was. Maybe it was some other St. Martin entirely.

The patterns of sunlight had shifted across the creek bottom. We'd been sitting and talking for quite a stretch. The green kids had finished building their city of bark, mossy mounds, and canals, and it was impressive. I asked them if it was a city in St. Martin's Land; first Abbie looked puzzled, and then she shook her head.

Ovid, what do you allow? Richard asked. You think you can help?

Your guess is as good as mine, I said, but I'm glad to try.

Richard fed me and the kids—Emma always took her lunch to the school, so that she could mind her pupils. Abbie and Jim didn't eat much: a stalk of this, a few leaves of that, and some beans. Then the two of them wandered back to the woods. We brought the saddles in under a roof, though it didn't look like any rain was brewing. Jack looked contented, grazing with the other horses. I wondered if horses talked it over when they got together like that. Did they tell each other about where they'd been and what they'd seen? Already in his young life, Jack was accumulating quite a mess of tales to tell.

I pitched in with Richard for the rest of the day on chores that needed doing around the place. He said the green kids were helpful when it came to sweeping up or toting water from the pump. They wore out easily when working outdoors, even in the shade. They were particularly handy in the garden. He added, It's like they got green thumbs. I could tell he'd been building up to that line, and I figured it wasn't the first time he'd said it. They tended the vegetables in the early mornings and when the evening shade was long.

Richard asked me when I thought I might expect a vision that would do us some good. I told him there was no expecting them. Visions came when they had a mind to, and more than half the time I couldn't understand what they showed me. That said, I'd noticed some patterns. They seemed to find me more often—and come fuller and clearer—when I was asleep and dreaming or when I was off by myself.

Emma got home, and Richard introduced us. He'd clearly talked about me a lot, on account Emma looked surprised when she saw me. She told me she thought I'd have a wild beard and blazing eyes, like John Brown—or maybe wear camel hair and ask for wild locusts for dinner, like that other John, the Baptizer.

I said, Afraid I'm pretty ordinary to look at, Ma'am.

No, no, she said, not ordinary at all, and we all had a good laugh at that. Then she was quick to make me welcome. Emma looked tired from her day, but not wearied from living.

She had a bright, round face, though she wasn't plump, and seemed at least ten years younger than Richard. I reckoned she must have a good bit of generosity of the spirit to take in the children.

Richard and Emma sat me down on their evening porch with some tea they kept cool in the well, and the two of them worked side by side getting supper ready. We elders had salted ham, taters, and greens. Abbie and Jim reappeared in time to set the table, like workers showing up for a shift. I noted that they hadn't run out of the woods to greet Emma when she came home, any more than they'd come to see Richard when he and I rode up. They didn't talk much as they ate their garden fare and some green soup Emma made for them.

After supper, Richard did the washing up, Emma studied her books and plans for the next day, and the kids sat by a lamp and lost themselves in books. Emma kept them well supplied with books borrowed from the school. She said they'd learned to read English faster than they'd learned to speak it. I'll allow it was a tad bit frightening to see the serious intensity with which they perused and turned pages, sitting in straight-backed chairs, hardly ever looking up, like they were a pair of countinghouse clerks with the boss watching. Do they like the books? I asked, which seemed to me at once a nonsensical inquiry and a genuine puzzle. Oh, yes, Emma said: They ask for them, and they're sad if I don't bring home enough. I've had to borrow books from parents and exchange with other schools to keep our library stocked.

I could see that the books weren't easy ones; they were full of history and literature and poetry. Abbie was immersed in *Paradise Lost*, which seemed fitting. Jim was reading his own book but had scooted his chair around so he could also read Abbie's book over her shoulder—two books at once.

There was just enough of a chill outside to make the fire cozy on the hearth. As Richard and Emma were both occupied, I got up to give it a poke. When I passed their table, I asked the kids if there were books in St. Martin's Land.

The two looked up at me impatiently. Jim went back to reading, but Abbie indulgently squinted and hunted for words. Yes, she said at last, but very many—no, very little. She went on: Some read, talk other, talk other. She made a spreading gesture, wiggling her fingers, and I imagined stories being passed from person to person.

I returned a smile and let her get back to *Paradise Lost*. The books, I thought, must be full of things the pair couldn't comprehend. But they were understanding something—plenty to keep them interested. I figure a reader always builds something together with the writer that's a different thing than what the writer has built. Who's to say what those green children were building out of *The Last Days of Pompeii*, or the Heaven and the Hell Milton wrote about?

I supposed it was a good thing that Abbie and Jim kept so much to themselves, even when they were together with the Decalnes. Their allegiance was to each other; they did not feel exactly like a part of the family, and the Decalnes did not labor to force any closeness. I supposed that both parties knew it would be easier this way if the kids could find a way to go home.

The children had a side room with two beds Richard had built for them. Richard and Emma were fixing to give up their bed for me, but I wouldn't hear of it. I had my bedroll, and the smooth, clean floor of the big room was a far fairer lodging than many I got. I fell asleep listening to the fire burn itself out and the whispers of trees outside. I wondered if the proximity of the green kids in the next room would allow me to dream on their behalf.

I did remember the fragment of a dream as the morning light woke me up, though it didn't mean anything to me at the time. There'd been pounding hooves, glaring sun, and a rising dust cloud. I also recalled seeing a quiet main street in a town—stores, water troughs, horses hitched up, wind off the fields . . . but in the middle of the street, a red stream, meandering in the dust. A stream of blood. I followed its course upstream, up the street. It flowed out from the front door of a building, splashing at the front step in a waterfall. A bloodfall. Above the door, a painted sign read BANK AND TRUST.

I didn't tell the Decalnes about the dream. I couldn't see how it applied in any way to the green kids. But over breakfast, I proposed that I ride out into the country and do some listening.

Whatever you think might help, Richard said. Just promise to come back.

I won't leave you high and dry, I assured him.

Jack was ready to get out and stretch his legs. He could tell by the lack of paraphernalia that we weren't going far. I took along the rifle and the Schofield, of course, and water.

It was a fine day, the sky still looking like summer, not yet sharp and desperate with light. We worked through a deep forest of shady oaks and maples, following a creek for several miles, then climbing onto a drier ridge where white pines took over. I surveyed the land from up there, the fields and farms and woods.

Down the far slope, we rode through a white chaos of bundleflower, the tangly blossoms folding up when Jack brushed them. As I glimpsed the flash of a river through the trees, something stirred in my mind, something like a mouse darting under the garden leaves. I headed that way through the dappled shade, trying to listen, keeping my thoughts quiet and loose. I could smell the ferns and the damp decay of fallen trees down in the wet. Along the edge of a meadow, we passed a bee tree. A few bees whirred in and out of its hollow, and a deep droning sounded in its depths.

We caught up with the river in open ground, down past a field of goldenrod. It wasn't wide or deep; I could see the rocky bottom straight across. The current ran clear, bringing a draft of cool with it from the forest. I swung down out of the saddle and walked with Jack through the foxtails and some knifey, ironlike waterweeds that I didn't know.

Right at the river's edge on the near bank was a magnificent lone tupelo, towering straight and tall, its dark, glossy leaves just breaking out in scarlet here and there. In another month, this old sour gum would be a sight to behold. I slid the Winchester out to keep at hand, then left Jack to graze at will. He wouldn't wander off. After a swig of water, I sat down with my back against the tupelo, the river at my right elbow as I faced upstream, where the water came out of the woods. After watching a red-tailed hawk circle high up, I closed my eyes and thought about home, about going home.

I was doing it for the green kids, attempting to think about other worlds under the ground, down below the deepest roots, down where ice-cold rivers thundered and the rock hung in icicles. That was what I attempted to do, but the home that filled my head was that old, tall house where I'd been raised in Illinois, the house built by my granddaddy out of bricks fired right there on his farm, where my dad had farmed the land after him.

Since the War, I'd gone back to that place only three times: once to tell my folks that I had to go away again, once to help bury my dad, and once to bury my mama. That's also when I'd bought Jack, a yearling, from Judge Broaddus. I didn't have the heart to sell the land, though I expected it would come to that. My good neighbor farmed the field; I was grateful to let him profit from what the land could provide in exchange for him looking after the house. But with every passing year, I wondered more often if I really had a home at all in this world.

The breeze rustled the foxtails and waterweeds. Now the sky was empty of anything but tufts of cloud. The hawk had gone off somewhere else.

Where should they go, Abbie and Jim? Where was St. Martin's Land? I shut my eyes again and listened.

All the books on the table in the lamplight had got me re-membering an old book I used to read about King Arthur and his Knights of the Table Round. Camelot was another sort of Paradise lost. There was a Green Knight in one of those stories—not just dressed in green, but green of skin from head to toe. I wondered if he might have come from St. Martin's Land. I couldn't recollect whether the story ever said, but I remembered how it turned out. That had stuck with me.

Sir Gawain learned that none of us has cause for any pride, on account we all fall short; yet it's important to go out and find the Green Chapel, to keep our word and choose to do the right things, for in the end, these things matter.

Then I heard it, behind the whisper of the breeze. Maybe it was only in my head, but it seemed to come from up the river, deep within the wood: the sound of bells, like church bells slowly ringing.

I opened my eyes, looking that way. It seemed that the tunnel formed of trees leaning over the water was aglow with green light, an ancient light that had not changed, and would not. It was the light of another land. Sitting there under the tupelo, I felt that I was right at the edge of the world, and that the river led somewhere else.

As if the vision hadn't told me enough already, the river beside me flowed green, bright green, like young grass at the doorway of summer. I'm pretty sure that was part of the vision, as it was still just a Missouri river. Jack came up beside me and nickered.

Yeah, I told him, that's the way we need to go.

Richard was excited when I told him what I'd seen, what I believed about following the river.

You think it's close, then? he asked me. The way into St. Martin's Land?

The kids watched us with wide eyes. We were in Richard's barn, where Abbie and Jim had been helping him shovel out the horses' stalls and put down some new straw.

I shrugged and told him I didn't know anything for sure, except that we were supposed to go up the river, up into the green woods.

How can it be so close? he asked. That old Doc Cinch took 'em all over. Have we been living all this time a few miles from where they came up through the ground?

It probably isn't the same place, I said. There are more weird kinds of doorways than you'd figure. But let's not get our hopes up too high.

Still, the possibility seemed strong . . .

Emma was happy to hear about it when she got home— sure enough, the kids heard her coming a long time afore we did, and this time they did run out to meet her. But she also had a few tears in her eyes as she watched Abbie and Jim through the evening. I knew she and Richard would both feel an emptiness in their place if the kids went home.

We had a big supper to fortify us. Emma was the praying type, which suited me fine—my folks had been, too. I talked to God all the time, though I usually did it in my head, where I didn't have to get the words exactly right or use words at all. After Richard's perfunctory blessing on the meal, Emma thanked the good Lord for bringing Abbie and Jim into their lives, and she asked that He'd get them safely home to their folks. The kids bowed their heads, too, and seemed to like that prayer.

Richard and I washed the dishes. Emma helped the kids pick out a few favorite books to take with them back to St. Martin's Land. I could tell there was one book they wanted to take that Emma wasn't supposed to part with; it belonged to someone else. After thinking it through, she let them pack it with the others. We'll work something out with Mister Reynolds, she said, and Richard smiled and sighed, shaking his head. Emma made sure the kids got baths, and she folded up their clothes for them to take.

It took me a while to fall asleep. I listened to an owl and the tree frogs, the whole late-summer night music. Then I had more strange dreams: water rushing, falling on rocks in the mist, and the sounds of guns being cocked, though it was only sound—no people. I felt like someone was behind me, which kept me rolling back and forth on that hard floor. I was relieved to wake up just afore dawn and to get out of those dreams. It took effort to sit up, on account my bedroll was wrapped tight around me like I was a bound captive.

After breakfast, Emma hugged and kissed the kids and Richard. She even gave me a hug, thanking me for what I was doing and telling me to look after them all.

Abbie and Jim were slow getting out the door, and then they both went back in several times to see Emma a little more. She had a school day ahead of her, but she came out to see us off. Richard brought along a pair of lanterns from the barn. We might be looking for a cave.

I rode Jack. Richard was on Wilkie, a sleek black gelding with a white blaze. The kids had learned to ride Peach, a skewbald mare of a good nature. They both climbed up into the same saddle, being slight enough that Peach didn't mind carrying two, even with their books, clothes, and a little daguerreotype portrait of Emma and Richard that Emma had tucked into their bag—So you won't forget us, she said.

We non't forget, Abbie had answered. For Abbie, no, not, don't, and won't were all the same word.

We had a clear day to work with, the sun rising through the oak leaves, and a robin brightly singing Lookit here! Lookit here! Mist curtained the low, wet places as the day warmed up fast. The cat took note of our departure, giving us a disdainful glance on its morning prowl. Three grackles in an organized line wobbled along through the yard, gleaning.

The green kids looked back at Emma for as long as they could, and she stood there waving and biting her lip, smiling bravely.

Back in the timber, a jay was doing some strident complaining. Woodland aromas replaced the yard's scent of hay. I murmured to Jack, asking his opinion on what the day would bring.

I had no trouble leading us as straight as we could go to the tupelo beside the river. Truly, it was no more than three miles from the Decalnes' place, if that much. I didn't change course until we swished through the goldenrod and ironweeds and got right up to that sour gum. Somehow, it felt like the starting point, like we needed to check in with the tree afore we set out for stranger places. That tupelo must have been sixty feet tall, just starting to think seriously about the autumn ahead, bringing forth its first tinges of scarlet.

Even from the saddle, even without clearing my mind, I could see the weird glamor of the woods up the river. I asked Richard if he saw that, and by his confusion, I could tell he just saw trees, water, and sky.

You see something? he asked me.

We're headed the right way, I said.

Up where the ground was still firm, I followed the bank out of the meadow, up the current, and into the embrace of the woods. At this hour, the light was purple and grayish, not yet lit up in emerald, but there was a church feel to the space, like a big holy sanctuary. Abbie and Jim looked eager. I wondered what the woods looked like to them.

As we got farther in, I started hearing birdsongs that I didn't know, and seeing strange plants and blooms that I didn't recognize, and that was all a confirmation of what I suspected: this was what I called an Edge, like I'd seen a few times afore, where different worlds came together and shared a border—a place where some things took root or nested that didn't originate in our world.

Abbie and Jim whispered in their secret language, pointing out things they saw. Richard noticed their heightening interest and nodded hopefully at me.

But suddenly, Abbie gave a soft cry and reined Peach in.

Both kids tensed, listening.

Richard and I stopped, too, and Richard asked them what they heard.

Abbie couldn't find the words. Careful, she muttered: Angry things.

I didn't like the sound of that, but when she nudged Peach forward again, I led the way onward. We wended through a grove of old, twisted willows, dangling their cascades of wands down to trail in the water. Some of them felt rotted to me, bad on the inside and full of nefarious thoughts. I could see trees better in places like this—I could see through to their hearts.

But there were trees here I couldn't begin to fathom or name, old dense trees with nubbly bark, and cloaked in unsettling vines.

Fall river, Abbie announced quietly, and in due course, I could hear far off the sound of a waterfall.

You still hear the danger? I asked her.

She nodded, making an expression I didn't understand.

Richard asked her if she had any other words for the danger, and Abbie said what sounded like Bird Snail, which didn't help us.

The riverbed got rockier, with spills of huge boulders on the banks and mossy islands forming in the current. Then the waterfall came into view, sluicing over a cliff afore us to thunder down on a wide shelf. The shelf curved around to join the banks, so that you could walk right up to the falls on either side. Dragonflies darted over the ripples. Now the sun was higher, and the woods were lit in glorious green, effulgent and hushed.

As I peered into that white curtain, I discerned that this was the center of what I felt; this was the Edge of our world. It wasn't farther up the river.

We're here, I said quietly.

Richard asked what I meant, looking this way and that for something significant.

Beside one of the rocks, down in a muddy hollow, was a pile of horse apples that didn't look more than a day old. I pointed them out to Richard and made sure I could get at my Schofield in a hurry. If horses had been here, it meant people had been here, in the middle of nowhere. Scanning the ground, I saw the track of a boot in the mud.

The kids dismounted and hopped around on the rocks, exploring. Richard rode up the near bank to higher ground, and I found a shallow place to ford and rode cautiously across and up the far bank, staying alert. We each had a good look and a listen, finding no other signs of anyone here now, though Richard saw more horse droppings in a grassy clearing where horses might graze.

There were other disconcerting things in the woods: unnervingly large spiderwebs among the limbs, and some plant pods that looked like something unwholesome might hatch out of them. I figured it best not to probe too far. Better to hurry up and take care of what we came for. Edges such as this, usually in lonely, wild places, were like corridors leading to various rooms, all close together but markedly different from one another. I hoped St. Martin's Land was here, but if it was, it probably wasn't the only other world.

Neither Richard nor I had wanted to be out of sight of the kids. By the time we joined them back at the waterfall, they were pointing at it and telling us there was a way in—they'd spied a cave straight in back of the falling water, and they'd heard bells ringing over the current's roar. They were eager to rush right in, but Richard told them to wait for us.

We left the horses saddled but didn't hobble or tie them; if some craither did come out of the woods, I wanted Jack to be able to run and kick. I'd seen him put some regret into a catamount that jumped us once. I slid the Winchester out of the saddle holster and told Jack he better not eat anything growing around here.

Afore we brought the lanterns, it made sense to see what we could from the cave's mouth. Richard had his twelve-gauge and his Schofield pistol. He told Abbie and Jim to stay close behind him, and he let me start first along the ledge.

The kids weren't afraid. I asked Abbie, Which way is the dangerous sound?—the Bird Snail? She pointed up the left bank, toward where Richard had found the clearing.

Just as we moved along the shelf, taking care to keep our guns out of the spray, the two kids turned and looked back down the stream. I assumed they were taking a final look at Blow Land, the world of crazy colors. I hadn't ought to have assumed that.

The cave opening was narrow, almost as high as the falls, but just wide enough for one person to walk in without turning sideways. The wet rock glistened, ferns and fungi sprouting from its crevices. Behind the cool breath of the river was a colder draft, the exhalation of the earth. It had to mean that the cave went a good way back into the hill.

It looked like one big room beyond the entrance crack, the floor a jumble of boulders and scree. Enough daylight flooded in through the falls and from some fissures in the ceiling to let us see pretty well, even afore our eyes adjusted. Someone had been here; there were a few burned-out ends of torches and an empty bottle on its side.

St. Martin Land? Abbie asked, looking worried. I could feel a draft, but there seemed to be no way out of the chamber except the cave mouth behind us and maybe the gaps overhead, opening to the outside. I didn't see a tunnel leading deeper.

I did pick out more details as my eyes got used to the dimness. A mound of rubble at the chamber's back seemed to have resulted from a cave-in; I could see a recession in the wall and ceiling from which rock had fallen. The draft came from one edge of the mound, cold air flowing around a slab. The huge, flat rock seemed to block an opening—imperfectly, but effectively. In some former time, the cave had continued here; a passage ran deeper into the hill.

Look here, Richard said. Tucked behind another rock were some large, bulging canvas sacks. I guessed afore he dug into one what they contained.

Banknotes. Paper currency, stacks of it bound with neat bands, and lots of it in wads, shoved hastily into the bags. A tremendous amount of money.

Richard looked up soberly. Bank robbers. That's who'd

been here. An outlaw gang was using this cave as a hideout. Suddenly I was less worried about Bird Snails and more worried about what I'd seen and heard in my night dreams— blood flowing out of a bank's doorway, guns cocking behind me . . .

Jim and Abbie put their faces up to the cracks at the slab's edge, trying to see into the opening behind. They tugged on the slab, but it was far too massive to budge.

Bells, Abbie said, sounding on the verge of tears. I could hear them faintly, too—like church bells, ringing in stony hollows deep inside. The ringing faded to silence. Had we come to the doorstep of St. Martin's Land only to find it sealed off?

Richard said, We got to find a way to dig past it.

Well, I advised, don't jump to conclusions yet. Maybe I needed time to listen and hunt for a vision. Maybe there was more than one way in. But my nerves were jangling being boxed in here. The bank robbers were bound to come back. Our best hope was that they were far away, getting supplies or hitting another bank.

We searched the space, hoping for some crack or pit that we'd missed. But there were no other drafts. The kids had entered our world through a cave; I guessed it made sense that a cave would be their passage back home. The visions had led us here, probably because it was the closest place where the worlds came together . . .

I was just about to go outside when we heard a gunshot.

The kids tensed, eyes wide in the gloom.

There was only room for one of us in the cave mouth, so I moved ahead of Richard to take a look. He came along behind me. I went with caution, doing my best to see anyone afore I was seen.

Peeking around the edge of the rock, out past the falls, I was looking right at a man with his rifle braced over the top of a boulder, sighted at me.

There you are, the man called cheerily. Y'all come out of there now. And don't be stupid. We got you from all directions.

I didn't raise the Winchester, but crouched quickly behind a rock on the ledge, a little farther out, from where I could see better.

A second man was perched on a boulder in the open, knees spraddled out like he didn't have a care. He held a silver pistol that he didn't bother to point at me, and he flashed a grin. Another man aimed a rifle from behind an oak trunk to my right, and I could see two more figures downriver, sitting on their horses in the riverbed, far enough down as to be out of effective gun range. The shot we'd heard, I figured, was to get our attention.

It was the Sunday gang, or part of them. I recognized faces from the posters, and I'd seen Ma Sunday and her sons once in Fort Smith, at a distance, as they rode out of town. I was pretty sure that was C.J. Sunday talking to me, over on my left. And one of those mounted was clearly Orma, the leader— known as Ma, wearing her signature bowler hat with dried posies around the band, just like in her portrait on the wanted posters. Judging by his long, reddish mustache, the man with her was George Bigby.

The grinning one had to be Billy Dance, and I figured him at a glance: he reckoned if I made a move, he could plug me dead with that silver Colt afore any of his compadres got off a shot, and then he'd keep reminding them how fast he was, how Ma relied on him above them all.

The man behind the tree looked like Frank McLaurel, whom I was acquainted with in Laredo afore he seriously outlawed up. I was standing right beside him in the crowd the day they hanged his brother Clarence. McLaurel had a hatchet face and jumpy eyes. His face always looked shaded somehow, even when he wasn't wearing a hat. When he got a good look at me, he recognized me, too.

Well, I'll be damned, he said. If it ain't the famous Ovid Vesper!

C.J. repeated my name and asked who Ovid Vesper was.

He's got a second sight, McLaurel said. He found them missing folks in East Texas.

Ain't never heard of him, C.J. said, and added, Ovid Vesper's gonna be famous and dead if he don't come out of that cave. All y'all come out. There's three horses, so there's gotta be three of you.

Good: he hadn't actually seen us—hadn't seen the kids.

There's no way out of there, McLaurel informed me. This don't have to end bad if you come out civil.

I knew it was going to end bad. We were inside their cave

full of money. We knew who they were and could tell the law where we'd seen them. They could just move along afore a posse came after them, but this hideout was too good to give up. They weren't going to let us go.

Trying to buy time and think, I hollered, Where's the rest of the boys? Where are Marvelous and Earl?

They'll be back soon enough, C.J. said.

From his rock, Billy Dance said, We can all play some cards and have a drink.

What do you think, Ma? McLaurel called out. We could use a man of Ovid Vesper's talents. I bet he knows where the nearest marshal is . . . and the nearest stagecoach.

Ma leaned over and spat into the river. I couldn't tell if she was chewing or not. Just get 'em out of there, she said. Stringy gray hair hung down around her face. I'd heard how she'd killed her estranged husband in Arkansas with a shovel. Her horse was a big, handsome bay.

I backed up quickly into the shelter of the cave mouth. You want to talk, I yelled, you just come on in.

Richard had been watching over my shoulder. He was scowling now, trying to cipher how we were going to get out of this.

I looked for the kids and saw them high up near the ceiling, crawling into one of the sunlit fissures that led to the surface. That was good. They could vanish into the forest, and they had the sense to get away. The Sunday gang never would be able to figure out where the third man had gone, and it would vex them for a good while. Richard met my glance—that gave us some satisfaction, knowing that the kids weren't trapped here.

I'll keep them talking, Ovid, he muttered. You climb up there, too, and look after those two.

I shook my head. You're their father, I reminded him. And think of Emma. I've got no attachments, except to Jack. I hoped Jack would get himself away—I hated the thought of him carrying outlaws around.

Well, you're being stupid, C.J. called.

Richard and I studied the blocked passage one more time, as if something might have changed. It was maddening to be so close.

What do you allow, Ovid? Richard asked me. When it comes down to it, blaze of glory?

I knew what he meant. If we went out blasting, we might take two or three of the gang with us, but they'd have us in a crossfire. If we surrendered like they wanted, they'd execute us; I saw no reason why they wouldn't. I had to concede that the blaze of glory seemed like our only option. The question, I told Richard, was the timing. I'd known of folks who got rattled and threw their lives away a little too soon. Depending on how smart the Sundays were, we might be able to maintain our standoff for quite a while.

Unfortunately, they thought of something.

We got some dynamite, yelled a voice that I was pretty sure belonged to Billy Dance. He was talking to us, not his cohorts. How 'bout we drop some in there, with a real short fuse?

I hoped he was bluffing about having dynamite, but most likely he wasn't; the Sundays were always blowing things up.

You could do that, Richard hollered back, except that your loot's in here with us.

That was met with a silence. Then the gang had a better idea—not better for us.

One of them, probably C.J., put a rifle shot in past the edge of the falls. The bullet whined off the entrance arch and screamed around inside the cave, hitting the rock walls at least three times afore it was played out.

Richard swore and ducked.

That hit anybody? C.J. called. I guarantee one of 'em will.

He had us there. We were fish in a barrel. There was no way to dodge ricochets.

Well, Ovid, said Richard, I'm sorry I got you into this. I'm sure I had this coming to me, but you deserve better. I'm sorry, and I thank you. You're a good friend.

It's all right, I told him, thinking that if you turned the clock back far enough, he was in this spot on account he couldn't leave the two kids chained up. After the War, we were both just trying to put the world back together.

I asked him, You want left or right? We'll go fast and keep shooting.

I never heard Richard's choice of directions.

Someone—it sounded like C.J.—commenced cussing and hollering, and straight above us, Billy Dance yelled, Fire in the hole! down through one of the ceiling fissures. Sure enough, a stick of dynamite came clattering and bouncing into the cave, its fuse sizzling right down through its last inch. Crazy Billy just couldn't resist one-upping the rest of the gang, being the cock-of-the-walk that brought things to a dramatic end of his choosing. He didn't care about the bags of money.

Richard and I ran. He slid through the entrance just ahead of me and sprang left, so I went right.

I cleared the edge of the falls and found Frank McLaurel—as providence would have it, just as he was moving closer, from his oak tree to a better position. He was in the open and didn't have a bead on me, though his rifle was coming up now.

He got his shot off at about the time I did mine. His bullet went just a little wide—it sang past my ear. I hit him in the chest. He spun around as he fell.

I kept moving, searching wildly for anyone else taking aim. There was shooting to my left—Richard and C.J. I glimpsed Ma and Bigby, a lot closer now, still down the stream.

In that instant, the dynamite went off. A fantastic spray of water shot out from the cliff face, and a shudder through the ground threw me off my feet. I sprawled down hard on two different rocks. I heard the detonation and felt rocks striking the earth, raining down everywhere, big chunks that tore through the trees.

Tree limbs snapped, debris rattled, and voices shouted.

More gunfire.

I expected to feel hot lead tearing through me, but that wasn't happening, at least not yet. I couldn't tell if I had any broken bones. When I lifted my head and blinked, I wondered if I were in the midst of a vision.

Huge shapes hurtled through the air—not dislodged rocks,

but flying things—living craithers. Only they were big as bears. I blinked and tried to focus my eyes.

When one of the shapes slammed into Ma Sunday and hovered for an instant, I saw that it was a bee—a gigantic, striped yellow jacket. Its stinger went into Ma like a spear, and as the bee flew skyward, she tumbled off her horse into the water. George Bigby was shooting at the monster and missing it.

Another bee swooped up and stung him from behind, hurling him forward over his horse's head. He flopped face down into the water and didn't get up.

C.J. was still blasting at Richard, who had gotten behind a rock. When a bee veered over the water betwixt them, C.J. scrambled up the bank and into the trees. The river was pouring down ragged from the altered clifftop. Richard was in the jets of water. It worried me that he wasn't firing back—either his guns had jammed, or maybe he'd lost them. I suspected he was hit, too—I didn't see how C.J. could have missed.

I rolled over with some pain and tried to get myself into better cover. Now I'd lost sight of both C.J. and Billy. One of the bees hummed over me, its shadow dark across the water's sparkles.

I saw Richard moving behind the boulder. He eased up over its edge, searching the tree line.

I caught a flicker of movement.

Billy Dance appeared on a high rock above what was left of the falls. He raised that fancy silver Colt pistol and pointed it down at Richard's back.

I swung the Winchester to my shoulder, but a giant yellow

jacket took care of Billy. It buzzed across the sun and hit him with its stinger full in the gut. The bee hung there a moment, yanked its stinger free, and zoomed away upriver.

Billy dropped to his knees, that fool grin finally gone, and then fell forward—down the curvature of the rock in a somersault, straight down into the roaring current, over the shelves, and on into the pool at the base of the falls. I will allow that Billy had his shining moment on center stage: he had the most spectacular death that day.

The woods droned with bees, and it was a terrifying sound, a roar that echoed among the trees. Downstream, C.J. became visible on the shore, mounted and riding away as fast as the brush would allow. I just might have had a shot at him with the rifle, but I wasn't inclined to shoot a man in the back. I knew he would tell his brothers all about this, and he'd got an earful of my name, if he remembered it. But that was trouble for another day.

Standing up carefully, I kept my eyes open for any yellow jackets that might swoop toward me, but the swarm seemed to have moved off. As I worked my way across the river to Richard, the buzzing slowly began to settle down. I couldn't see our horses. Ma's and Bigby's climbed out of the water and wandered along the bank.

I guessed my bones were intact, though I'd skinned my arm and would probably have some bruises.

To my great relief, Richard wasn't too bad off. He had a powder burn on his face and two grazes—one along each side of his ribs. One had torn a little deeper and bled considerably,

but we eventually made a long bandage out of Billy's silk shirt
and bound them up tight.

Richard was trying to wrap his mind around yellow jackets that big, and where they'd come from.

I started to explain, but suddenly the bushes rustled. Jim
dashed toward us, his face scratched and smudged. Tears
shone in his eyes, and he was alone.

Abbie.

My heart pounded.

Richard caught Jim by the arms, asking where Abbie was.

Jim pointed into the trees, stammering, trying to say something. He gave up and tugged on Richard's arm, wanting us
to follow him.

We hurried up the bank. I kept the Winchester ready and
my ears open. The birds were still. Ahead, I could hear a gut-
tural growling and a deep, savage barking.

Jim motioned for us to hurry and ducked his head, going
quietly around a stand of wild raspberry bushes.

On the other side, a pair of four-legged things leapt and
snapped, trying to reach Abbie, who was hugging the limb of
a tree. She was about twelve feet from the ground, and the
two dog-craithers were almost reaching her; one caught the
hem of her skirt and tore a shred loose. The things had no fur.
Their skin was bumpy and looked like wrinkled leather. Long,
lizardish tails dangled behind them.

They must have heard or smelled us, on account they
stopped jumping and turned their heads. I saw their piggy eyes
and lots of teeth.

Then they charged us.

We just had time to get our guns up, aim, and shoot. By grace, it worked. The things died so close that we could have touched them, if we'd had the inclination. Wherever they'd come from, it wasn't the world we knew.

Abbie climbed down, agile as a squirrel.

Wincing at his injuries, Richard threw his arms around both kids, and they hugged him back. Abbie told us how she and Jim had wriggled out of the cave and followed their ears to the hive—I supposed they were fascinated as well as full of dread, overcome by curiosity.

I got it then: not Bird Snail. Abbie had said Birds Nail. She didn't know the word for bee or yellow jacket, so she'd put Birds together with Nail—the stinger. Angry, she'd said. Forming a crazy, desperate plan, she and Jim had pelted the hive with stones and branches, then raced back toward us when the swarm came out. Just afore the bees overtook them, the kids burrowed in under some bushes, and the swarm passed overhead, full of fury. They'd found Ma and Bigby sitting in the riverbed, and Billy Dance standing proud on his high rock. The kids had saved us. But they'd been sniffed out by the dog-things.

We found our three horses and were mighty glad to see them unharmed. One of the gang's horses had been stung to death. We rounded up the others.

The dead outlaws were a fearful sight. Frank McLaurel was simply dead from my shot. It was another thing I'd have to live with. The other three—Ma, Bigby, and Billy Dance—were purple and swollen up so badly they hardly looked human. The poison of bees this size would likely kill a man five times over. We laid the bodies on the riverbank and would take them back to Woolpit over their saddles.

The other Sunday boys might get here any time—we couldn't dawdle. But we had to see what had become of the cave. The entrance crack had widened considerably, so that the falls were farther back now, dumping over what had been the rear wall of the cave. We saw no sign of the money bags; if any of those banknotes hadn't been blown to shreds, they were all buried under rubble now, somewhere under a deepening pool, or else washed away. Maybe some fortunate soul would be fishing, miles from here, and see a whole school of greenbacks floating past.

Down betwixt two separate courses of the falling river, a pit had opened up. There was enough of a rubble rim that the water didn't pour into it, but instead came past on both sides.

The passage! Richard cried out.

The slab had been blasted apart. It no longer blocked the tunnel. We all waded to the threshold and peered inside. The deep earth's breath washed over us, cold and pure. From down in the stony dark, we all heard, far off but clear, the sound of bells. The kids' faces lit up.

I don't know where the bell sound came from. It had led the kids from St. Martin's Land to our world, and now it was leading them back, though there wasn't a bell close by out here or in there. Maybe that's just the sound that some worlds' Edges make.

We remembered to unload the kids' packs from Peach, and then it really was goodbye. Richard and I went with them far enough to be sure the passage would really take Abbie and Jim home. We tied a rope around a boulder to follow back, just in case the way was confusing. We also lit the lanterns.

After a dark, winding stretch, the tunnel seemed to be running uphill, not down, and then the chill earth-draft turned into fresh, outdoor air. The stone channel grew brighter— with a rich, green light.

We climbed up over some roots and shelves, emerging from the ground as if coming up from a cellar. And it truly was someplace else, a world all green, with grassy hills, green rocks and mountains, an emerald sky. Abbie and Jim laughed and spun in circles. Now they couldn't stop chattering and pointing, tears on their faces, not needing to speak English at all anymore.

We were on the top of a high hill. There was a green forest, even the trunks were green. Abbie tugged on our wrists and pointed. Far away, light shone down through a rift in the dimmer clouds, resplendent on a bright and mighty river. Beyond it was a shining country where the sun seemed to blaze, golden and warm.

Blow Land, Abbie said fondly.

She and Jim had been there, to that unreachable place. The direction and distance we were looking made no sense, but we'd been there only minutes ago, and would be again soon. And now we were in the Land of St. Martin, where the breeze was comfortable. The kids knew the way to their own

house from here. It was time for them and us to go. They flung
their arms around Richard, squeezed my hands, and dashed
away, their packs bouncing on their backs, two little bundles
of grayish-brown in a land of green.

Richard and I had no trouble following the rope back. We
came out again into the ruins of the cave, where nothing else
had changed.

As we were getting set to head out, I got a funny tingling
on the back of my neck, and the daylight seemed to dim just a
little. Then I felt that strange pulling and compression. Even
afore I turned around, I knew what I would see.

Back in the shadows across the stream, the Craither was
watching. I could just barely make it out—a ripple, a warping
of the light—but it was looking right at me. It *wanted* me to
see it. I stood and stared back. Richard was busy and didn't
notice me.

Weariness swept through me. I wanted to tell the Craither
to leave me alone—it was sucking strength right out of me, so
that I had to sink onto a rock, a chilly sweat breaking out on
my face and neck. I felt something else from the thing besides,
some powerfully unpleasant emotion: Displeasure? Anger?
Close around it, the leaves of trees curled up, withering on the
branches, as they'll do if a large fire is burning just beneath them.

It occurred to me that the Craither came around when
death was in the air: the battlefield, those hills of the cannibals,

and the great Dragon from the stars . . . now the fight here. Back during the War, it was clumsier, mostly shapeless. More like a newborn animal in what it could do. It seemed more defined now, slightly more humanoid in shape, with more distinct limbs, a trunk—like it was *learning* to move in this world . . . *adapting* . . .

But why the rage, if it was rage I felt?

Abbie and Jim.

Was it unhappy that they had escaped? Was it hunting them?

No, that was speculation. I didn't have enough to go on. I didn't understand the Craither, on account it was nothing like a person, not like any craither of this world.

You dreaming, Ovid? Richard called out. You all right?

I'm all right. I was just thinking, I said.

About what? Richard asked.

Nothing, I said.

I turned my back on the Craither and left it to itself there among the trees. I wished it would stop coming around.

Richard and I didn't talk much on the ride to his place, each of us content to dwell in our own thoughts. As soon as I was away from the Craither, I recovered quickly. I saw Richard drying his eyes once, and wondered if he was thinking of the green kids or maybe of his brother, Robert. Maybe for Richard, Robert didn't feel quite so far away now, or quite so lost.

Emma was happy to hear the kids got home, but she also looked sad. She got Richard fixed up better. That evening, he and I took the outlaws' bodies, horses, and what we could salvage of their gear to the sheriff in Woolpit. When he and others saw the corpses' condition, we told them we'd had to contend with some angry yellow jackets, which was true enough. As it happened, a federal marshal was in the sheriff's office, a man named Chervil Dray who was tracking the Sunday gang. The marshal looked familiar—we had met in Laredo, Texas. He hadn't been a marshal then. Dray was interested in what Richard and I had to say. We didn't mention taking green kids back to a land under the ground. We were just two old comrades in arms, riding along the river and catching up on old times, who accidentally discovered the Sundays' hideout. If the law wanted to go dig through the rubble for the banks' money, they certainly could, but we told them to be careful out that way—it was an uncanny land.

There was a sizable reward for the dead outlaws. I didn't care to be paid for shooting Frank McLaurel or profiting from folks' deaths, no matter how notorious they were. When Richard wouldn't take my share, I gave it to help care for orphans. There were plenty of kids, not just green ones, who needed a home.

I stayed on with the Decalnes for a while, doing the hard chores until Richard could bend and lift without pain. Finally, he and Emma sent me on my way with much gratitude, which I also felt toward them.

About three weeks after the kids went home, in the first

days of October, I was in Corinth, Missouri, getting my bear-
ings and some supplies afore I headed farther west again. I
came in one afternoon from a ride with Jack to the news that
the Sunday gang was in town. They'd arrived that morning,
led now by Ma's son Marvelous. I was fixing to ride out quietly
afore they heard I was here, too. But as I was saddling Jack up
again in the livery stable, a cowpoke told me that the marshal
was on his way here; Chervil Dray and his posse had been
sighted, approaching from the east, and the Sundays had got
wind of it. Things were about to get ugly in Corinth.

Well, that meant I'd better stay around. The marshal could
use another friend, and he needed to be warned of what he was
riding into. I turned toward Jack, intending to slip away north
out of town, to circle east and intercept Dray.

But afore I could mount up, I heard the first shots. Leaving
Jack in the stall, I came out of the stable and found myself facing Marvelous Sunday. Away behind him, though I hadn't the
leisure to focus on it, the church bell hung in its steeple, not
ringing today.

Somewhere, I knew, bells were ringing, bells heard but
not seen, and the light was gleaming on the river and on that
brighter place that's not under the shadow where we are now.

The Shootout at Furniss-Wells Saloon
Corinth, Missouri—Wednesday, October 3, 1883
Approximately 2:20 p.m.

[From *The Wild of the West*, chapter 4, "The Shootouts,"
by Jonathan Havilland and S.T. Cox, Fountainhead-
Fulcrum Publishers, Inc., New York, 2004.]

BEFOREHAND:

The Sunday gang, led by Marvelous Sunday following
the death of matriarch Orma "Ma" Sunday, had
robbed the bank in nearby Bartleby and killed young
Abner Millhouse during their escape—the latest
exploit in a three-year spree of robbery and murder
which left sixteen innocents dead. Federal Marshal
Chervil Dray heard from an informant of the Sundays'
plans to lie low for a night at the home of Edward
Tallman, north of Bartleby, and then to move on to
Corinth for supplies. Having pursued the Sundays for
months, Dray took his posse of three men to Corinth,
intending to arrive a day ahead of the Sundays and to
enlist ample assistance there to arrest the outlaw gang.
Unfortunately, the information proved inaccurate:
the Sundays proceeded straight to Corinth and were
already there when Dray and his men rode openly and
unsuspecting into town along the main street. The
Sundays had expected pursuit. With his gang staked
out and watching the road, Marvelous Sunday ate a
leisurely lunch in the saloon, boasting of the reckoning
he would deliver to Chervil Dray if the marshal showed
his face. At the sounds of shouting and the clearing of
all traffic from the street, Marvelous moved to gaze out
through the saloon's front door.

THE ENCOUNTER:

Marshal Chervil Dray and his deputies James Eastham, Hector MacBride, and Charles Lovewell ride into Corinth from the east, vigilant but unaware of the Sundays' presence.

C.J. Sunday is positioned in the shelter of a small, covered porch at the southeast corner of the Furniss-Wells Saloon, covering the street. His brother Earl "Gimp" Sunday is behind a stack of barrels at the southeast corner of the adjacent T. Machlin dry goods store. Their cousin Cassius Evers is inside the blacksmith shop of Thomas Hollis, directly south across the main street.

Seeing the posse arrive, Marvelous Sunday steps out of the front door of Furniss-Wells, two pistols raised. Without preamble, he shoots James Eastham, probably mistaking him for Dray since Eastham is riding in front of the others. Fatally wounded, Eastham falls from the saddle to the street.

Wanting both cover and mobility, Marvelous retreats to the southwest corner of Furniss-Wells, about 15 feet away.

C.J. Sunday shoots at and misses Chervil Dray on horseback.

Dray returns fire with a buffalo gun and kills C.J.

Earl Sunday shoots from the far front corner of the dry goods store and wings Dray.

Deputies MacBride and Lovewell return fire at C.J. and at Earl.

Earl, spooked, flees north and west around the back of the dry goods store.

MacBride pursues Earl up the alley on the near side of T. Machlin's, between it and the saloon, hoping to outpace Earl, who has a limp.

Earl opens fire behind the dry goods store, forcing MacBride to take cover against the store's west wall.

Meanwhile, immediately after the first shots from Marvelous, Cassius Evers shoots at MacBride and Lovewell from the front area of the blacksmith's. One of his shots hits Lovewell's horse, which has to be put down. The blacksmith, Hollis, unexpectedly strikes Evers with a sledgehammer, breaking Evers's right arm. Apparently intimidated by Hollis, Evers stumbles out into the street, fleeing eastward as Lovewell fires at him. Evers attempts to take cover behind a water trough.

Dray, now dismounted, shoots Evers with the second barrel of the buffalo gun. Wounded and with a shattered arm, Evers falls behind the trough and surrenders when Lovewell approaches with his pistol cocked and aimed.

At the beginning of the encounter, Ovid Vesper emerges from the Knowles Livery Stable, immediately west of Furniss-Wells, into the alley between the two buildings. Knowing the Sundays were in town, he had been preparing to leave quietly. Alerted minutes before that the posse was coming, he decided to stay and assist the marshal as necessary. Vesper hears gunfire

and sees Marvelous Sunday appear at the southwest
corner of Furniss-Wells, taking cover from those in
the street. Vesper, his Schofield pistol raised, accosts
Marvelous from behind, ordering him to drop his guns.

Marvelous whirls and fires at Vesper.

Vesper fires twice. Both shots strike Marvelous,
who stumbles, cursing, back out into the street and
falls dead.

Gauging the location of the main encounter by the
sound of gunfire, Vesper moves eastward, around the
back of Furniss-Wells.

Earl Sunday wounds MacBride in the right leg but
is also shot in the side by MacBride. As MacBride falls
to the ground, Earl flees westward behind Furniss-
Wells, directly toward Vesper.

Vesper and Earl see each other from opposite ends
of the rear covered porch of Furniss-Wells. They
exchange fire. Vesper fires three times, hitting Earl
twice. Earl falls but is not killed. The semi-conscious
Earl is apprehended.

THE AFTERMATH:
Cassius Evers recovered from his wounds, stood
trial, and was hanged. Earl "Gimp" Sunday, pending
trial, convalesced in a room on the second floor of the
courthouse/jailhouse in Freeling, Missouri. One Lucy
Farraday, hearing of his presence there, marched into
the courthouse with a Colt pistol. According to a clerk
who witnessed the event, the attending deputy advised
Farraday, "Lucy, you'll hang," to which Farraday
replied, "Then I'll hang for Melvern." [Melvern was
her late husband, shot dead in Trumpet City by Earl.]

When the deputy turned his attention out the window, Farraday climbed the stairs and put three bullets into Earl Sunday, killing him. Lucy Farraday was never brought to trial. She relocated to Chicago and raised her three children, one of whom became an Illinois State Representative.

INTERLUDE

Sometimes when I pondered about the Craither, it led me to think about the times in life when I'd been scared. It seems to me that there are at least three kinds of fear. One is the kind a person can't help but feel when death is about a half step away, when bullets are flying or you're tumbling off a horse or the ledge is giving way; that's the type designed to help keep us alive, on account it impels us to get away from the peril, or get through it. Another kind is the dread of what might happen, when the worst future outcomes flash in our heads.

But then there's a third type of fear. It's the sort we feel when faced with the unknown or the uncanny.

One winter's day, when I was about three or four years old, I was terribly afraid. My mama had taken me with her on some errand to the home of an elderly widow. I believe it was somewhere far away from our town. The house was two or three stories tall, and crammed full of old fancy furniture and figurines and gewgaws. Even as we approached it along a lane, I knew I was going to remember the place, on account it was an octagon house. It was like a big, fancy cake among the trees, painted in shades of dusk and fog on the outside, with two stairways leading up and around at the sides of the front porch.

I remember my mama having tea with the frosty-haired lady. When I'd gotten bored, I wandered off by myself, intrigued by all the objects in the quiet, lofty rooms. Nothing there was like the prairie houses and cabins I was used to seeing. One room led me to the next. There were lots of windows, some of them stained glass, lighting up the rooms in ruby and emerald, deep sapphire and gold. I remember angels painted on the ceiling. I came to a closed door that seemed to be calling me to find out what was behind it.

The brass doorknob was cold, and I was so small it was at about the level of my head. I got both hands on it, turned it, and the door opened with a long creak.

A frigid draft met me on the threshold. It was a bedroom; in the dim gray light coming through closed curtains, I could see a wide bed neatly made and covered with a white bedspread. In my mind, it was a room no one ever came into. I couldn't imagine our elderly hostess ever setting foot here; in fact, I wasn't even sure she knew about the room's existence—I was a kid.

A writing desk stood to my left, and I think a closet faced me on the room's far side. But on my right, at the foot of the bed, was a vanity of dark wood and the panes of three tall mirrors.

All the mirrors I'd ever seen had a single pane of glass. You looked into them and saw yourself looking back, appearing weirdly backward. If you had a slingshot in your right pocket, the slingshot in the mirror was directly across from it and seemed to be on your reflection's left side. Still, there was a kind of order to it, once you accepted that right and left meant nothing; at every point, the mirror showed what was straight in front of it.

But that mirror in the rich woman's closed-off, freezing spare bedroom had three panes: one facing me and one on either side, at an angle. I realized those mirrors could look into one another, which boggled my mind a little . . . but more disturbing by far was that they could see more than one of me.

There I was in the straight mirror, looking back at me like usual. But to the right and left were other Ovids turned a little to the side, not looking at me at all. Worse, when I got really close, I saw what seemed a kind of endless hallway in either side panel—and in them were endless repetitions of me, getting smaller and smaller in the distance, none of them looking at me exactly, none of them aware.

I fell over my own feet backing away, for by then the bedroom's chill had settled into me, and I was shivering, my heart racing. I scrambled out of that room, yanked the door shut, and ran back to my mama. It didn't matter that she scolded me for wandering off and made me apologize to our hostess for exploring her house. I was overwhelmed with relief that there was just one of me. I knew it was all just a trick of the mirrors, produced on account there were three mirrors together.

Still, it made my scalp prickle for a long time afterward whenever I thought of that cold bedroom behind the closed door, that room of silent gray light where no living person went. I wondered if those mirrors were still full of countless Ovids turned to the side, regressing to infinity to the right and to the left, all of them forever three or four years old.

That was how the Craither made me feel—that same unsettlement of something I could not fathom.

Another time I felt it was in the year after helping Richard Decalne get those two green children home. I spent much of 1884 in the desert, wanting to be good and warm, out in the country of the Navahos and Hopis, where I could see things coming from a long way off.

One day I came upon a Hopi boy who was off by himself and had gotten snakebit, and he'd just sat down against a rock to die, on account he didn't have the strength to get himself back home. I figured it was too soon to give up, so I did the usual things, cutting an X across the bite marks and sucking and spitting out the poison, which I know is a risky endeavor and not a cure at all, but better than leaving all the poison in.

I got the boy up on Jack's back and took him to his pueblo, where some folks knew better how to treat him. He was sick for a while, but he pulled through, and he even kept his foot.

Long story short, I made friends with two of the boy's older brothers, who called themselves Joseph and Tallman. We had some high times tending their crops, riding, swapping stories, and camping under the stars.

I remember that they showed me the sacred mesas off in the distance. The Katsinas lived there, they said, on the flat tops. They explained that the Katsinas weren't like people, but another kind of being; they lived among the Hopis for the first half of each year, coming down from the mesas. The Katsinas, they said, brought the rain and made the corn grow.

When I was leaving that part of the country, something made me want to go closer to those mesas. Of course I had no intention of getting too close, on account I knew that was sacred land, and no people went up onto the mountains. But I was drawn to them and had to see them a little closer up—I suppose it was the same urge that had led me to that closed door in the rich woman's house.

I ought to have known better both times. In the hour just after dawn, on the rim of the mesa above me, I saw what looked like a bright cloud just perched on top of the high wall. I didn't see anything exactly, just the cloud. But I felt that same disquiet, that freezing of my blood as I beheld something too much for my human mind. The Hopis were made to live in the Katsina land, to learn and benefit from them, under their care, but I was not.

Jack was on the edge of panic, too, but he kept himself together and stayed steady until I agreed that it was time to go back into parts where we had business being.

I've often remembered how Abbie, the green girl from St. Martin's Land, called our world Blow Land, showing us what she meant by blowing on a dandelion that had gone to seed. Like that, she'd said, after she made the seeds fly. I think she was trying to describe our world of all different colors, which to her seemed a state of chaos, the solid green of things swept away in an ocean of hues that were all disharmonious with one another, everything off in its own direction, disjointed, nothing safe or whole—a scattered world.

There were countless Ovids in the mirrors, off in the cold silence . . . Dragons from the stars asleep in the ground, men in blue and gray who slaughtered each other, people hurting and hurt and hurting some more, and a Craither that was never far away, which I did not comprehend, sucking energy from me whenever it got close.

As Jack carried me under the sun, I said to him, Jack, we are in Blow Land.

CHAPTER FOUR:
WIND

KANSAS, 1886

The wind is what moves out there on the plains. It pushes clouds across all that vastness of sky. It pushes soil, stripping it away, bringing barrenness. In the long winter, it drifts up the snow. It rages, knowing no master and brooking no fools. It laments more profoundly than the sorriest of wretches, crying like the damned. The wind pushes people, too, blowing them about over the face of the Earth. If we plant ourselves somewhere and try to put down roots, the wind makes us fight to stay in place, our heads bowed and our eyes squinting against the grit.

I've often thought, out there in the open, that if we ever glimpse the shape of God, or see His footprints, it's in watching the wind in the grass. The prairie hasn't changed in uncipherable thousands of years. It's a canvas old as time, and God paints revelations on it, like when He stuck Moses in that cleft of the rock and passed by, showing Himself only from the back, for no mortal could look upon His face and live.

The wind had pushed me nearly to the end of Kansas, to

the town of Lennox, and I was digging postholes for a new fence that a good woman needed, for the old fence was in sorry shape. We both needed that fence, Nancy and I, to mark out the boundaries of the corral and the pasture, something to show that it was a farm, a home. We needed something that didn't move.

I knew when Jack and I rode into Lennox that we weren't going to get out of Kansas like I'd intended. First, I'd come at the suggestion of Chervil Dray, the marshal I knew from back in Corinth, Missouri, and from even afore that, when we met in Laredo. Chervil had turned in his marshal's badge and had settled in here as the local sheriff, a position that he'd been welcomed into and that so far had been quiet, just like he wanted.

Nancy Mavornen had lost her husband some two years previous. On account she couldn't farm the land by herself, Nancy had been working as Doc Sheibel's clerk and assistant— she'd been trained as a nurse during the War, back East in the thick of it. She'd been a girl then, too young to see the things she saw, which was every stitch as bad as what I saw; she'd held soldiers still as the surgeons sawed off their legs and shoved their guts back in and sewed them up and cauterized stumps.

Nancy still spoke with a soft, prepossessing Tennessee lilt, having grown up down there in a place called Dark Hollow, though she'd not been back in the South for many years. She was quietly pretty, with long dark hair and gray eyes that some-how retained their warmth amidst the sorrow. Those eyes saw me, which was what told me to dig in my heels against the wind and take the saddle off Jack. I'd plowed the Illinois soil afore the War, and it was time to take up plowing again.

Folks regarded Nancy well. We kept things quite respectable. Until such time as we fixed on a wedding date, I bunked in an enclosed lean-to against the back of Chervil Dray's place, riding out to visit Nancy during daylight hours and escorting her home from church on Sundays.

I kept busy with odd work for whoever needed it, hammering and digging, wrangling, chopping, earning my keep. Also, Chervil deputized me, though he hardly needed a deputy most times. In the year I'd been in Lennox, we'd had to lock someone up for a night or two only twice—once when there was a dispute about a card game and Shoat Sievers made his point with a bottle and then a chair broken over two pokes' heads, and once after some trouble at Grover Sabine's ranch. Nothing that a fine or two and some time for repentance didn't fix. It was a far cry from that time in Corinth.

When she showed me the barn, Nancy pointed to some haystraws that a twister several years back had driven into the outside wall. They stood straight out, embedded like arrows. A few went clean through the boards, and you could see their other ends sticking into the stall inside the barn. A twister was a terrifying visitation, when the wind took a shape that you could see, unless it came in the dark. You could always hear it, its awful roar, and the house groaning and shuddering, things crashing down, and you just hoped your home and your barn and all that you owned wasn't right in the twister's way. For there was no rhyme to it, no wherefore, just a power like no other in nature, and an unspeakable caprice, rubbing out silos and centuried oaks as with an India rubber gum. The way it spared only certain things was an inexplicable mercy, if it was mercy: like how Nancy was left alive if not unscarred, alone afore she was old . . . like how both of us had been spared to come out of all those fields of death back in Pennsylvania, in Virginia, in Maryland . . .

The first thing Nancy's husband had built after the house was finished, afore he raised a barn or the sheds, was a storm cellar. It looked like a little green hill, grass growing over it, with a heavy plank door that could bolt from the inside.

When we came out of the barn, a sickle moon had risen, gleaming and clear. A warm west breeze stirred the sweet corn, making it whisper. I flicked away a June bug that had alighted in Nancy's hair. She yelped at it and had me look for any more and told the bug to get itself lost. Nancy was well used to the hard work of life on a Kansas farm, and acquainted with grief, as Isaiah the Prophet would say. But in those days when we were courting, I could still see the girl in her, a shyness in her smile.

Doves were settling down in the hedge, their gentle calls in the dusk making me think of charcoal, if charcoal were given a sound. It was almost full dark, so I expected I'd best be getting back to Chervil's, as we didn't want to be fueling the town's gossip. Nancy said it didn't need fuel, that it would burn just fine as long as the town was there.

I took her slender hand as we strolled along the lane. We couldn't see buzzards anymore; earlier, we'd watched some circling away past the creek, somewhere back of the pasture. Nancy said what she disliked most about buzzards was how they showed up afore something died, while it was still hobbling. Even then, the buzzards gathered and watched with cold, smug eyes, thinking inside their bald, pink heads, Oh we've got time. Oh there will be death by and by, there will be feasting. Carrion prophets, Chervil had called them once, the buzzards.

On the creek bank beside the lane, a thick stand of salt cedar leaned every which way, full of scrabbly soft noises as the breeze shook it. A big, hard oak stump was back among the stems, and there was still just light enough for me to descry a large heart shape carved into the bark, with the letters J and N cut out inside it. I could tell that Nancy was sorry I'd seen it and both sorry and not sorry that she'd seen it, too. Her eyes misted.

I meant to let her hand go for privacy's sake, giving her freedom to feel everything that the carving made her feel, but she squeezed my fingers tighter and didn't let go.

Jubal was a good man by all accounts, I said quietly. I hear nothing but good about him. Nancy smiled, and we kept walking.

I'm surprised you know his real name, Nancy said. No one called him Jubal except me. He was always Rosey in Lennox.

Rosey Mavornen.

I allowed that was the name I always heard for him, until one day I asked Chervil how he'd gotten a name like Rosey. Chervil didn't know.

So I put the question to Nancy.

All I can figure, she said, is that it was on account of his disposition. He could find a rose in a field of jaggers, and the rose was all he saw.

I said I reckoned that was a good way to be.

She stopped walking and stepped closer, looking me in the eyes. It is and it isn't, she said. See them or not, the jaggers are there. It's usually better to dig them out than ignore them. After a pause, she added, I think you dig things out, Ovid, when they need digging.

I took a breath and carefully asked what had happened to him.

Something went bad in his stomach, Nancy said. A tumor, I guess. Doc Sheibel could not help with much but the pain. Jubal couldn't eat, and he got thin, and he died.

I said I was sorry.

She pulled me close. I held her for a while in the deep shadow of the salt cedars, and then we moved on again.

Nancy was like that sickle moon above us, lovely and luminous, riding high above the emptiness, and much of what she'd been was sliced away.

Were you ever married? she asked.

No, I never was, I said. I farmed with my folks, and then there was the War.

It's been a long time since, she said.

A long time, and not so long, I said.

It felt in some ways like time stopped with the War, that our nation and all of life were like a chord that a fiddler had been playing, and then the bow just slowly dragged off the strings, dropping, the sound sagging into discord and then nothing. I couldn't settle back into farming, at least not right after it was all finished. I had to get out into pathless country that had no memory, where the roar of nature ever fierce could drown out the roar of cannons and the cries of men . . . and where the silence was louder still, comforting and dreadful.

The visions in my head clamored, too, pulling me onward. I wasn't sure for a long time what I was looking for. Maybe this.

Chervil Dray thumped on my door early the next morning. I was up and dressed, on account I'd heard horses out front and men's voices. Outside my window, the light of dawn was like a splash of wine poured into water and swirled in the glass, all rosy and suffused with gold. Not that I'd seen wine in a long time, but my Aunt May had used to have bottles of it shipped from somewhere out East, and she'd put some in water like that for me as a little tad, in a crystal glass, or flute, as Aunt May called it. I don't know why I was thinking of Aunt May as I looked out at Chervil's yard that dawn, with Chervil blustering around the kitchen. Maybe the quiet and the dew on the purple scurfpeas along his fence were reminding me of happy early times when the biggest vexation in my life was a cow that always needed milking and chickens in want of feed and full of determination to tell me about it.

A long time since, like Nancy said. And not so long.

I got to the bucket and doused my head and ragged my teeth with Doctor Eason's powder. The men and horses had come and gone. Chervil said, Sit down here, Ovid. Eat these eggs and biscuits. We got to ride out to James Foy's place.

I was glad for coffee. The rosy winelight slanted in through the kitchen window, setting aglow a delicate stained-glass gewgaw that Chervil had hanging there—the image of a church in brown and white, with emerald trees and azure hills. What's doing with James Foy? I asked.

Some varmint got into his cattle last evening, Chervil said. Killed three of them. Foy says we got to see it, being's it ain't natural.

Ain't natural? I frowned. He sure it's a varmint?

Foy looked mighty queer about it, Chervil said. He came himself, with his boy Vernon. They had to go on into the store, but they'll meet us out there.

Something low and unpleasant started ringing in my head, that unsettling inclemency I had sometimes when things were about to turn bad.

I saddled up Jack, checked my Winchester rifle, and we got on the road to Foy's. As we left the yard, the wind picked up, and the hayloft door banged open and shut, its latch broken loose again. Got to wire that down better, Chervil said—that whoopla will drive the horses crazy. The vanes on the windmill spun and squeaked, like a giant cricket fiddling in the air. Storm coming, Chervil said. Likely to get wet afore we get home.

The early light was a little too red, and there was an ugliness brooding in the northwest sky. Chervil cussed as a gust hit him, nearly taking off his hat. The blue alfalfa along the lane was pressed flat and shivering. Ain't no stopping that wind, Chervil said.

No, there wasn't. Some things couldn't be stopped, and some could be. In a corner of my mind, I wasn't ready yet to let go of those memories I was having, those thoughts of home and the old folks. Something about the wind in my face gave me a sudden recollection of my mother, the schoolteacher, who saw to it that I got some education.

I was seeing in my head a day nigh on forty years previous, when a big, wild, midnight horse named Acheron got loose from his handler at Judge Broaddus's place, up the road from ours. Acheron was supposedly broken, though he remembered it only sporadically. That horse had Hell in his eyes; he had nostrils that looked like they might spew brimstone. That day, he knocked his handler end-over-applecart and jumped the corral fence and burned his way down the road, heading for our place. Judge Broaddus's men came after Acheron, way behind, hollering for him to stop like he was going to listen, like that big devil horse was going to say, Oh, beg your pardon, Sirs, I am being refractory and I shall desist.

I was carrying a basket of washing for my mama. She had stopped pinning clothes to roll a new cigarette, like she did betwixt baskets. I watched from under the clothesline. Through the bellying nightshirts and britches on the line, I could see Acheron coming as if in a dream. First he was at Broaddus's, then a sheet flapped in front of me and whisked away, and Acheron was halfway to us, looming like one of the Four Apocalypse Horses that didn't need the other three.

Then I saw my mama out at the wild rose hedge along the front of our place. My heart about stopped when she went out through a gap, directly into the road in front of that Hell beast. Mama raised her left hand—I can still see it, plain as the nose on your face—she was left-handed, and had a pinky finger that wasn't quite straight, and knuckles already getting big with the arthritis.

At the top of her lungs, Mama hollered, Whoa!

I've often wondered if that horse heard the word as Woe. Woe is what Mama's students got if she ever had to set them straight. I'd gotten a dose or two of the Woe myself when I needed it. Whatever Acheron heard, or whatever he saw in Mama's eyes to compare with the Hell in his own, that horse threw on the brake and leaned on it hard. His hooves plowed ruts in the road and raised a long cloud of dust, and he stopped dead with his nose right in front of Mama's. They stood there looking at each other and breathing, neither twitching a muscle. Smoke curled up from Mama's cigarette, and I imagined some of the smoke was coming from Acheron's nostrils.

I don't know how that glaring contest might have ended—I've tried to imagine the various outcomes—but finally Judge Broaddus's men came up pale and full of apologies. They got a rope around Acheron's neck and made sure Mama was all right, and they led him back up the road. Missus Broaddus sent us a peach pie big as a full moon. Folks said Mama could have been killed. After my initial start, though, when I had time to think on it, I knew my Mama was in no danger from that horse or any other. She was indestructible, and would remain so in my reckoning for a long time.

I let that memory dissolve, on account Chervil Dray was replacing it with another as we leaned into the wind.

I got this ominous feeling, Chervil said, like that day.

I knew what day he meant—the day back in Corinth. I won't repeat what Chervil said then into the wind; he inserted a short and unnecessary imprecatory prayer betwixt Corinth and Missouri, a prayer that was not really a prayer, though I've no doubt it was sincere.

We'd stopped the Sunday gang that day—there was another thing that could be stopped. Chervil said, I should have known when we rode in that the street was too quiet. I didn't see it.

It wasn't pretty, I allowed. But it eliminated the pussyfooting.

It got Jim Eastham killed, Chervil said.

I paused then, out of respect for Jim Eastham. Then I said, Business like that, you don't get into if you're set on staying alive. It could have been bad no matter how it went.

I'd never seen the like of what had got into James Foy's cattle. The three dead ones were far apart, like they'd been chosen with a purpose from among the others—good steers coming into prime weight. They'd each been slashed across the throat.

I pictured some hairy pirate of the Spanish Main, eye-patched and peg-legged, dispatching those steers with his cutlass.

The blood-chilling sight, though, was the chunks that had been taken from the dead cattle—big, deep crescents, the way you might cut a slice from an apple. The best parts of beef were slashed away and missing, the wounds' edges perfectly clean and straight, as if some surgeon had butchered them with an uncannily large scalpel. I couldn't imagine that this was the result of many small cuts, or any sawing motion. The cuts went through bone and muscle with precision. None of us knew what to make of it.

It's got to be thieves, Chervil muttered. Ain't no varmint that could cut like that. Someone wanted the meat.

Truth told, I wasn't sure a person could cut like that, either. It was a wasteful way to slaughter cattle; though hefty slabs of the good meat had been taken, much was also left behind. Nor would the cuts have been ideally choice, as they contained bones and organs. The butchery seemed at once so slipshod and so impossibly clean.

Could it have been the mischief of *the* Craither? I pondered it, and I didn't think so; it might be some unnatural varmint, but it didn't feel like *that* Craither was particularly close by.

Something wriggled in me, making me anxious. I couldn't help thinking of Nancy and worrying about her. Something was out here that I didn't understand. I felt a jitteriness that was also like an ache. Other than fellow soldiers and men with me on the trail, I'd never had someone to protect from danger—not like this.

The first big raindrops spattered in the white thistle around the steer. I had the inclination to ride fast for home, but Chervil wanted to study the ground, looking for tracks or other signs. He wanted to go along the fencerow, sifting through the weeds.

He let us give up after a time, when the bruise was spreading over the sky and the clouds above us were rolling in faster and thicker. Thunder growled. As Chervil had predicted, we were well soaked long afore we got back to his place. I took care of Jack in the barn, giving him a good brushing down while rain drummed on the roof and made rivers in the yard.

Nancy had a fine and abundant garden of vegetables, with which she did spectacular work cooking, and she sold some produce at the store run by Corker McPhee. But a day or two after Foy's three steers got slaughtered, she announced that we were going to plant flowers. June was a little later than most folks planted, but she said that way the flowers would bloom into the fall, when we'd welcome the cheer and color.

It was fine by me. I took considerable satisfaction in kneeling beside Nancy, digging in the dirt, breathing the fragrance of alfalfa and turned soil. We put in marigolds, cosmos, zinnias, sunflowers, and nasturtiums. Nancy got them from McPhee's store in little hard-paper boxes with shiny labels. These flowers need lots of direct sun, she said, but some afternoon shade won't hurt them. We had to keep them from the wind, so we put the garden in the patch out from under the oaks, with the shed on the west. We'd be able to see them from the windows and walk past them going in and out.

Nancy knew I was stewing about those cattle, and she also knew that one of the surest remedies for worry was what we were doing here, scratching in the dark earth and planting something worthwhile. You know all the trees and flowers, Nancy said. Even the wild ones. That's unusual.

I smiled at that. I read a lot, I told her. When I could get hold of them, those were the books I fancied—ones with the detailed sketches of the stems and all the parts, and the names the botanists called them and the names regular people called them. Sometimes a plant or a tree could have four or five different names, like a person, depending on who was talking. I like to know what to call living things, I said—flowers and trees, animals, people—doesn't it seem that names are mightily important?

I expect so, she said.

I reckon those are the best stories, I said, if you're going to put something in a book: the stories of what grows in the earth. They're ones that always end happy. Spring comes. Things grow most everywhere.

She looked at me then with the kind of look I most cherished from her.

We lost our first Garden, though, Nancy said.

That's true, I agreed: An angel with a fiery sword kept Adam and Eve out of it—Eden was lost. But we get it back, I said, and then some. Just a matter of time.

Just a matter of time, she said quietly, thinking.

Sometimes when she was happiest, Nancy would remember something about Jubal, and she'd start to tell me—how Jubal had said a word funny or could never remember something, or what he thought about bumblebees. Then she'd stop, looking troubled and sad, like she thought hearing such things would hurt me. When I figured out what was going on, I took her hand and asked her to tell me the rest.

The Nancy I know and love, I told her, is the Nancy that was Jubal's wife. We're among the living, but we oughtn't lose the dead. I pointed to her heart. Jubal belongs in there like these belong here, I said, pinching gently on her ears.

I wanted to treat James Foy's dead cattle like a passing bad dream that we'd all woke up from. But they weren't the end of it. It happened to some of Grover Sabine's herd, too—five steers killed in the same way over two nights. Sabine found them in the mornings, those same precise cuts. Sabine's pasture was about six miles southwest of Foy's.

Chervil and I rounded up some men and hunted along the creek and out on the prairie. We didn't find any tracks or signs that gave us pause. It wasn't any way a man rustled cattle, and it wasn't any way a known animal killed them.

Then came the news that we dreaded. Out along the west road, the stagecoach ran across a saddled horse grazing idle, and nearby was one of Carl Vogel's ranch hands, a kid named

Luther Miles. When Chervil and I saw him, he was lying among the pink prairie clover, arms and legs flung out like he was comfortable, but his mouth and eyes wide open, and his entire chest and belly missing—the wounds' edges clean as razor cuts.

I told Chervil I'd seen this kid yesterday at the feedstore. He'd been full of vinegar then, slinging two big feed bags up on his shoulders.

Chervil swore a blue streak and lunged at the two buzzards that were eager for us to move on. They hopped back indignantly, just barely farther than they thought Chervil could kick. Chervil waved his hat and called imprecation on them and their progeny. I remembered what Nancy said about buzzards, and I wondered if they'd been here waiting afore this kid had his innards lifted out. I wondered what they saw, riding up there in circles on the wind.

I took Nancy for a good dinner that evening at the Blue Bonnet, what Clarence Chance called his saloon. It was always the best place to hear what folks were thinking and saying, and Chervil liked us to maintain a presence there, both to listen and to set a peaceable mood. Even when the jabjaws got liquored up, they were less likely to be stupid if Chervil or I were around. Folks passing through might have wondered why I'd brought a lady there, among the cards and the other ladies who worked upstairs. Truth was, Nancy and the other women of Lennox could handle themselves just fine, and no poke in the place would lay a finger on them anyway.

It was a fine repast: Maude's chicken and taters and greens. Despite the speculation flying around about what had happened to Luther Miles and what was tearing up the cattle, folks were carrying on mostly as per usual. But men as had shooting irons had them along, and most errands outdoors were getting finished afore dark.

Jilly Pickens was at the piano. The kid could make that piano sing. Jilly always wore a bowler hat with a bright red feather in the band, scrunched down over his long yellow hair. He'd learned music at a fancy school back East and come out here to work with his old man in the milling business. Folks said he should have played in an orchestra. Chervil said Jilly was our Morale Officer, soothing the savages and keeping spirits up.

Around the time we were ready to take our leave, old Ezekiel Smith shuffled in and made his way through the crowd of pokes and farmers to a little table tucked back in a dim corner against the stairs. It was the sort of table I'd often preferred, a vantage from which you could see the room with a wall at your back. I'd gotten much more accustomed to light, open spaces with Nancy laughing beside me and touching and bumping into my arm. Funny how often you bump into a person you like.

Something at the corners of my eyes shimmered as I

watched Ezekiel Smith trudge past us in his buckskin coat. The fringe on the coat swam and glimmered like the edges of my sight, and I knew the quiet ringing in my head was the beginning of a vision. When I got them, it was time to pay attention.

What is it, Ovid? Nancy asked me.

I said, I think we've got to talk to Mister Smith there.

Nancy knew about my visions, the hunches and images. When I got them, I had to be patient and focus until revelation came.

I got up and went over to Smith, who tipped back his chair on two legs until he was leaning against the wall. He squinted up at me from under the brim of his silk hat, which had seen far better days. His face was like a ruddy withered apple among a wild thicket of tobacco-stained white beard.

Evening, Mister Smith, I said.

Mister? he said, and gave a wheeze that I supposed was a laugh. Mister Smith was my pa, he said, and you won't find him here.

You earned the right to be addressed as Mister about a hundred and fifty years ago, I said.

Smith wheezed again, his mouth stretching in a wide smile.

You drinking whiskey? I asked him.

I ain't drinking nothing yet, he said.

Hold on, then, I said. I went up to the bar to pay Linus for our dinner and for a bottle. I asked for three glasses.

Nancy hadn't made it all the way to Smith's table; as usual, she'd found several folks to exchange pleasantries with along the way. But when she saw me coming back, she joined us and slid over two empty chairs from another table.

Ezekiel, you know Nancy, I said.

Since she was knee-high to a barnyard cat, Smith said.

You didn't, either, Nancy chided him. I wasn't around here then, and neither were you—not within a hundred miles.

Smith cackled.

I held the chair for Nancy and got her settled.

Smith watched me pour the drinks. Ovid, he said, you and me, we got something in common.

What's that? I asked him.

He tapped his head and made a two-fingered gesture like rays shooting out from his eyes. We see things, he said. Things that others cain't. It's why you come over here. It's why I knew you were coming. It's why I come in here tonight.

To talk to me? I pushed the glasses around to where he and Nancy could reach theirs. I could tell that Nancy was intrigued. But just then, one of the schoolteachers, on her way out with her husband, came by to chat with Nancy about some bake sale event.

While Nancy was distracted, Smith said in a conspiratorial tone, It's called scryin'. We're scryers.

I didn't know Smith that well. I'd spoken with him a few times, here and in McPhee's store and out on the prairie one day, when we both stopped to help a farmer who'd broken an axle. I knew Smith had been a sailor once. He'd crewed merchant vessels, some of the first to trade with Japan when the ports there opened up. Smith said he'd known Commodore Perry, or seen him at least. Smith flew a flag on his buckboard—a flag that was mighty threadbare now, like his hat—on which there was ornate Japanese writing. I'd heard a cowboy one day ask Smith what the flag said, and Smith said it was Comanche for Kiss My Backside.

We all raised our glasses to one another. Nancy was free of distraction again. She and I sipped; Smith tossed back his whiskey and shook his head with a happy exhalation. I poured him another one.

I asked Smith if he knew, by his visions or any other means, what was out on the prairie killing cattle and now a man.

He thought on it, and he reached up to scratch his head under his top hat. He answered with a surprising question. You ever hear tell of my Windwagon? he asked.

Nancy was shaking her head. She hadn't heard of it, but somewhere, I had.

Was it you, I asked him, who rigged a big sail on a wagon and sailed it on land like a ship? Some kind of a race, was it?

Smith laughed again. He didn't have many teeth, but the ones left somehow looked merry, like proud survivors. It weren't no race, Smith said. My old Windwagon's been gathering dust in the barn for many a year. Lucky if the tarmites ain't et it by now.

You sailed a wagon? Nancy asked.

That I did, he said. I figured if the wind can blow a ship across the sea, why cain't it blow a prairie schooner across the sea of grass? One thing we got plenty of out here is wind. I was gonna have myself a shipping company. Give Wells-Fargo some competition. And I wouldn't need no horses. Low overhead, see? Just some boys to load and unload, and a high time for the driver in betwixt—just me, riding the wind.

Sounds jolly, Nancy said. Did you do it?

Well, he said, finishing another glass. I refilled it, and then he slowed down. Well, the wind's a fickle mistress. She'll beat you half to death and then make herself scarce when you most want her around. She blows hard out there in the wide country, but she's not too good about taking you 'xactly from door to door. Leave you becalmed.

Horses are an expense, I said agreeably, but they're pretty reliable when it comes to it.

Smith nodded. It seemed he was fixing to say something, but then he crossed his arms and looked off across the room, gnawing his lip.

Nancy glanced at me, and I hoped my expression was reassuring.

I been in some empty places of the world, Smith said. Under the wide sky, in the grasses . . . out on the black ocean under the stars, or under no stars and no moon. It gets mighty dark . . . Dark ain't always empty, he said.

I nodded and said, Very true.

But these slicers, he said. There's two of 'em—a male and a female. Smith leaned an elbow on the table, and his gaze was clear. I seen 'em up here. Again, he tapped his head. He spoke in a low voice, though no one could hear us, not with Jilly playing and all the murmur of conversation.

Nancy watched and listened, taking him seriously.

Slicers? That's what you call them? Then these definitely aren't people, I said, trying to grasp what Smith was telling us.

They ain't people. And then, out of the blue, he said: Japan. He nodded sagely.

I raised my brows.

Nancy asked, Did you say Japan?

I went ashore, Smith said. You bet I did. I didn't cross that whole ocean to stay aboard swabbing decks. I was starved for conversation, too. You know what seamen talk about?—nothin'. They don't talk about nothin' but how to run the ship, how to keep it clean, who's on the poop and who's in the nest and when everyone's gonna change places.

With a sly smile, Nancy said, Not about their sweethearts back home?

Smith's eyes sparkled, and he wheeze-laughed again, and picked up the bottle himself to refill.

Could you talk to people in Japan? Nancy asked. Could you understand them?

There was some. Smith held up his glass demonstratively. When you got some of this, or what passes for it there, men find ways to make themselves understood. He winked. Now, that Tokugawa Show Gun, he didn't cotton to us. Not at all.

I'd heard of the Tokugawa Shogun, who didn't like the idea of Japan having trade with the West.

When we come 'round, Smith said, that Show Gun was always showing his guns.

I said, I don't think that's what shogun means.

Now, which one of us was there, Ovid? Smith said. Let me tell the tale.

Let him tell the tale, Ovid, Nancy said.

I nodded and extended my fingers toward Smith.

He told it: But there was one feller that did like me, some crazy coot down along the docks that was happy to show me where to have a good time. He was more like the Tokugawa Show Fun. Yeh . . . Smith's shoulders shook with mirth at more memories.

You know, I cain't even remember his name aright, Smith said. Kitchy or Itchy . . . something like that. There was more to it, I think. He told me how to say friend: Tom O'Datchee. Anyway, he used to tell me about ghosts. Japan is full of them, you know. Ghosts . . . and ghost can mean a lot of things. Sometimes what we'd call a monster, they'd call a ghost.

Are you telling me we've got Japanese monsters or ghosts here in Lennox? I asked him. Did you bring them back with you?

He studied me, looking very sober. They got the wind in Japan, too, up in the mountains. Sharp winds that twist around the corners and shiver the bamboo. Sometimes, when someone's out alone, out in the quiet places, the wind will just cut him.

Nancy looked uneasy. Cut him? she asked.

Cut him, like with a sword. A big gash will open on a man's arm, or across his chest . . . or his face. Only nothing is there. Just the wind. They call it the Comma Tachi. It means the sickle-weasel. Smith turned his shaggy head and seemed to be looking out through the wall of the Blue Bonnet, out into the night. He said, Out there, Ovid, we got big wind. What we got here, these slicers, are a far sight bigger'n weasels.

I sat back and finished my drink. I'd been hoping for an answer, and Smith seemed to have one. If I trusted my own visions, it seemed I ought to give Smith's the benefit of the doubt. Folks don't begin to fathom what all is close by but hidden. It's better that they usually don't know.

Smith continued: I'll tell you the real reason the Windwagon is sitting in my barn full of mouse nests. This is gonna sound clabbered to you.

The clabbered starts now, does it? I asked.

This world we live in . . . Smith said. It ain't just one world. There's a mess of unseen worlds, all taking up the same space, more or less. But they ain't all moving at the same speed. We go fast enough, or slow enough, and we start to see into different ones.

That sounded reasonable enough. I knew a person could go slower than standing still; I'd known folks who could slow down their own breathing, the coursing of their blood. They did it to get into other kinds of reality.

Like a different vibration, Smith said. He pointed at Jilly. Like how the high keys on that pie-anner sound different from the low keys. When we go faster than we ever go, we begin to *catch up* . . . We start to see . . .

Like we go up an octave, Nancy said, still thinking about the piano.

Fast, I said. Like the wind can blow.

Smith nodded. Out in the wide open, in the wagon, with nothing to stop the wind, going so fast I thought my axles might burn clean through, I could see things . . . After a while, I didn't want to see them no more.

Nancy asked, Did you see . . . sickle-weasels?

Some of what I seen could well have done that to the cattle . . . and to that Miles kid.

All right, I said. But then why could things from that fast place take chunks out of . . . our world? Did they slow down? Why hasn't this happened afore? Why's it happening now?

Smith rubbed his beard. He continued: I don't like to say this. But in my experience, when something big and bad is gonna happen, something awful, then littler bad things happen first, sorta leading up to it.

Portents, I thought. Signs of things to come. Like buzzards that know when something is going to die.

Things get out of kilter, Smith said. I don't know why. Worlds bleed into each other. That's what I seen in my head.

What's going to happen? Nancy asked.

Smith shook his head. That, I ain't seen. You, Ovid?

I hadn't seen it, either. I said to Smith, Tell me about these two . . . slicers.

A male and a female, Smith said: In my head, I call 'em sickle-wolves. They hit three places now—they're staying; maybe they're stuck here. Can't get back to the fast world, though they're faster here than we can see.

Monsters that moved faster than we could see—what a pleasant thought. They'll kill again, I said.

Smith agreed. They're taking hunks of meat, 'cause they're eating. That means real varmints, flesh and blood.

Flesh and blood can be killed, I thought.

If I could get going fast enough, I said—speaking quietly and carefully—fast enough to see them . . . could I put a bullet into them?

Ovid. Nancy took hold of my wrist. She didn't like where this was going.

We might be listening to the speculations of a man who'd been in the wind too long. But if Smith was right . . .

I ought to see if there's something to this, I told Nancy.

You see what Chervil thinks, she said.

Chervil sees the world one way, I said. He'll tell us we've been eating locoweed. And someone else will get killed.

Maybe he could help you, Nancy said.

The fact was, it was dangerous—it was bound to be. I didn't want to ask Chervil or anyone else to do it. Out loud, I said, Chervil's at a loss like I was. Hearing this wouldn't help him solve the problem. But it might just help me do it.

Nancy shook her head. Ovid Vesper, she said, you don't have to solve every problem yourself, alone.

I glanced meaningfully at Smith. Nancy was right: I couldn't do this alone.

Ezekiel, I said, are you willing to get that Windwagon out of your barn? I have to ask you for a ride.

He returned my gaze, uncharacteristically quiet.

That night, the visions reached me. I knew, with the strange omniscience that comes in dreams, how we would find the two monsters out in all the vastness of the prairie. When we reached their speed, they would see us. They would be drawn to us like iron to a lodestone. The monsters in my head were blurry, but I saw they were like no other beasts I knew. They ran on four legs, hairy and vaguely like wolves but much larger.

Sickle-wolves.

Something about their forelegs looked unnatural . . . The vision darkened, fading.

A male and a female. Lightning in the sky. They ran in howling winds ahead of a great black mass of storm.

I let Chervil know I was going up to see Ezekiel Smith at his place northeast of Lennox, in case he needed me in a hurry. I didn't tell Chervil much beyond that. I figured I'd better move quickly, afore someone else turned up dead.

It was hard taking leave of Nancy. She knew Smith and I could get ourselves killed. If a rotted, rickety Windwagon itself weren't hazardous enough, it might just put us eye to eye with what had slashed up Luther Miles.

I hoped I wasn't saying goodbye for long or for good. On the fine June morning, we walked under the oaks and along the ravine at her place, where the pale blue butterfly pea and milkweed grew. Stone outcrops above the stream sprouted with white puffballs. Some scent reminded me of the side room at McPhee's where Corker kept the seeds and had herbs drying. I liked that Nancy's piece of ground had this variety: a stream that sparkled and chattered, some dark hollows and old, thick trees. Such places were a relief in Kansas, where most everything was wide open and the land had no secrets.

My mama loved it down there, Nancy said, looking into the hollow, by the stream. It was Mama's special place, a little bit of Dark Hollow.

She was here? I asked, trying to figure how that could be.

She came out with Jubal and me, Nancy said. Jubal promised her a holler, and here it was, amidst all this grass. Mama was happy here . . . happier than she'd been since my papa died. Nancy seemed on the verge of tears. I haven't shown you their graves, she said.

Not yet, I said. I want to see them.

They're in the cemetery, she said. Side by side.

I wanted time. Time to go there with Nancy and see the graves. Time to hear every story she had to tell me . . . but there wasn't time today.

She wore a cotton dress the color of lilacs, with a print of tiny blossoms. I pulled her close in the shade. She had her hair tied up in loose knots, but locks of it were coming free and falling around her face.

Ovid, she said urgently, I want to get married in August.

That was coming fast, but I reckoned it ought to work. There wouldn't be many folks traveling from far away, not too many letters to write. Our folks were all gone, and we had enough friends nearby to fill the church and make it a lively day.

Weather'll be at its warmest, I said, which I meant as a good thing.

Mama's and Papa's birthdays were both in August, she said. The fifth and nineteenth. And I want us to be married before it turns cold, so you can keep me warm when it does.

We kissed for a long time, the trees sighing each time the breeze picked up and the stream murmuring on. The weathervane swung around with a squeak, and out in the light, the wind stirred the filaree with its feathery leaves and its flowers like pale lavender stars.

To make it an official promise, I got down on one knee and kissed her hand. August, I said.

She wanted to laugh, and she wanted to cry, mad at my stubbornness and happy and just plain worried. Get up, she said, tugging me to my feet. Now you listen to me, Ovid. You get yourself back here. I mean it. She kissed me again.

I knew we were both thinking of Smith's words, his suggestion that the sickle-wolves had appeared as a portent of something more awful that was going to happen. And I was thinking of my dream in the night. Maybe I should have thought about it harder.

A field mouse ran for cover as Ezekiel Smith slid open the shrieky door of his spidery barn. Like most farms, his place had outbuildings that were added over the decades, and none of the barn's stalls matched, all reinforced with odd lumber—a project of generations, maybe of different families. I'd seen a big round floor of cobbles behind the barn and thought, Once there was a silo here—it sounded like a poem. One outer wall of the barn was so covered in vines that the hatch windows were sealed shut. There were no horses inside; Smith had a newer one for them and his mules. This one housed only the Windwagon, and a big gray tomcat that looked irritated at the flood of daylight. The close air smelled rich with time—fermented air, laced with the essences of wood, of old manure and straw.

It wasn't too hard to push the wagon across the yard to the edge of the empty field. It was a little smaller than I'd imagined. When we got it out into the open, we walked all around it, checking it over. The wagon looked sound enough to me. There were no rotten boards, no rust on the metal parts. I began to see how it worked, and how he could keep it indoors.

First, it had long outrigger spars on both sides, in the wagon's middle. These were jointed and hinged, folded up against its sides like a nesting bird's wings. When we got them fully extended, he fastened them straight with splints of iron secured by steel bolts straight through the spars. Out at the end of each spar were three more wagon wheels. I had wondered what kept the Windwagon from flipping right over when the first crosswind hit the sail; these ought to do it. A long spar slid from underneath the wagon, pointing straight out in front, where a team of horses would go ordinarily. It had a heavy steel wheel with a wide, flat rim out near the tip, and another about halfway back. This prow spar would keep the wagon from upending over its front.

The mast was made of separate pieces, too, raised by an elaborate pulley system. One man could hoist the sections one by one, but it was better with both of us pulling the rope. Smith crawled up a ladder and locked the sections together with more braces and bolts. Then we carried the mainsail and the jib out of the barn and checked them. Mice had shredded up one edge of the jib's corner, but it wasn't too bad; it helped that Smith had rolled them up tight when he put them away. He had to correct his work only a few times when he hooked it all up, with the ropes and pulleys connecting his tiller. It had been years since he'd assembled the thing, but he'd designed it himself and then used it a lot in those months long ago when he'd raced over the plains in this contraption.

It was getting on toward noon when we were about ready to set off. Jack had a good corral to graze in, plenty to eat and plenty of water. I nuzzled his face and patted his neck, telling him not to worry, and I'd try to get back soon in one piece. Smith was just putting a foot on the wagon's step when he thought of something and tramped off to his other barn.

He came back with two flags—the tattery one from his buckboard wagon with the Japanese writing on it, and another that looked in better shape. It wasn't new, either; its writing was more complex but shorter, just two complicated symbols. I helped him fix them to the flagstaffs above the corners of the wagon's seat.

What do they really say? I asked him. And don't tell me it's Drink My Piss in Comanche.

Smith hooted at that one. This here one that I fly all the time says Thanks for Looking After Me.

It says that on a flag? I asked.

That's how we gotta live, Ovid. Take care of others, and know they're taking care of us. Let's go take care of Lennox and fix what ails it.

All right, I said. What about that other one?

This here one is short and simple, and I guess it's right for this mission: God Wind.

What's that mean? I asked.

Smith hauled himself up to the seat with a prodigious grunting and scooched around, getting comfortable. It means don't fear, he said, and made a swishing gesture: The Divine Wind will sweep our enemies away.

I clambered up beside him and found a safe place for the Winchester rifle.

Don't take up the whole seat now, Ovid, said Smith. Thanks for Looking After Me.

There wasn't a cloth roof on the schooner, nor even the hoops that made a frame to hold it up; we weren't making a long journey. We had no cargo.

Smith handled the controls. He said, I gave the whole system a good oiling yesterday.

I saw several pedals and levers: brakes for the main wagon and for the wheels on the outrigger spars, a tiller for the wagon's front wheels, and a tiller for the jib.

He studied the treetops in his yard. There was a kind of oppressive humidity, a heaviness to the air. We got a pretty good breeze, he said. Get ready. When I start to raise this sail, we're gonna move. Turning sideways, he unlocked a winch drum that held a chain. As he turned a crank, the sail crept up the mast.

Sure enough, the wind caught the sail like a giant kite, and with a bump and a squeak and a smooth glide, we were rolling out of the yard and into the pasture. Smith steered with one hand as he cranked with the other, the sail steadily rising. I couldn't hold in a laugh. We were moving under wind power.

Hoo, hah! Smith hollered. It's down to the sea and a barrel of your finest!

We left Smith's yard with the wind behind us—he knew what he was doing. Out in the open, he brought us around and headed into the wind, just like a sailor could do in a boat; he had to tack back and forth in long arcs, letting that wind push us across its face one way, then the other. We rose and dipped with the contours of the land, just like ploughing over ocean waves.

Gigantic white clouds were piled in the sky, slowly morphing. Gaillardia flowers bobbed in vibrant red-and-yellow sprays like little suns. I told Smith that the Kiowa say those flowers are good luck. He said we'd need that.

Smith laughed and carried on as the joy of it came back to him. I could tell he reckoned he'd had the Windwagon put away in the barn for too long. Notwithstanding what frights might be out in the wind, there was exhilaration in this mode of travel that was nothing like riding a horse. There was no rumble of a train, no smoke of an engine, no steel rails controlling where we went. There was no team of horses we had to think about and not wear out. It was effortless—just the bellying sail and the jib swinging to and fro, the wash of grass past the wheels, that grand unbroken sea where some unseen spirit danced afore us and beside us, parting the grass with fantastic feet.

We rolled through hairy buffalo grass, goat grass, a current of giant foxtail flowing in like a river joining the sea. We raced right into the waves of big bluestem, taller than a man in some places.

Only way to ride! Smith hollered, guiding us along a rise, heading deep out into the plains. In all the tacking, I began to lose my sense of direction with the sun so high. If we got lost, I figured we'd find our way back eventually.

Smith started quoting Scripture: Your eyes will see the land that is very far off, he said. Your heart will meditate on terror. Where's he who counts his towers?

Where's that from? I asked.

Book of Isaiah, he said. A place in which no galley with oars will sail, nor majestic ships pass by! He laughed and swung the tillers, bringing us back across the wind. I don't know if he was laughing at the ride or at the joy of words from the Good Book, or maybe those were bound up together. The wind was music, the voice of the desolate and lovely places where grass stems and flowers without number sprang up and drank the sun and died, their seeds going back along the breeze and into the soil to sprout up again. Where is he who counts his towers? There was no counting out here, no time, no construction of man or human habitation.

There the majestic Lord will be for us, Smith proclaimed. A place of broad rivers and streams!

Rivers of grass, streams of air, floods of light, and always the wind.

I filled my lungs and hung on to the seat, hung on to the sideboard, feeling frail as a moth in the face of such vastness and speed, yet feeling also like a giant, or like that tad in the old fairy tale, striding across the land in his seven-league boots.

We soared over the brow of a ridge and came upon a miraculous sight. Ranged out afore us, dark against the grass, was a herd of buffalo, which started running in the direction we were going, as if the sight of us made them want to run. Golden sunlight gleamed on their horns, their great shaggy backs.

I told Smith that I'd thought they were all gone from these parts. He agreed that they mostly were. Not many of the big shaggies left, he said, steering so as not to catch any of them with our spars. This might be the very last of 'em in Kansas, he said. You're looking at the Last West.

Some of the buffalo raised their huge heads and watched us as we careened through their midst and outdistanced them. Maybe they figured they were seeing a miracle, too.

You sure we're still in Kansas? I asked, to which Smith only laughed.

All right now, he said, pulling his battered silk hat down tighter and starting a long, gradual arc. You ready for this, Ovid? You ready to run with the wind?

Ready as a mortal ever is for anything, I said. I was conscious of the pops and creaks of the Windwagon, of the fact that it was a contraption of boards and nails—nothing at all against the force of the wind. It was entirely possible that our fellow pilgrims on Earth would never see a trace of us again.

We hung there a moment, almost motionless in the turn. Your heart will meditate on terror.

Smith brought us about, and now the wind was full at our back. The sail and the jib stretched taut. The forward spar bent low, pressed down hard; even with its length holding us, our tail end felt light.

We picked up speed, the wagon shuddering, the grasses whisking by. I imagined us setting the grass on fire as we blazed across the plain.

Smith commenced to singing some old hymn, but I couldn't register words then. Besides, I think his words and his tune were five miles behind us by the time they cleared his mouth. I wasn't sure the human constitution could survive such speed. It seemed I had no breath. Could the heart beat? Could the blood find its way?

Even the light seemed to change.

Then I began to glimpse it, that other world Smith had spoken of, those things that moved on a faster vibration. I can't describe any of it well now—it has faded over the years like a dream fades in the morning, and I'm not sure what was vision, what was there, and what might be altered by my memory of other strange things I've seen since.

Shadows fell across us from living craithers that towered over us, so big I could only see their bellies, like the sky, so big their legs were the pillars of the world. There were things without shapes, presences that seemed only swatches of color in the air, globes of brightness with wings, spiral beasts with uncountable feet, hoops within hoops, skittering in many directions all at once.

I wondered if that Craither from Antietam was out here—could it move this fast, or faster? And what would it look like now?

Just when I thought I couldn't stand the sight of it all any longer, Smith worked the tillers, and we veered off the wind and began to slow down. We didn't come anywhere near stopping, but we moved at a fathomable speed again, and the Windwagon was still in one piece. The world as I knew it began to look more substantial.

Now he believes, Smith hooted, talking about me as if I were some third person. No more Doubting Thomas! Now he knows.

My heart was pounding, my hands gripping so tight that the knuckles were white and they ached. I unclenched and gave them a shake.

But we could see something that concerned us. A darkness roiled along an edge of the sky, very real—a summer storm blowing up quick. Lightning filled the clouds, a black wall far away but racing toward us.

That don't look good, Smith said. Thought I could smell that afore we set out.

I remembered that weird humidity in the barnyard.

Which way's it heading? I asked.

Toward Lennox, he said. Might help us out, though—the wind'll be picking up. We got to keep moving fast now. We done kicked over the slop bucket. Those sickle-wolves seen us pretty clear, I reckon. They'll be coming. You best have that rifle ready.

The thought of another run with the wind scared me as much as it thrilled me—I felt like all my insides were squashed. But worse would be sitting and waiting, knowing those sickle-wolves were barreling toward us, fixing to slash us like they'd done Luther Miles.

I hoped I'd see Nancy again. But then there was no more time to hope or wonder. Smith brought us about, and again the sails bulged out and we went like a greased lightning bolt. It seemed to me that if we'd hit a rock just wrong, if we'd come to just the wrong dip in the ground, there'd be nothing left of us but wooden splinters for ten miles, and maybe a silk hat coming down out of the sky in the Rockies, an old, tattered flag caught on a fencepost in San Antonio saying, in Japanese, Thanks for Looking After Me.

There they are, Smith said.

As the world shifted again—the plains becoming not quite the plains we knew—as weird shapes strode across the distance, I saw two wild beasts running, fearsome and powerful, pounding over the grasses in a blur, zigzagging, each crossing the other's path as they angled toward us. I had no doubt that these were the sickle-wolves. Hooking out sideways from the joints of their forelimbs were curving, wicked blades of bone. These craithers had razors growing out of their skeletons. They had broader heads than wolves, jaws sprouting with pointed teeth. And the biggest natural wolf wouldn't have come up to their shoulders.

As they veered toward us, I sighted and fired the Winchester, guessing that shooting at this speed would take some learning.

I could almost see the bullet in the air—maybe it was my imagination, but that bullet seemed to spin out slow from the bore and drop away to the left as we all outran it. Did I feel it ricochet off the lateral spar behind me? I chambered and shot twice more, taking care not to shoot straight out in front of us for fear of what might happen.

I glanced at Smith in vexation, beginning to think the rifle wasn't going to do any good.

One of the sickle-wolves leapt straight over the forward spar and streaked away to our right.

I lost track of the other one and looked all around, having the eerie sense that it might be straight under the Windwagon, or maybe pouncing right now, unseen.

Then an impact shuddered the seat. I turned around to see the wolf—the big, silver-coated male—scramble right up into the back of the prairie schooner.

Smith hollered into my ear. He fought to keep the tiller steady.

I saw that sickle-wolf's massive paws gouging furrows

in the wagon bed as he struggled for purchase. Then he was up in the bed, completely filling it, bulging over its sides, his nightmarish head rising behind us, and his forelimb coming up, bringing his bone-sickle to bear.

But I had the Winchester's barrel right in that feral face, and this time our trajectory was on my side.

The shot shattered that wolf's skull. He let out one choking yip and tumbled, spraying blood. I hit him with a second bullet as his huge gray shape rolled and slid off the wagon back, into the grass.

Smith whooped, That's one! and thumped me on the back.

As I held on and looked around for the female, my hat went flying away. Smoke was rising from the wagon's axles. I searched the grasses, which grew darker and darker. Something was blocking the light, swallowing it up.

Then I saw what it was. Black clouds churned. Rain and hailstones stung our faces, sizzled across our chests—not falling on us. We were crashing straight through them, the raindrops and hailstones, which seemed to hang suspended in the air.

Smith let out a wordless cry.

Ahead of us, glowering and writhing, was a twister—far bigger than any I'd seen, and I'd seen some. It was like a colossal tree betwixt Earth and Heaven, winding, its base a livid haze of destruction. More twisters around the big one, like its unwholesome children hatching, came snaking down out of the clouds, looking at first like loose ropes reaching for the land, groping downward, finding the earth, gaining substance and power, darkening until they could drink light from the air.

Smith's top hat sprang away and shot toward the cyclone.

We couldn't speak. There was no voice but the voice of nature, the endless and elemental roar.

Smith tried to move the tiller, but it wouldn't budge. The wind had hold of us, and we were at its mercy. He struggled with the winch, attempting to lower the sail, but the wind wouldn't have it; unmeasurable tension held the sail up.

The jib tore away, pieces of its rigging and its lines spinning free, lost in the tempest. I heard the prow crack, its braces warping as the wind forced it hard against the ground. Our wheels couldn't turn fast enough; we were skating, outpacing their spin.

Now I saw the female sickle-wolf charging ahead of us, leading us straight into the midnight vortex. I knew she was cunning, leading us to our doom. She knew we could no longer turn aside. But neither could she. Her paws slid. Her sickle-bones sliced the prairie, and her legs splayed out. Then she was flying, howling, though I could not hear her, trapped in the elements of our slow and unforgiving world. The twister sucked her in.

Beside me, Smith laughed, a soundless wheeze, and gripped my shoulder. He gave my back a thump, grinning through his thicket of white beard. He took his hand off the tiller then, his feet off the pedals, and leaned back, arms stretched out, inhaling the thin air—happy with the land and the day the Lord was showing him.

I saw the Craither then, the one that had followed me since the War. It was just barely visible, right at the foot of the twister. Mostly I saw the two glittering eyes. It was very still, watching us. The maelstrom didn't affect or concern it in the least.

The prairie grass dropped away below us, our wheels no longer on the earth. I thought of Nancy and fixed my gaze on her gray eyes and felt the touch of her warm hands in mine.

I don't know how I survived. I reckon it just wasn't my time to go yet. All I know is that I opened my eyes and found myself looking up into a clean sky just past dawn, with the sun warming up a golden mist. I was in a patch of twistflower, the dark purple blossoms opening up among fiddle-shaped leaves, and the high bluestem grass all around me—grass as far as I could see. The breeze was calm, and the whole world smelled like a garden, its pathways neatly swept.

I was lying atop the barrel of the Winchester, which dug into my back. I'd have to clean that rifle out well—hard telling what dirt had gotten into the bore. I still had the Schofield pistol in its holster.

There was no sign of Smith or the Windwagon. I contemplated briefly whether I might be in Heaven, but I figured if I were, I wouldn't be bruised and sore and gouged up from hailstones and flying grit.

I've had a long time to think about that wild ride and the man I rode with. You may have heard stories about Windwagon Smith, and I guess I had a lot to do with getting them started when I told folks what had happened. It always made me smile when, later on, I'd hear about him in some far-flung place and wonder just how the tale had got there. As far as I know, no one ever saw the man again. That legacy would have given him glee.

I had a great dread in me of what I'd find when I made it back to Lennox. Smith had said the storm was headed that way. It took me about three days of walking. I knew the compass directions from the sun and stars, but I didn't know where I was. I found some sand plums and a few yucca flowers to eat, and there was water from a spring on the second day. Finally I came to a trail and caught the attention of a farmer in a buckboard, heading for Lennox to check on his cousin. He'd heard that the cyclone had hit Lennox hard. That soul was kind enough to give me water and take me the rest of the way and to drop me where the lane ran out to Nancy's place. With a wave, the farmer went on toward his cousin's farm. I hope he found relief and not sorrow.

My heart sank as I saw some trees down, fences broken or vanished altogether. I ran the rest of the way, praying. Nancy's house and barn were gone. The gray and the chestnut mares she kept were grazing in a fenceless pasture, doing all right, and another horse I didn't recognize. There was also a buggy that wasn't Nancy's lying on its top, its wheels in the air.

But there was nothing left of the two sheds or even the storm cellar that Jubal had built, that green swell of the ground and its brick dome beneath the soil. I'd never seen a storm cellar destroyed by a storm. But it was just a big hole in the ground now, a foundation and a packed-earth floor, and bricks scattered all the way down to the creek. I felt numb as I stared down into it.

I hoped Nancy hadn't been home. Maybe that was it. With the storm coming, she would have worried about someone in town, maybe Lou Ella Pearce or Grannie Merton. It was like Nancy to worry and rush off to make sure folks were safe. But then why were Nancy's horses here? Maybe someone came to get her—maybe Doc and Missus Sheibel worried about her.

I lurched my way into town, sides stitching with cramps. I hadn't seen such devastation since the War. Fully two-thirds of Lennox had been obliterated. The school was a pile of boards. McPhee's store was sideways on its foundation, the front door now facing southeast. The Blue Bonnet was half caved in. Town Hall and Chervil's office were an open pit. Boards and shingles and furniture lay strewn everywhere. A Schuttler wagon was up in the limbs of the one oak tree left standing.

Everywhere, people were carrying things, digging through wreckage or sitting among it, their gazes as lifeless as the town. Horses wandered in confusion, wondering why corrals no longer had fences.

I saw Jilly Pickens with a wheelbarrow and was about to go ask him what I wanted to know when Chervil rode up on his horse. He swung to the ground and caught me by the arms just afore I fell down.

Chervil's face was hard and dark, like someone had chiseled another Chervil out of granite. He looked older. Twister come up fast, he said. No warning. We got sixteen dead that we know of. Still digging out bodies.

You seen Nancy? I asked.

He didn't want to answer. I'm sorry, Ovid. She's gone.

You mean she's dead, I asked, or no one's found her?

She didn't make it, Chervil said. I was out on the road by her place, coming in from Ellis's when we saw the twister. The Sheibels were out that way, too, in their buggy. Nancy took Doc and Missus to her cellar. I hightailed it back here.

That explained the overturned buggy and the strange horse in Nancy's corral. So she was home when the twister hit.

Chervil said, I looked all up and down the creek out there and out in the fields. I'm sorry, Ovid.

I couldn't say anything back. I fell more than sat on an upturned water trough, leaned the Winchester against it, and remained there in the heat of the day. Chervil watched me for a while, then mounted and rode up the street. The air here wasn't nearly as clean as the sky out on the prairie. Up in the oak tree, one wheel of that Schuttler wagon was slowly turning like a windmill. Away behind me, I heard a piano key ding, and then another note, and then a few chords. I guessed Jilly had dug his way down to his piano.

Having found a horse to borrow, I rode up to Ezekiel Smith's place. Jack was fine, and mighty glad to see me. I took care of Smith's animals and got them all back to town where they'd be looked after.

I stayed a few weeks in Lennox, sleeping in my lean-to room at Chervil's, waking up in the night, hoping it had all been a dream. I always watched the distance in the daytime, hoping to see Nancy come walking through the heat waves. I prayed she might have woken up somewhere like I had, far out in the grass, that the twister might have laid her down gently, too, and she just had to find her way home. But she didn't come.

Eventually, we had everyone scooped out from under the jagged boards, out of the dirt, and we dug new dirt and put the dead in new holes. I stayed around to help folks rebuild, those that had the heart for rebuilding—temporary shelter and functionality, at least; the real rebuilding would take more time and lots of new lumber. It was good to keep busy, to move alongside people. Even stricken with grief and loss, we were a community, our voices and hammers drowning out the muttering of the wind.

But when that first wave of construction was done, I told Chervil I had to move on. He asked where I had to go, and I told him I didn't know, but I couldn't stay there. I was seeing Nancy everywhere, feeling her in everything, and it was killing me.

Chervil said, I reckon I understand that. But you're depriving me of the best deputy I ever had. No, the second best, he added. Charlie Lovewell was about thirty percent better than you.

What happened to Charlie Lovewell? I asked him.

Last I heard, Chervil said, he was ranching Appaloosas up in Montana. Chervil gave me his hand and said, You take care, Ovid. I hope I see you again.

I hope I see you, too, I said. Chervil, we had us a good run.

We had us a good run, he agreed.

I stopped by Nancy's place on my way out, though there was nothing left of it, except for the trees, so rare out there in the grasses. Most of them had survived, not without their scars and losses—a familiar story. The salt cedars whispered, and the creek still chattered down in the ravine. Out past the creek in the open, the filaree still danced like pale lavender stars. Some ladies from church had come out to tend and harvest the vegetables, what ones of them were left. That was good—folks around here needed food. I'd heard that Jubal had a sister in Arkansas, and this place would be hers to decide on now. I was glad of that, that there was family to decide on it, at least. It would make a nice home for someone.

While Jack cropped the grass, nosing his way and snuffling contentedly, I knelt beside the garden plot we'd put in. They were all coming up now, the marigolds, cosmos, zinnias, sunflowers, and nasturtiums. I gave them plenty of water and built a careful wall out of the debris south of them, far enough away that it couldn't fall on them, to give them some afternoon shade. Some of the flowers would bloom on into the fall, like Nancy had intended. They were ours together; we'd planted them on that good day. They would bloom here lovely and alone, with no one to see them. I guessed that was all right, and anyway it couldn't be helped. I figured it was supposed to be this way, that Jubal and Nancy had ought to be together again, sooner rather than later.

INTERLUDE

At the time of the vernal equinox, when the day and the night were of equal lengths, I saw a blinding fireball in the sky away to the east of me. I knew it wasn't the sun, on account the sun was overhead, descending toward the west at midafternoon. Also, the fireball did not linger long. It rolled upward from the ground into the blue sky and flew apart. Even as it vanished, an enormous plume of flame shot up beneath it, as if the Earth were burning. And then came a mighty wave of force—like a wind, but not wind. It staggered Jack sideways, and we toppled into a silvery salt-bush. The prickly branches weren't pleasant, but they were springy enough to cushion the fall. Jack and I got back up. Neither of us had broken anything.

When I looked again, the fire was gone. Only a weird, bluish smoke spread up and outward, and I saw trees and bushes down, their tops pointed toward us.

Agitation made Jack jumpy. Calming him down, I tried to imagine what had exploded. I hadn't heard a blast, which was baffling—only a *whooooshh* and the noises of things falling over.

Standing beside Jack, I felt something whack against me, and when I looked down, I saw that the stirrup on that side had swung up and was stuck against my holstered Schofield like a nail to a lodestone. I pulled the stirrup loose from the pistol. After a half minute or so, the magnetic attraction faded away.

Images whirled in my head as if a vision were coming, but then my mind quieted down, like when a storm cloud blows over.

I didn't like any of it, but I had to try figuring out what had happened. So I climbed back up into the saddle and turned Jack toward where the fireball and flames had arisen. I wondered if some kind of geyser had burst from the ground . . . Maybe an explosive vapor had ignited. But I couldn't account for the magnetism or why the phenomenon had set my head to seeing things.

The center of the strange event turned out to be over a mile away. Closer in, the trees were incinerated, some of the trunks now just long mounds of ash that the wind was scattering. Then I began to think that a burning rock had fallen from the heavens—I had heard of such things, and seen craters. But surely I would have seen a shooting star as it streaked earthward, and there ought to have been a loud noise, a tremor through the ground.

Something seemed to weigh down the air, making it heavy. It felt like my teeth were ringing, and the hairs on my arms stood up, tingling. I passed the remains of a fence, a cabin that had blown down and been consumed in the fire . . . and lying in the field, noxious and smoking, the blackened husks of a man and a mule, the framework of a plow, its blade still barely glowing red-hot. Someone else had been in the dooryard of the cabin—maybe a woman, though it was impossible to tell.

Ahead, I saw the center of the emanation, whatever it had

been. There was no crater, no fire now . . . just a bare, ashen patch on the ground, from which the destruction fanned out in all directions. I reined Jack to a stop afore we got there. I didn't think it wise to be right in the middle of it.

I felt something then—a rushing beneath me, down under my feet, and I got the odd sense that I could see through the soil. There were lines of light like rivers underground, shining pathways in the earth. I didn't know what they were, except that they represented part of its structure, like the bedrock and the mountains, the rivers of water on its surface. Maybe they fed the force of gravity; maybe they controlled the tides or the winds . . . or gave life to the seeds of plants, or drew baby birds instinctively from their eggshells. Maybe those lines even called to the moon and tethered it in place and swung it around like a sling through day and night. Whatever they were exactly, the lines were powerful, and three of them, running in different directions, crossed under the precise middle of the silent explosion deal.

As I pondered that, another awareness came to me, and I understood a little better—for now I felt again the drain on my strength—and the anger, the mad frustration of the Craither.

Lifting my gaze, I saw it. Straight across the emanation's center from me, far enough out on the other side that it had some intact charred tree limbs to hide among, the Craither skulked and glared at me. It looked more like a man now, with arms and legs, though still with no features but the eyes—still no more than a shadow. It was even more vexed than it had been back in the woods near the cave from where the green children had gone home.

The Craither had caused this destruction—I was certain of it. And whatever it had been trying to do, it had failed. It wanted something . . . something that the power of the Earth-lines could do for it. The Craither didn't care who was in the way of its objective.

But *what*? What had it wanted?

A family was dead here, burned to cinders by the power the Craither had released from the intersecting lines.

And Nancy was dead. Had that been a natural twister, or had this Craither somehow caused it, too?

What I did next was one of my life's most foolish antics. I slid to the ground so as not to put Jack in more danger. Snatching up the rifle, I tore off on foot, charging at the Craither. It's not often that I lose my temper, but I'd had it up to the neck with that infernal thing that had followed me from Antietam and didn't belong here and wouldn't go away.

It was you, I told the Craither in my head. You took Nancy away!

I ran across the center of the weird blast zone, not caring, my feet kicking up gray ash. The soil itself seemed to have turned to ash. I hollered like a crazy man and sprinted onward. Of course it was pointless. By the time I got anywhere close, the Craither had hidden itself, yet still it sucked life energy from me, so that I dropped to my knees, gasping, my hands shaking. Was it trying to kill me?

Somewhere nearby, the unnatural thing lurked unseen. It would keep following me, biding its time.

CHAPTER FIVE:
THE GOOD HOUR

MONTANA TERRITORY, 1887

I went out the front door to find Hat Toynbee waiting astride her snowcap Appaloosa with a second horse in tow, a snowflake, and across its back the bundled-up corpse of Hat's husband, Edward, whom Hat had dug up out of his grave. Hat was betwixt fifty and sixty, an iron rail of a woman, straight and bony and tall. Her Christian name was Harriet, which folks in Dravo had shortened to Hat. It wasn't to oblige them, but she always wore a black felt Stetson, even in camp at night, her ankles crossed in their sturdy boots on a rock, as close to the fire as she could get them without setting flame to her dress.

Mister Vesper, she said on that early September morning, tipping her hat to me, I'm obliged to you.

I took off my own hat and nodded, not sure what else to say as I looked at that woman and her two horses and the parcel of her late husband, with the early honey light slanting through the pines. Somewhere in the branches, a bird seemed to be warbling in human speech: Staaaart up. Start up start up start up.

As summer wound down into fall, I was working for Charles Lovewell on his Appaloosa ranch. He had good, experienced men doing the real horse work. I was not loath to shovel out stalls, to brush and feed those beautiful animals and give them plain exercise. I shored up roofs and fences and laid in wood, getting the ranch ready for winter.

Lovewell knew me from Corinth, Missouri. He'd been a deputy of Chervil Dray's on that day when Chervil settled things with the Sunday gang. Here outside of Dravo, with the Rockies towering across the western sky, Lovewell and his wife, Annabelle, were glad to give me a place at their table and a bunk with their wranglers. Lovewell said he was indebted for the help I'd given that day in Corinth; he said things could have gone a lot worse without me. I replied that we'd seen the grace of God then, and we kept a silence for James Eastham.

Lovewell understood that I was looking for something—something that I hadn't found yet, though I'd drifted far and wide looking for it. He told me to take all the time I wanted in his employ—he was happy for the extra hands. I guessed what I wanted for the present was Montana.

That Montana Territory was an astonishment—not quite a state yet, and I wondered how such a place could become a state; it felt like any star representing it might be too big to fit on the flag. Up that way, the great plains ran into the mountains, and the forests rose in colossal green waves, tumbling down to river valleys and meadows ablaze with color. And the

sky . . . it seemed to me that God had left the ceiling off the
world in those parts, that we were looking straight up at Him.

Then there were the Appaloosas. They looked like they'd
all been standing round when a powder keg had gone off inside
a shed full of white paint. They were spotted and snowcapped,
blanketed, leopard and few-spot leopard and snowflake, roan
and marble and varnish roan, mottled, frosted . . . Some of
their hooves had stripes like a magical shell you'd pull out of
the sea. I figured they had to be colored so wild in order to
show up against the backdrop of Montana.

Lovewell told me with pride that these were Nez Perce
horses; he'd bought the ranch from Colonel Strathairn, who'd
rounded up the herd after the Indians lost them in the Nez
Perce War. There were many among this herd, Lovewell said,
that were living then. We were out by the south corral when he
told me, in the ruby light at sunset. Lovewell patted the neck
of a mottled horse. Who knows? he said. This boy, Billy, is
twelve now. He might've been rode by White Bird or Looking
Glass . . . maybe Chief Joseph.

The thought made me sad. That was hardly a war; it was
more in the nature of a crime, and Lovewell knew it as well as I
did. But the horses were the horses. They didn't have to go live
inside a little circle we drew in the dirt for them in Idaho. They
got to stay and run in this land where they'd been sired. At
least Lovewell was keeping the horses in fine shape, breeding
them so that they'd increase and flourish, and he remembered
whom they'd belonged to.

It was the night when August rolled into September, after

dinner by the fire, that Lovewell broached the subject of Hat Toynbee and what she was fixing to do.

I'd thought it curious that Lovewell had asked me to sit a while after the meal, when Annabelle was cleaning up in the summer kitchen and their four boys had gone off to late chores and bed. Morning started early on the ranch, but Lovewell handed me a cup of brandy and settled with his into his chair.

You know Harriet Toynbee, he said.

I know Hat, I allowed. She'd lost her husband in the spring. They lived in a cabin up north of Dravo, mostly growing what they needed. Edward trapped and hunted, I recalled, and came into Dravo to sell hides and pelts now and again. I'd met him only once, I thought: a giant of a man, what my people used to call a cloudsplitter, with a prodigious silver beard. I remembered when they had the funeral at the church. Lovewell and Annabelle had gone to the service, on account they were friends of the Toynbees, or of Hat at least; it was Hat who came to town more often. I hadn't gone, knowing the little church could only hold so many, and I didn't know those folks well.

It happens, Lovewell told me, that Hat has gone and dug Edward up.

I wasn't sure I'd heard him right.

Hat says Edward wasn't resting in the ground, Lovewell told me, and her conscience was eating her up. Seems she promised Edward afore he died that she would lay him to rest up in the mountains where he was born, in a particular place. Says she made the promise on account she was certain she'd die first. Edward was never sick a day in his life, strong as an ox, and younger than her. Says she thought if it ever did happen, she could cross that bridge then. And now it did happen. Says she held her breath and waited to see if Edward would take to the churchyard with those pretty birches and the bell ringing on Sundays, but he doesn't like it and he can't rest there.

I took a drink of brandy, letting that much sink into my mind. Isn't it breaking the law to dig Edward up? I asked.

It is, Lovewell said. But he said the sheriff, John Springate, had told her, Hat, I don't want to lock you up or make you pay a fine. If you give me your word that you'll get Edward back in the ground this week, we'll call it good. You find a place where he can rest, and get him in the ground.

That's compassionate of him, I said.

Lovewell smiled faintly. He said, Hat Toynbee knows the principle that to get what you want, it's better to ask for clemency after the fact than to ask permission. There's people deserving of the weight of the law, Lovewell said. John Springate knows Hat ain't one of them. She's a grieving widow trying to do right. Lovewell went on: John asked her if she needed help. Hat said no, she didn't want to tie up his men on her personal business. Said she'd take care of it. Besides, Hat told him, the hard part was done.

The hard part. I put myself to imagining Hat out there in the churchyard up on the hill. The birches and some junipers made a curtain along the east edge, so even if she'd had a lantern, Hat conceivably could have worked through the night with no one seeing her. I expected she worked by moonlight.

But the grit it would take . . . even the sexton didn't dig graves
by himself. Hat, alone among the stones and crosses, would
have all that dirt to turn back, enough to get the lid off that
pine box. Then she had somehow to get Edward up out of that
coffin where he'd been for nigh on four months. I didn't like to
think of the shape he would have been in, her Edward, the man
she cooked for and talked to and lay beside through the years.
She must have looped a rope around him while she stood in
his coffin and tried not to put a foot through him and tried not
to leave part of him behind. I guessed she'd used her horse to
haul Edward up out of there. Next, she would have wrapped
Edward all up in the blankets she'd have brought and laid out
ready. She must have used a good many blankets, and maybe
tucked in some herbs to alleviate the smell. Not wanting to
leave her mess for other folks, she'd have put that coffin lid
back and shoveled all the dirt back in there and tamped it
down. Finally, she'd have had to contrive a way to get Edward
up across the horse's back. If it were me, if he were too heavy
to lift, I'd have hitched the rope around him again, passed the
line over the saddle, and tied the other end to a tree or a stone;
then it would be a matter of walking the horse steadily away
from the anchor and guiding the bundle as the horse did the
lifting and Edward sat up, then straightened up like he was
standing, then slid up into place. That's probably how she'd
done it. Yes, that would all take some grit and determination.

Lovewell said, I can see why John would be agreeable to
letting Hat rebury Edward quietly on her own. Better not to

have three or four men grousing about how they had to drag Edward Toynbee up a mountain after he was good and buried in May. John himself might've had to answer questions.

Yeah, I agreed, best to keep it quiet if a person's going to do something like this.

Lovewell looked carefully at me then, and I knew we'd come to it—the reason he was telling me all this.

I knew afore he said anything else what Lovewell was going to ask me. But I had a question for him: Hat says her husband wouldn't rest in the ground, huh? How does she know that?

Lovewell poured us each another little splash of brandy. Well, Ovid, he said, she says Edward's been standing beside her bed in the night. Or she'll see him out in the garden in the moonlight, just looking straight at her through the window. Hat says he doesn't speak—just looks at her with reproach, on account she didn't keep her promise.

I nodded. That was how she knew: nothing ambiguous about that.

Ovid, Lovewell said, Hat finally figured out that she was going to need another person, someone to help her get up to the high country. Unfortunately, she had the bad sense to approach Colson Forbush about it.

My nose wrinkled of its own accord. That was a bad decision. Colson Forbush was here and there around Dravo; I understood he hadn't been in town much longer than I had, and he'd first showed up as some kind of peddler, selling musical instruments he called dorcimers that he made himself. Trouble was, they weren't very musical, these things he built. They had a dull, unlovely tone, and even I could see they weren't glued together straight: there was one specimen hanging on the wall at Robichaud's, the saloon—Jock Robichaud had bought one, but it stayed on the wall except when someone wanted to squint at it, turn it round, twang the strings, and tell Jock he'd been taken.

Finding the dorcimer market in Dravo mighty poor, Forbush had turned next to weathervanes that he ordered as kits and made a grand performance of putting up for folks, a process which took a good two days and cost too much. It usually involved ladders dropped in the posey beds, maybe some shingles torn loose, a broken window or two. His weathervanes mostly fell over and damaged roofs further, or else, no matter what the wind was doing, froze in place with the cast-iron rooster gazing forlornly in one direction forever. He sold maybe a half dozen afore the blacksmith advised him to stop it. From the time I met him, Forbush drifted around town from job to job, doing each one until an irritated boss let him go.

Why'd she talk to Forbush? I asked.

Lovewell shook his head. I give Hat credit for a lot, he said, but she don't always make the best choices. She never wants to put folks out, and I figure she thought she could borrow Forbush for a few days and no one would miss him. What else has he got to do?

He's a strong-looking kid, I allowed. But an ox was strong, and a good deal smarter.

Lovewell sighed and said, Forbush, for his part, was mighty eager to go with her, especially when he heard that Hat has a map she intends to follow up to this secret place, this home of Edward's where he was born and wanted to rest forever.

This all came down the pipe today at Sandy's, Lovewell said, where I was buying feed. Hat was talking to Forbush out front, and he was nodding and grinning. I heard this just as John Springate come up from the other direction. John wanted to tell Hat that her husband's grave had been disturbed—he wondered if she knew anything about it. I loaded up the last of my feed sacks and joined the conversation.

I had to smile at that. Charles Lovewell was the one who could Straighten Things Out in Dravo. I knew Sheriff Springate relied pretty heavily on him, just as Chervil Dray had, and Springate wasn't the only one.

Lovewell said, I told Hat she wasn't going off with Colson Forbush into the high country.

You told her? I said.

I damn well told her, and John backed me up. I told Forbush, too, that he wasn't going with her, and John made that an official order.

But she's going? I asked. I'd thought we'd established that.

Lovewell nodded and looked sheepish. He admitted: I told John and Hat that I'd ask you.

Have mercy, I said, scratching my head. I watched the pine logs popping and the flames dancing in Lovewell's hearth. Well, I told Lovewell, if you think it's best, and if the lady needs help, I can do that.

Truth was, I felt a bit honored. Lovewell was beginning to rely on me like Chervil used to, like Mister Bowdler had out on the trail. Another truth was, this was the sort of mission I seemed born for: escorting a dedicated woman, a courageous and possibly crazy one, up to a secret location in the Rockies. It was bound to be a good sight more interesting than patching the roof of Lovewell's west barn.

Thank you, Ovid, Lovewell said. I'd go myself, but we got the auction on Friday.

You got your hands full, I agreed. He had picking and pricing to do. And time was of the essence. If Edward Toynbee hadn't been resting afore, his condition most certainly was not improving now.

Lovewell seemed to be looking through the fire into something beyond it. Hat wouldn't say too clear, he said, but I think she aims to go up by Harper's Dome, somewhere up there. It's not just wild and unforgiving land. It also has the reputation for being ghost country.

Ghost country? I said.

Witch trees and spirits of the dead. All those things that drunk white men claim to have heard from sober Indians about a place. But rumors of bad medicine usually come with enticements, too. Lovewell chuckled. They talk about lost treasure up there—caverns of gold. That's why Forbush was itching to go along.

Gold left there by whom? I asked.

Hell, I think it just grows in the earth, Lovewell said, laughing harder. Already minted and stamped with Latin phrases. Property of King Solomon, rendered to Caesar.

The logs settled, sparks rising in a flurry. We finished our brandy, and I bade Lovewell good night. He said, I really do appreciate it, Ovid.

I nodded and thanked him for dinner and the brandy and good conversation. This sojourn with Hat Toynbee would be interesting—the good kind of interesting, I hoped, not the bad kind.

Missus Lovewell had insisted on sending me off with a good breakfast in me, so I had come round early. John followed me out the front door when Hat came by. We exchanged pleasantries there. I had Jack saddled up and ready, and I'd cleaned the Winchester lever-action rifle and had it in its leather holster athwart the saddle, and of course my Schofield pistol. The Lovewells had fixed up a chuck bag with food to last us seven or eight days. Lovewell figured that would be more than enough. It looked like Hat was toting supplies, too, and she was armed. We had our bedrolls, and Lovewell sent along a roll of oiled canvas that we could stretch up for an awning in case it rained.

Lovewell told us to be careful. I tipped my hat to him and Missus, and we rode out northwestward, over the stream and past Clemson's cattle barns on the south, then across an open stretch and up past the church where Edward couldn't rest in the ground.

The morning light looked auspicious. There was nothing to indicate bad weather. The sun behind us slowly pushed back the purple shadows, making the grass gold and the pink sky bluer and bluer. We scared up a big, speckled grouse who rose in a fury of wingbeats and swooped away from us in a long glide.

Hat didn't say much for a time. She sat straight and tall, and I guessed she was partly getting used to me and partly a mite embarrassed to have imposed. Not talking was fine by me; quiet was more my nature than chattering was, but I also tried to let her know with cheeriness that she wasn't putting me out, that I saw no burden in riding Jack up into the Rockies in the first gold of September, with summer hanging on but the earliest undertones of chill in the air.

She asked Jack's name and how old he was. I learned that her snowcap mare was named Early, short for Early Thaw, and she was eight—a striking, pretty horse, with a white patch over her hips. Hat had the second horse on a long, easy lead. That one was a gelding called Satchel, six years old, a snowflake, mostly dark with white spots, like he was farthest away from that paint shed when it blew up and painted all the Appaloosas—and, of course, the corpse of Edward over his back, all wrapped up in blankets and tied secure. Hat had him wrapped well. I couldn't smell too much of Edward—just once in a while, when the wind was right.

Hat had a few polite questions for me as the morning went on: where I was from, how I liked it in Dravo, where I'd been. She and Edward had mostly stayed put all their lives. They'd both been born out here—she herself was from Idaho—and the War hadn't changed things too much for them.

We stopped to rest and unburden the horses in the midafternoon. Working together, we lowered Edward to the grass. In the light shade of some red cedar and fir along a creek, we ate beside a patch of white trapper's tea. There was yellow tansy along the water, too. A chunky longspur was out pecking in the tussocks. Clouds of shining white slowly rolled and stretched. Not talking then felt awkward. I could eat and ride and sit beside a man for hours on end, and neither of us saying a word would be perfectly natural. But sitting with a woman and not saying or hearing a word was disconcerting, like wearing a hat that someone else has clapped on your head or having your boots on the wrong feet.

What's that pistol? I asked her at last. This here's a Schofield.

She showed it to me, and it was a surprise. Hat's was a LeMat revolver, that we used to call a Grape Shot Revolver—a gun the Rebs used. Nine-shot cylinder that fired through the top barrel, and a smooth, one-shot barrel that was essentially a one-hand shotgun. You flipped a lever on the end of the hammer to switch betwixt pistol and shotgun. Hat's looked like a later one that used ordinary bullets and shells, not the weird big ones from when they first made it. Where'd that come from? I asked her. She said it was Edward's, that he'd got it somewhere.

We loaded up and went on, the ground rising all the while. When we got up high, we passed through a sea of beargrass, still hanging on though its season was done—tall, bushy blooms on stems as high as the saddles, whitish with a hint of yellow. Jack seemed to enjoy plowing through it, snorting and knocking it with his nose.

Hat had this first part of the route learned by heart; she didn't even get out her map on the first day. It was just a matter of following the rise of the country, of getting us up into the mountains. Jack was used to walking. The climb seemed a little harder for Hat's horses, but we were in no hurry. I'd learned long since not to think too hard about where Jack and I were going, on account it took forever to get anywhere, and I didn't want to spend all my days fixated on places where we weren't. It's far better to look around where you're at, the one place you're passing through in that moment.

I remembered this bit of philosophy by the fire that night, when Hat asked me what I reckoned the best part of my life had been. She got more loquacious at the end of that first day. I guessed she'd decided I was steady, that I wasn't going to balk at a long trail. Or maybe she just felt freer out under the stars, away from the little circles of day-to-day living. The open country can have that effect. Maybe she felt calmer now that we were far enough along to see our purpose through, happier now that she was keeping her promise to Edward. We were going to get him up there, where he could rest.

I didn't have the kind of answer Hat wanted. The time courting Nancy was the best, when it had felt like I was home; it came with none of the anxiety of usual courting, as it was clear Nancy and I both knew our minds. But I didn't want to bring all that up—the memory hurt too much. Other than that, there wasn't any one time in my life that stood out as better than all the others. I'd rather not have had the War; that stood out as being the worst. There were joys and disappointments all the time, and usually there was some kind of work to be done. I guessed that if you forced me to name something, the best times were those moments that came every day, when I could take in what was around me, what was moving or growing on the earth, the way the light was finding and showing it, and what it all sounded and smelled like. It's always seemed to me that God has put us in a glorious garden. We may have lost the first one He put us in, but the one we're in now is a pretty fine suggestion of what it must have been like and of what's to come.

Hat said she'd liked it most when she and Edward were a little younger, when the rain didn't make joints ache, and when the coming winter wasn't such a dread. Mainly, she said, she just liked it best when Edward was alive, when they could sit and talk and be together, watching the same dusk.

Mister Vesper, she said, it's such a short time we're here and when it's all in balance, like a sundown when the whole world is lit up in gold. When our people are here and we know what place we're in. You know? It don't stay. She watched me, her arms folded, her boots propped on a rock, one ankle over the other. She said, I reckon we get one good hour on the Earth.

I nodded, figuring she was right. Even if we lived a hundred years and it was all mostly good, it was just about like an hour—that's what it felt like. I told her that she ought to call me Ovid, and she said all right, and that I should call her Hat.

When we'd first stopped for the night, unloaded, and seen

to the horses, Hat had said she'd start the fire, so I occupied myself with gathering wood. We hunkered down near a big bur oak, with some pine and red cedar ranging along a creek. We each did some of the cooking—coffee, real buttermilk biscuits of Missus Lovewell's that just needed heating, some smoked beef and fried taters.

I kept the Winchester within easy reach. We heard wolves howling, a mournful sound. The moon was not much past the full. Closer at hand, a nightjar churred in the branches, engaged in his nightly hunt, I supposed. We could hear him fluttering around up in the oak leaves. The air was perceptibly chillier here than it was down at the ranch. We'd come up a long way. Hat and I each wrapped up in a blanket as we sat there appreciating the hot coffee.

Hope them wolves don't get any closer, Hat said.

After a silence, I figured I could ask her a personal question, so I inquired how Edward had died.

Tore open his arm, she said, when he was fixing the roof. Probably a rusty nail. He kept working, thinking it wasn't so bad. That's the harm in not minding pain much—Edward had a high tolerance. He didn't clean it up till that night, and then it got angry, and he was too stubborn to go see Doc Clayton. I brought the doc to him when Edward was burning up and couldn't walk. But then it was too late. And suddenly he wasn't there no more. She looked into the fire. Then she said, It was like if these Rocky Mountains just wasn't here some morning.

I shook my head, feeling sorry, thinking how folks could die in such unnecessary ways.

After a respectful pause, I asked her how Edward had come to be born up in the mountains in the middle of nowhere.

That's where his folks lived, she said. His daddy was Alban Toynbee, and his mama, who went by the name of Emma, was an Assiniboine woman whose real name was Under-the-Ground. I don't know the circumstances of her leaving her people and marrying Alban.

I'd heard some stories of the Assiniboine. They called themselves the Nakota or Nakoda, which meant The Allies.

Hat wrapped her fingers around her coffee cup and peered at me through the steam, from under her Stetson's brim. Now Alban, she said, was a bear-witch.

What's that mean? I asked.

The way Edward told it to me, she said, was that Alban was fixing to shoot a grizzly bear one day, and the bear spoke to him. Somehow, he could hear what that bear wanted to say. It said that if Alban would spare its life, it would give Alban part of its spirit and part of its blood, and he'd be kin to all the bears. Moreover, it said, the bears would send him, for his wife, a beautiful princess who cooked with stones.

I thought about that, sipping my coffee. The beautiful part made sense, but I wondered why cooking with stones was to be desired in a wife.

Well, Hat said, Alban let the bear go, and sure enough, within the year, he was hitched up with Emma, and the first time she was cooking meat, she heated up stones in the fire and dropped them into the kettle to boil it. That's the way she learned from her people. And the bear was right about the other things, too—Alban was a bear-witch now.

You mean he turned into a bear sometimes? I asked.

I never heard that was part of it, she answered. But he was stronger than other men, and not afeared of nothing, and he always felt the bears protecting him when he went about in the mountains. My Edward got the bear-witch blood from Alban. He was big and strong, too, and hairy like a rug, and his snoring would raise the dead. He'd have just slept all winter if I'd have let him!

We both had a laugh at that. So that grateful bear had granted to Alban and his progeny hairy hides and the power to sleep and snore mightily.

Hat wasn't done with her story. For their home, she said, Alban and Emma found a place up behind Harper's Dome—a place that was already there, and Alban said it was a gift from the bears.

What kind of place? I asked.

It was safe and it was secret, Hat said. Edward could never remember it too well, she said. He was barely walking, scarce more'n a baby, when his mama died. Without Emma, Alban didn't want to live up there no more, so he brought Edward down and raised him closer to other folks.

Hat could see that I was sorry to hear about Emma's dying, and she shrugged. They had one good hour, she said, like everyone else. Anyway, Edward's mama gave him a Nakoda name that meant Comes-Home. She told him that wherever life took him, his home was up there behind Harper's Dome, in that secret house where he'd been born and lived with his Nakoda mama and his bear-witch daddy.

Hat built up the fire and prodded it, and the shadows around us danced back a little. The wolves had stopped howling.

What did Edward remember about that secret house? I asked.

That it was big, she said. It went way down into the ground, into the heart of the mountain. He and his folks lived only in the tippy-top part of it. And it was old.

A cave? I asked.

No, it wasn't natural. Hat narrowed her eyes, thinking. Edward said nothing there seemed made for people—the stairs was hard to use, the way walls joined was not like on the buildings we make. He always guessed giant bears made it way back in lost ages. Alban drew Edward a map so he could always go back there if he wanted to. That's the map we got with us.

Well, that's a wondrous story, I said. I told her that I was glad we'd get the chance to see this secret house where Edward was born.

Now, fair's fair, Hat said: I told you a tale. Next I want to hear yours.

So I told her about things I'd seen and done, letting her questions guide me. She seemed to relish getting to see into another life, even for a little while, even secondhand. I was glad that we human beings had the gift of words, through which we could give each other a lot.

Hat studied her map the next morning, checking the peaks we could see and the shapes they made, which old Alban had taken pains to sketch and describe. Alban had names for the mountains I don't think anyone else used, except maybe the Nakoda: Dark Face, Big Knee, Stormy Back, Cloudy Knife, White Hat . . . The weather was still holding fine. We spied an eagle, dark against the cornflower sky. After breakfast, we loaded up and headed a little north and west, climbing up over a saddle and down into an open valley full of aspens. Just starting to turn yellow, the leaves quaked and rustled in the breeze, so that it felt almost like we were in the midst of a yellow river that whirred and dazzled over pebbles. The air was clear and fresh, too, like the scent that wafts up from a deep, pure well.

Hat said the land was watching us. She pointed at the aspens, and I saw shapes on the narrow trunks, shapes that looked like eyes peering out of the green-white bark. The marks were where limbs had been; as the aspens grew taller and their canopy shut out light, they pruned themselves, losing those limbs. Being looked at by the trees reminded me of what Lovewell had said, that we were up in the ghost country now.

Deer paths proved useful to us. Animals knew where to go up and down in this steep country. In a meadow, we watched about twenty or more mule deer, big-eared and brown against the green. Some of them were pronking with their heads down, backs arched—all four feet going up and coming down at once, like they were bursting with joy. Hat said, The mamas will be weaning them fawns any day now, and the bucks will be scrapping with each other. Autumn for the blacktails! The notion made her laugh. I hadn't heard her truly laugh yet. It was a good sound.

We climbed again, dismounting to walk the horses up a long, steep grade. Coming to a flat place atop it, we stopped to rest them, and Hat took another look at her map.

Away behind us, a flock of some kind of birds burst upward from the leaves. They were too far away for me to tell what they were, but I looked long and hard at the trees. The back of my neck was tingling, and I could see little stirrings now and then through the firs. I told Hat that it looked like someone was on our trail.

She asked what we ought to do.

There was a big jumble of rocks up the shoulder to the north of us. I figured we ought to get up into the rocks, a defensible location, and wait to see who came up the long slope.

We led the horses up carefully and found a good vantage. I had the Winchester ready.

I said to Hat, You and I both know who's going to come out of those trees.

You reckon it's outlaws? she asked. She honestly didn't know.

I said, It's going to be that ornery beanhead who was told he couldn't come along.

Sure enough, Colson Forbush emerged from the firs, bent low in the saddle, squinting at the ground for hoofprints and scuffs that showed him which way we came. He was riding a strawberry roan.

What's he want? Hat said.

Instead of climbing off and walking his horse, Forbush prodded that roan straight up the slope, cussing as the horse struggled. He was fortunate it didn't lose footing. When he got almost to the top of the slope, I hollered, What do you want, Clodhopper?

Forbush dug in his knees and made his horse rear up like it was standing over a rattlesnake. He went over its rump and sprawled down in the goldenrod.

Hat shook her head, disgusted and embarrassed for him.

Forbush came up calling me names worse than Clodhopper. We worked our way down to meet him on the open flat.

What're you doing up here? Hat demanded.

Howdy, Missus Toynbee, Forbush said. He had an insolent grin, the kind that a kid wears when he's saying I ain't going to steal nothing, while he's fixing to loot your house. At the same time, I could see relief in his face. I guessed he was quite happy to have come across us so he wasn't lost up here.

I come to help you, he said. Being neighborly. You can't have too many helping hands up in dangerous country.

That depended, I thought, on what the hands were helping themselves to. He had a pistol on his belt. I noticed he was avoiding looking long or directly at me. There was nothing I liked about his demeanor, and I'm predisposed to like most folks until they show me I hadn't ought to.

Well, you're here, Hat said. Mind your manners.

Now, Missus Toynbee, he said, just t'other day you were asking for my help.

This is today, she told him, and we got one job to do. I won't refuse honest help, and I thank you. You hadn't ought to have inconvenienced yourself.

He said, No inconvenience, Ma'am. And now, when she turned away to mount, Forbush showed me a sly grin like he was saying, Women, right?—like he thought I was on his side.

I gave him a glare and swung up onto Jack.

Hat led the way, still towing Satchel with Edward's bundled body across him. I took my place behind her, and Forbush fell in behind me. If a catamount or grizzly came up behind us, it could eat him first.

There was something unsettling about this country. Just when I'd have liked to give it my full attention, we had Forbush to keep an eye on. Here and there, white bark pines clung to the rocks—short, twisted trees, ominously resembling human figures in contorted, pain-racked postures. There was Indian paintbrush even up here, its crimson splashes at first glimpse making me think that something had been slaughtered.

There were more places where we found it prudent to get off and walk; it was just too steep for riding. Even Forbush showed some sense.

Hat kept a careful watch on her map and the landscape. When we came around a brushy shoulder, Harper's Dome rose up afore us against the dazzling sky. There were no clouds at all now, as if the Dome wanted to be alone up there in the endless blue.

We spent the rest of the day threading a tortuous course around its feet, where hidden chasms opened suddenly beside us, dislodged pebbles clicking and echoing into the depths. I saw more eagles and at last, just afore we stopped to camp, the tremendous light burnishing the whole country, waters sparkling and ink pooling under its boughs. It was like we were up on the roof of Montana, beside the highest steeple.

Now, that's a sight, Hat said.

I allowed that I saw why her Edward had wanted to come home.

According to Hat's map, we were pretty close to the old secret house, but there was a last tricky stretch like a maze, and we were out of daylight. So we found us a camp at the edge of an upland forest of pine, juniper, and fir that filled a valley like a wide, shallow bowl. The Dome towered straight above us. Back in the trees, a freshet sprang out of the rock and flowed into a pond, from which a sluice escaped by a ravine through one side of the valley and coursed away down the mountainside. We had good water and the gentle sighing of the branches, and enough open sky at the Dome's feet so that we could see the stars blazing in all their glory. The moon rose and cast a silver glow down through the trees and over the face of the rock.

Forbush had some dried beef and beans to add to our stock. We weren't hurting for food. When Forbush went off through the trees to relieve himself, I said low into Hat's ear that she'd better roll up her map and sleep with it in her bedroll, and she heard me; she tucked it in there afore Forbush got back.

We talked about the hairy bittercress growing around us. Hat said it was a kind of wild mustard.

Forbush came back spooked, saying that the whispering trees sounded like they were talking with voices and words. He kept glancing over at the body of Edward, all wrapped and bound up in the blankets. It made him jump when an owl hooted, and it didn't help any when the wolves commenced to howling again, some to the north answered by more to the south.

Them wolves are on both sides of us, he said.

You wouldn't a had to come up here, Hat told him.

Forbush looked up at Harper's Dome, chewing on his lip like he was ciphering.

Why did you come up here, in truth? I asked him.

Well, he said, to help out, of course. But also, he elaborated, there was this feller who passed through once, a prospector. I heard him jawin' with some of them at Robichaud's. He had this map that looked a lot like that one of yours, Missus Toynbee. And he had an old book besides, with some mighty queer stories and pitchers in it. Made me think.

About what? Hat asked.

Well, Forbush said, this feller said his partner had been up here on Harper's Dome and found some big cave that wasn't a cave exactly. It looked like it had been dug out, like a mine, and went way down under the ground. He didn't have the right equipment with him, so he could only go in a little ways. But he come back out with a few pieces of mighty strange gold. Not ore—real gold coins, with funny dents in them like some kind of writing that used dents instead of letters. Forbush said, The partner made a map and intended to go back proper. But he got the gangrene in his leg afore he could go back, and when he was dying, he give the prospector the map and this book he'd been studying, which told all about these caves of the Old Things under the mountains. Caves fulla gold.

Well, Hat said, we're not here after gold, and we're not explorers. We got one thing to do, and then we're going home. You hear me, Forbush?

Yes, Ma'am, he said. But I could see that smirk of his in his smile. I knew he wasn't going to get this close and not take a look inside that secret house.

Now, look here, I said to Forbush. There's no mountain of gold up there at Mister Edward Toynbee's house, and you know how I know? On account if there was, Hat would be living like the Queen of Sheba. Edward would have left her a big fortune. Hat, do you care to confirm or deny that?

Edward wasn't rich, she said, and neither was his folks.

I could tell Forbush wasn't persuaded. He had the idea of gold fixed in his head, and there was no room for logical thought. He was set enough on the notion of gold that he'd followed us all the way up here.

Another thing I didn't like was that the wolves were getting closer. They were calling and answering, and now there were some to the east, too.

We better get a bunch of wood, I said. Build up this fire.

Forbush was too unnerved to go back far into the trees, so he messed around at the edge of the light, picking up little twigs and straining to see into the dark. I saw Hat drag Edward up close to the fire. She wasn't going to let the wolves get him.

Jack was edgy, too. His ears were going back and forth, and he was scuffing his hooves and giving voice to his unease. I wondered if we should take the horses up to higher ground. But we had the fire here, and by the sounds on all sides of us, I guessed we didn't have much time until it came to it. We could only pray that the fire and some shooting would drive the wolves away. It didn't look good, though; this many converging could only mean that they were hungry enough to take us on. Or maybe it was the shadow of the country, this ghost place. Maybe the land itself was sending wolves against us on account of our trespassing.

All we could do at this point was give it our best. I gathered up as many big dead branches as I could carry, and I was a good ways back under the trees when I saw, in the moonlight filtering down through those needly crowns, something uncanny.

All around me, high in the biggest trees, there were platforms built. I knew they hadn't been there a moment previous. They were platforms of logs with bundles on top of them— tomb platforms of the Nakoda. That's where they buried their dead: up in the trees, where the wolves couldn't get them.

I knew those platforms weren't there in the real sense, or not in our present time; I was seeing ghosts. As the branches shifted, the platforms faded in and out, there again, gone again. And faintly, behind the stirring of the boughs, I could hear voices chanting.

Though I didn't see it, I felt it: Somewhere out in the dark, the Craither was watching, and it irked me. It was waiting for opportunity, waiting for something to feed on, like a bald-headed buzzard.

We aren't doing this for you, I told it in my head, feeling my strength begin to drain. Stop drinking me dry! I shouted at the Craither mentally; at such times, I knew my mortality like a lead weight inside me, pulling me toward the ground. Yet there was the constricting pressure, too—forces pushing and pulling on me at the same time, tearing me apart. In this ghost land, its power was purer, more deadly.

Of course, we might not make it through this night anyway. It would serve the Craither right if wolves ate me up afore it got whatever it wanted.

The howling got louder, and I hastened back with the wood and helped Hat make a big blaze. We brought all the horses in close to the fire, and I kept talking to them and trying to calm them down. Forbush had already shinnied up a tree. He was gazing wildly around, searching for the wolves. What he apparently couldn't see was that he was sitting on a Nakoda tomb platform, the bundled dead on it right against his back. Like the other platforms, it was there for a little span, then it was gone again.

You might want to get yourself up a tree, too, I said to Hat.

What about you? she asked.

It would feel like I was abandoning Jack if I climbed a tree, and I wasn't going to do it. Go on up, I said to Hat. You'll have a better vantage for shooting.

You, too, I hollered to Forbush: Don't forget that you got a pistol. When they come at us, you use it for all you're worth.

Aw, Hell, Hat said. I ain't going if you ain't. She drew her LeMat and picked up a flaming brand from the fire and held it like a torch. I made sure I had the first bullet chambered in the Winchester, and we put our backs to the fire and watched.

We could see the eyes now—glowing pairs of wolf eyes, drifting among the tree trunks and up through the shadows by the escarpment.

I wanted to get Edward home, Hat said.

I said, Well, you as good as did. I reckon he can rest here just fine if he has to.

Hat smiled a little. Once the noise stops, she said.

That was the moment when we heard the first of the deep growling, and then a roar that made my scalp prickle.

Most of the wolf eyes winked out as they turned their heads. There was a crashing somewhere in the brush, and a wolf yelped. Then came more deep-throated, rumbling roars. It was on all sides of us, too.

Only one craither made a roar like that. There were grizzlies around us, out in the dark.

I saw the bewilderment in Hat's face.

Branches snapped. Savage snarling . . . heavy impacts . . . and another wolf wailed *Yi-i-i-i* in pain. The eye sparks all vanished. Thunderous roars, brooking no defiance—and the lighter paws moved fast, over the carpet of needles.

Howls in the distance, regrouping, farther away now.

I knew the sounds of retreat.

There followed a long silence, broken only by gasping and whimpering from Forbush, like there wasn't enough air up in the treetop. I could also hear the whispering of the boughs.

We waited to see if we were about to face starving grizzlies next. But we weren't. Of course we weren't. Those bears had come to protect us like they'd protected Alban Toynbee on his forays through the mountains. They knew we were escorting Comes-Home, the bear-witch's son.

I was greatly reassured by the way Jack and the Appaloosas calmed down. Hat looked at me, and we didn't have to say a word. We both knew what had just happened. It was a long while afore Forbush came down from the tree, and when he did, it was apparent that he'd wet himself good. Eventually, his discomfort overcame his fear of the woods, and he went off to the stream.

We bedded down then. Knowing that we were under the protection of the bears, I slept better than I had in a while. I had a bittersweet dream about Nancy.

I sprang awake at the sound of voices. Agitated voices.

Instantly angry at myself for being so deeply asleep, I jumped up by instinct, trying to see what was going on.

Hat and Forbush were pointing their pistols at each other and hollering. For once, she had her hat off, her iron-colored hair in disarray. His pistol looked like a Smith & Wesson 3. The strawberry roan had its blanket and saddle set on its back but not cinched up. That fact told me that Forbush had meant to make off quietly, cinching it properly when he was well out of earshot. Forbush had Hat's saddlebag at his feet, and the Appaloosa Satchel had a bridle on with the lead looped around the roan's pommel. So he'd meant to steal Satchel.

I regretted jumping to my feet. The Winchester was on the ground beside where I'd been lying, as was the Schofield in its holster. I glanced down at them, but Forbush swung his pistol toward me, yelling at me not to move.

I caught him making off, Hat said. Trying to slither away. She kept the LeMat trained right on Forbush, who held his pistol wavering back and forth betwixt us. Even if I moved fast, I might not get the Schofield in my hand fast enough. If I tried it, I'd be giving him reason to shoot me. So I stood there and asked Forbush what he was doing.

I'm just leaving quiet, he said. Borrowing this horse, which I'll send back to you, Missus Toynbee.

No, you ain't, she said. You ain't doing that. She thumbed the lever from bullet to the shotgun barrel.

I put it together. Forbush was going after the gold he thought was up there in the secret house, and he didn't want to divide it with us—didn't want us in his way at all, now that he was essentially on the doorstep. He was purloining Hat's saddlebag on account he thought the map was inside it, and he wanted the extra horse to load with all the gold he believed he was going to scoop up.

You want to go, Hat told him, you take your own horse and go. You never shoulda come. We need Satchel to carry

Edward. And that saddlebag ain't no good to you, so leave it. She sighted along her barrel. I mean it, she added.

I saw the understanding sink into Forbush. The map ain't in it, he said. You got it! He sounded accusing, like Hat had done him an injustice. You give it to me, Missus Toynbee. You give me the map!

It was an ugly situation. They were standing so close that neither of them was going to miss. If I went for my gun, I'd get shot, but it might give Hat the opportunity to put Forbush down. Maybe that's what I should have done.

Colson Forbush, Hat said, you going to make me shoot you dead?

You just give me the map, he said, and shook his gun for emphasis. The motion put just a little too much pressure on the trigger. He had the pistol cocked. It went off, and his shot caught Hat in the ribs.

She stumbled backward a step and sat down hard.

I scooped up the Schofield, and somehow I got it pointed at Forbush without getting shot, but I saw he wasn't trying to shoot me.

Forbush was calling on the Lord and shrieking, his eyes wide and the color draining from his face. I'm sorry, Missus Toynbee, he wailed, I'm so sorry! I didn't mean to do that! He called again on the Lord. I didn't mean to do that!

Well, you done it, Hat said, hunching over with her arm against her belly.

Forbush dropped his Smith & Wesson as if getting rid of it could somehow distance him from what he'd done. He fell to his knees, crying now, holding his head with both hands. I ain't a killer, he said. You got to forgive me, Missus Toynbee.

I lowered my pistol.

Hat sat up straighter and looked at her hand, which was covered with blood. A stain was spreading down her side. She looked appraisingly at Forbush, who was sobbing and sniveling and rocking back and forth, now asking no one in particular what he was going to do.

Hat raised the LeMat and let him have it with the shotgun shell. She hit him square in the chest, and he flopped straight over backward, skidding a ways. He jerked and wriggled a little, and he tried to say something, and then he stopped moving.

I watched Hat as she lowered the pistol and put her hands back over the wound. I was trying to figure out if she'd shot him for revenge. Sure, he'd had it coming, but he'd thrown down his gun.

Had to do it, Ovid, she said. He never would have gone back, not after doing me like this.

I guessed that was true. If Hat died—and it didn't look good for her—they'd hang Forbush.

He'd a run, Hat said. He'd a run off, somewhere betwixt here and the time you got back down to Dravo. And that wouldn't have been justice. He might've killed you, and that would be worse. You might've had to shoot him, and you don't need that on your soul. I'll be meeting God anyway. I can explain myself.

We'll get you back down to Doc Clayton, I said, crouching beside her. People can live through all sorts of stuff.

She shook her head. You got one thing to do, she said.

After you get me my hat. You take Edward home. Do it now, and maybe I'll still be here when you can tell me it's done. She pulled the map out of her pocket and pushed it into my hands.

Hat, I said, I can't leave you here like this.

You got to, she said. It's all right. It's what we come for. Go quick now, and I'll wait. She reached toward her hat, and I went over and got it for her. She settled it on her head. Now pull me over to that rock, she said, so I can look out at things.

There wasn't much else I could do for her except what she asked. I felt sorry for towing her, her bootheels dragging in the dirt and brown needles. As gently as I could, I got her situated with her back against a boulder and her face toward the west, where there was a gap twixt the woods and the rock face. It was a fine view.

You take care of Early and Satchel, she said. And I want you to keep this gun of Edward's, which you find interesting. You can remember me by it. She grabbed my arm, looked toward Edward, and nodded to me. You take care of things, she said.

I saw that it was the only thing I could do. She wouldn't make it down to Dravo.

An important question occurred to me. I asked her, Do you want to . . . to rest up here with Edward, in his house?

No, she said. This mountain is his province. We'll be to-gether right enough, no matter if our bones lie separate. I want Christian hymns floating over my grave, not the howling and the wind. Take me back and put me in the hole they dug for him.

It took a little doing, but I got Edward up onto Satchel's back and secured him in place. Working with him close like

that, I caught more of the odor, but that didn't matter. I put
Forbush's saddle on the ground again for the comfort of his
roan, tied up its reins, and saddled Jack. I didn't expect the
way ahead was flat enough for riding, but I just wanted Jack
along. I made sure Hat had a full water bottle. Then, following the map, I led Jack and Satchel up through the rocks and
the crevices toward the summit of Harper's Dome.

The last part of the map was marked out in extreme detail,
on account the way was so convoluted. But after a few hours
of winding around and picking our way up some grades that
made us dizzy, we came to a flat, open hollow in the rocks,
around behind the top of the Dome.

There, in the middle of this open space with high walls
on three sides, was a pit like a well, some fifteen feet across.
Leaning against its side was a long, stout ladder that I figured
Alban Toynbee had made. The morning light showed me a
level floor down in there, and what looked like a chamber that
widened out.

I unhooked my rope, got Edward onto the ground, and
tied the rope securely around him. Then I sat for a pause to
rest and to work through the particulars of the task.

So this was Edward's secret house. The flat-bottomed hollow on the mountain was like a little garden. Saxifrage grew all
around, the flowers done now, but the mosslike clumps looking
peaceful and softening the hard lines of the rocks. Saxifrage,
whose name meant stone breaker. Some folks called it rockfoil.

All right, Mister Toynbee, I said aloud. Let's go in. With
help from Jack as my anchor, I lowered Edward down over the

rim, down into the throat of stone until he rested on the floor. Then, taking it slow and careful on the old ladder, testing each rung, I climbed down to untie him.

I looked around with great vigilance on the way and when I got down there. The light didn't go very far, but I could hear the echo of a vast space, and what I could see didn't look like any natural cave. There were patterns of indentations in the walls, like you'd get if you pressed a bowl into mud. It made me think of Forbush's story about the weird gold coins.

I untied Edward, and I guessed I'd better leave him bound up in his blankets. But I pulled him away from the ladder's base, back into the dark where no rain would fall on him. I pushed him over to the base of the wall, which met the floor at a curious angle. Maybe I should have said some words or a prayer, but instinct was telling me not to linger. Besides, this didn't quite seem a Christian burial, or a place for one.

A chill was creeping out of the depths, feeling like more than the cool of the deep earth. A few steps farther on, something lay on the floor. Too far into the dark for me to see, but it looked like an open book, or what had been a book, but the damp had taken its toll. I was not inclined to pick it up or even to take those further steps into the secret house. I didn't know how Alban and Emma had made a home down here, but I supposed if they believed this place was a gift from the bears, then they found a way. That book, though—maybe the prospector from Forbush's story had gotten this far. If he'd left his book, that didn't bode well for him.

Just as I turned to go, I heard something back in the dark—
a shifting, an ominous sound. I went up the ladder a good deal
faster than I'd come down it.

It was past noon, judging by the sun, when I got back
down to Hat. She was still alive, but she was pale and had lost
a lot of blood. She was mighty glad to see me. I described it all
to her, which made her smile and sigh.

When I got to the part about how it was done, how Edward
was at rest now in his old home, she said she already knew.
Edward was here, she said, Edward and the bears. She gazed
off down the slope into the tangles of brush. I could have asked
her more about that, but it didn't seem necessary. I reckoned
I was looking at true love in this old woman on the ground.

Part of me still wanted to try getting her down to the doctor, though it was clear she wouldn't make it, and I knew she
wouldn't go. It would only have been cruel to make her die in
pain on a horse's back. So I saw to it that all the horses were
content, and then I sat with Hat.

I brought her more water. That was all she wanted. We sat
there watching the light change and listening to the wind in
the trees. We talked on and off through the afternoon about
all sorts of things. She wanted to hear more about places I'd
been, and she told me about Edward, the things he thought
about and said, the things he could make with his hands, the
little kindnesses he'd always shown to Hat.

I coulda been nicer to him, she said. There was times when
I spoke ungently.

I said I guessed we could all say that about the way we

spoke. I felt the truth of that: we never say all we ought, all we want to say, to people while they're with us. Then they're not, and we can't.

I feel bad about keeping you here, Hat told me. She was thinking about how I'd have to get her and Forbush back into town, me and Jack and the two Appaloosas and the strawberry roan—quite a parade that would be, and I couldn't start it until she died.

It's not a hardship, truly, I said. Don't you worry.

Thank you, Ovid, she said. She patted my hand.

An eagle passed betwixt us and the sun, its shadow touching us for a flicker. The distant peaks gleamed, and the far-off plains shimmered with haze. There was gold tinting the country, the first footfalls of autumn, which brought both a dying and a ripening.

It's a pretty land, Hat said.

It is, I replied.

When the hour of sunset came, Hat crossed her arms and smiled. I could see she was fading now, not feeling the pain, going out like a candle that has burned itself down to the last wax.

This is a good hour, Ovid, she said to me. I'm fixing to see that tree of life that grows on either side of the river.

I just held her wrist, and nodded.

Then she leaned her head back against the rock, and there seemed nothing around us but the breathing of the wind, and gold everywhere.

INTERLUDE

The closest I ever was to the Craither afore that last time was in the blazing early summer of 1888, right around the time an old and true friend of mine left this life, though I didn't find out about that until about four years later.

First I was in Flagstaff, and things were going rough. A bigshot with the name of Cyril Bellamy, who'd gotten rich on a dry goods business, had heard about me and made it his business to teach me a lesson. I learned the facts later, when I asked around.

Bellamy had been a Reb captain, and he clearly still considered me the enemy. I never did understand why he had it in for me—it had to have been more than the War. It may be that the man had some secrets, and he was afraid my visions might show me something about him that he didn't want known.

Anyway, he and a band of his men waylaid me in front of a stable, and I believe they meant to thrash the tar out of me and finish up with a bullet through my head—I could see murder in their eyes, and no amount of fast-talking was persuading them otherwise.

That part of town was strangely quiet, like there wasn't a living soul nearby. Bellamy was pretty much running Flagstaff, unofficially. I figured his intentions regarding me were known, and no one wanted to cross him. His bunch had me ringed in. The sun beat down like a hammer. I heard a fly buzz somewhere close by, and I recall how those men and their horses had practically no shadows at all, on account their shadows were straight below them.

I had my feet on the ground. I gave Jack a final pat and whispered my thanks into his ear. I hoped they'd treat him decently. There was no point going for the Schofield pistol. I might have been able to shoot Bellamy at least afore they got me, but I saw no purpose to it. I had no animosity for the man and no reason to be his executioner when it made no difference.

I looked him in the eyes and waited.

And right there, under that hot sun of midday in Flagstaff, Cyril Bellamy and his men just withered afore my eyes.

They shriveled up like husks, and at the same time fell to pieces—the men and their horses, too. I don't mean they turned to dust. I wish it had been that; it wouldn't have been as awful to see. Pieces fell away. Skin peeled off them and crinkled up. Innards jiggled out, wet and glistening, and were practically nothing by the time they hit the ground. Everyone teetered in place for an instant, limp like scarecrows, and then they fell. All that remained were the things not alive: guns, saddles, clothes, boots . . . and foul, oily pools where men and animals had been. I heard more flies buzzing then.

It was like in the Good Book, the pestilence that walketh in darkness, the destruction that wasteth at noonday. Or again like when Judas Iscariot flopped down in the Field of Blood and his bowels rushed out. I was shaken to the core, unable to wrap my mind around what had taken place.

A stir of motion caught my gaze, and I saw, through the stable's open doorway, back in the dark, a pair of glittering eyes. I felt the presence of the Craither.

It had done this: somehow, it had killed Cyril Bellamy and his men, and I expected to be next, as I felt the thing crushing and yanking on me something fierce.

But *why?* Why?

In another moment, the Craither vanished again. The effects on me diminished, and for the time being, I could breathe again.

I've never forgotten what happened in those few seconds. It still comes back in nightmares sometimes, and I never have seen anything else like it.

I did find a sheriff afore I left town, and I told him what I'd seen. He had very few questions for me. The man didn't want to look at me; he mostly talked to my boots and the wall beside me. I figured he was ashamed of himself for not stopping Bellamy—and scared at the same time, on account he'd seen what was left of Bellamy's bunch and heard from some quaking witnesses who'd been peeking through curtains and seen what went down. He knew I was telling the truth, but he didn't know who I was, or what. Probably he thought I had somehow brought the wrath of God down on those men and might do it to him. I could tell he wanted me out of Flagstaff. So I went.

Over the next week, I rode about eighty miles, right to the rim of the Grand Canyon. I needed some peace and some

inspiration. All I could suppose was that the Craither had protected me. It had not wanted me to die then, in that way. I
didn't know why—why had it gone from seething anger at me
to keeping me alive? Or was I misinterpreting everything?

It was the sort of weather Chervil Dray had called hotter
than four-barrel Hell. At the end of a long, dry day of riding,
with Jack and me having to tote any water we fancied drinking, we had the reward of that sight: the canyon in the evening
effulgence, the rainbows of those rocky walls and towers, one
of the world's most magnificent artworks, wrought by God's
chisels and paintbrushes, made from a river and a long, long
time. In the light reflected from it all, the cares of life settled
into their proper perspectives. If I were about to die, I would
not regret moving on. I'd lived deep and full, and I'd be going
at last to that better place. I'd quite like to see Nancy again,
and my folks, and lots of good old company who'd never made
it home from the War. I wondered if George Buckles would be
there, playing his Aeolina.

That night, well back from the rim, I fell asleep watching
the meteors, which were frequent, and the brilliant stars, the
bright clouds among them, and the bottomless dark around
them. I wondered if Nancy Mavornen, now in that life after
this one, could see the stars from where she was. If so, I wondered whether they were the same stars. I wanted to believe so,
on account that would have been something that connected us
still. But then I thought no, she was with Jubal now, the husband she'd lost, and I expected that was all she needed. The
thought did not make me feel less lonely.

Sometime in the dead of night, I sprang awake to find the Craither looming right above me, bending close, and it felt like my soul was peeling right loose from my bones. The Craither seemed big as the saguaros around my camp. Its bulk distorted the veil of stars.

It was hard to tell just where the Craither was, to the right or to the left—it wavered like a flame. At the same time, it seemed like it might be out behind the stars, millions upon millions of miles away, bulging through them, wrapping itself in the heavens—and it seemed to be leaning right over me, an arm's length away.

Part of it reached toward me, something like an arm, with shadowy extensions that might have been fingers. Though the thing seemed vast, the hand of it was hand-sized.

I threw back the flap of my bedroll and seized that hand. If the thing were going to finish me, it was time to get on with it. But when I grasped the hand, I felt nothing solid, as if I were attempting to grab onto smoke. And yet I did *feel* . . .

An electric wave coursed through me. But the flood that came next was a monstrous, volcanic yearning, more powerful than the tearing pain and pressure. The Craither wanted something, and for some reason, it was looking to me, as if I could provide it.

WHAT? I screamed aloud, alarming Jack. WHAT DO YOU WANT?!

But the Craither couldn't tell me. We could no more communicate than we could touch hands.

My heart raced and I sat there gasping, writhing,

wondering why I couldn't die already. But suddenly the thing was gone again, and my heart kept beating. Breath came easier. I wept in the darkness, blubbered like a baby, begging that Craither to let me alone. Then I thought I'd better lie still and listen, on account that cursed visitor usually came with peril. But there were only the sounds of the night, and Jack all sympathetic and anxious, nuzzling my face.

Sitting up, I leaned against his head and talked to him till he was reassured. Then I settled back and tried to sleep, while the infinite and unfeeling stars kept their secrets.

For some reason, a tune was wandering in my head, one that George Buckles had used to play when we were driving cattle with Mister Bowdler, and another cowboy they called Alabama used to sing along with him:

> Kingbolt Bob's a-goin' home,
> Nevermore with us to roam;
> Wants no more of the ramblin' life,
> Aims to settle down and take a wife.
> Oh, there's no bed or wife for me,
> No rest for my back but a willow tree,
> No shelter warm though the cold winds come,
> But Kingbolt Bob's a-goin' home.

I don't know what I've got to give you, I told the Craither, wherever it was: I can't think of one blessed thing.

CHAPTER SIX:

SOMEPLACE COOL AND DARK

NEW MEXICO TERRITORY, 1889

I was feeling the drain on me of the Craither's proximity most of the time now. It wouldn't let up. At times, I was so dizzy that I could barely stay in the saddle. This situation had to end soon. Something in my mind told me that it would, one way or the other.

How do you have a showdown with an alien thing you can hardly see?

It was more like an illness than an enemy. But then, illness is an enemy in the body, and the Craither was an illness in the world.

We never know till we get there how close to death we are. But we rub shoulders with death all the time, even those of us without a Craither; we might sit down next to it for a spell in some unexpected place, and it might glance at us and nod. Or it might brush past us on a street or on some lonely trail fifty miles from nowhere, stepping right betwixt us and our shadows.

I haven't quite come to the last one yet, though I figure I

was about as close as I'd ever been one time in the New Mexico
Territory. It started with me dangling on the end of a rope—
no, not what you're thinking.

Charley Rim was holding the other end of that rope for me,
paying it out, and my boot soles were walking down the wall
of a cave shaft that went straight down into the whispery pit.
There was depth to this cave—the torch in my hand billowed in
the draft, throwing red light across rocky knobs and holes that
led off into black dens that looked like they might go on forever.

Where Charley was standing had been a whole ledge full
of rattlesnakes, big fat ones lying there in the dark, shaking
their tails. We took care of the snakes, but there were worse
things below me.

I'd been venturing deeper into caves in recent months. The
visions in my head seemed to be suggesting, more and more
often, that what I was looking for lay under the ground. I was
going on as if life stretched on afore me—as much to help
Charley as to help myself . . . though if there was help for me,
it was more likely to come this way than if I went to a doctor.

As I worked my way down that rough wall, though, with
the rope gnawing my palms, biting into my waist, I was getting
another picture in my head. There was a woman in a garden.
And yet there wasn't. It was all like I was looking through fog,
though the light was bright and green, sunlight through the
leaves of trees—I could sense her, with pleasant flowers and
blossoming vines beside her. It was full summer in the vision,
but instead of hot and sticky, I could feel that the garden was
cool, like this cave, with water flowing. Something prowled

behind her, too, among the thickets, its eyes glowing green. I thought it was a big black wildcat, bigger than a painter. It wasn't stalking the woman but seemed peaceable, a friend to her like Jack was to me. I could see big slabs of stone peeking through the foliage. The place didn't look like it was anywhere nearby. I wished I could see the woman better.

Ovid, Charley hollered, you all right?

I shook myself out of the vision. This was no place to be vanishing into my head. Yeah, I told him, just don't let go of that rope.

My sweaty shirt felt like ice. It amazed me how it could be so hot up above and so cold down here. Of course, it wasn't just a natural cold. There was cave cool, and then there was this.

The shaft opened out, and I swung down into an open space and touched ground on a boulder atop a mound of debris that was probably once part of the ceiling. A few dead rattlers were strewn around my feet, half-cooked, still smoking from the bath we gave them in burning oil. Nothing alive and wiggling—I made sure.

I held up the torch and squinted around this big gullet of the earth. It went back a good ways, as I'd suspected. Tunnels led off—or converged here, depending on how you looked at it. Fissures yawned betwixt heaps of loose rock. Easy to lose your footing and fall to China. Dry needle-rocks hung like knives from the ceiling, and the nose-blistering stench told me I wasn't alone. Hadn't figured I would be.

I also saw that the map we'd been following was right: this wasn't just a cave. The flickering light fell on the carvings now, the designs with the dots that I'd been seeing more and more of lately, the angles you couldn't wrap your mind around, geometry they don't teach at the schoolhouse. I'd been at the Edges of such places afore, and they drew and repulsed me in about equal measure. This was another pit where the Old Things used to be, those as wallowed in the canyons and slithered in the moonlight when the mountains themselves were young.

Thing about the Old Craithers: they fancied gold just as much as modern folks do, and they'd been good at finding it. Either they'd mined it, or they'd made others do it for them. I wasn't sure, though I'd read some mighty disquieting stories in a worm-eaten, crumbling book that must have been a translation of some tome vastly older. I won't even mention where that book was, on the chance that it might still be where I came across it. I don't want you or anyone else to go and find it—believe me, it's better if no human eyes look on that book's blasphemous words again. I do wonder, though, if that was another copy of it, or a similar book, that I saw in the half dark up in the secret house on the mountain when I helped get old Edward Toynbee back there to rest—him that his Nakoda mama had called Comes-Home. That copy, whether it was or wasn't the bad one, will be long rotted away by now, and not a danger to anyone. At least, I hope so . . .

The Old Things flattened the gold into coins long and oval, not too regular, and marked with little dots and notches. Gold coins were piled up in glinting mounds down there in the cave—more than I'd ever seen. More than Charley and I could have toted out in fifty trips.

Charley felt my weight was off the rope, but he had the sense to keep quiet. He knew I'd got to listen.

Sure enough, I heard them stirring and snuffling, back where the light didn't reach. The sound echoed, and my torch wavered, making rock shadows jump left and right. The varmints felt the heat, and they smelled me. I wondered if I was as rancid to them.

They weren't stupid. The first one rushed from behind me.

That particular Hellhole had an infestation of what I called the pig-spiders. That's what they looked like: fleshy, jowly things that moved around on black, jointed legs, the knee hinges higher than their bristly backs. They were just a little smaller than a full-grown hog. And they had a fringe of short tentacles, too, along their bellies—white, boneless grub arms that were always wiggling. I didn't know why the pits of the Old Things tended to be chock-full of nightmares like those. Maybe it was on account there was no place up under the sun for a pig with spider legs.

I drew my Schofield, but afore I shot, out of curiosity, I used the toe of my boot to flip a dead rattlesnake right out in front of the pig-thing. Good to observe and learn; ain't that what they teach you?

The porker wobbled to a halt. They didn't actually skitter—too heavy for that. Their legs creaked as they went, which for some reason gave me the willer-jeebies more than anything else about them.

There was grunting and creaking all over, behind the boulders, off in the tunnels.

Piggy bent his head down to sniff at the fried rattler—I could see the wrinkles in his neck—and then the front tentacles scooped up that snake and shoved it into his piehole. He chomped and sucked it in, crunched the rattle but didn't even spit that out, and then he glared at me with his beady eyes.

We weren't friends just on account I gave him dinner. Pig-spiders always looked pissed off, and I guessed that was only right. We always met like this, me shoving a torch at their snouts. I cocked my pistol.

Charley, I yelled, loud but calm.

Yeah? he said.

I need to come up fast, I told him. Ciphering from the sounds, there were way more than sixteen of these things, and I only had six shots in the Schofield and ten more in the LeMat that Hat Toynbee had given me.

Just as the first one started to charge, I put a bullet betwixt his eyes. He squealed and went down in a wreck of legs and wigglers. But now they all started to scream—they didn't much care for the gun blast—and they came running. It was a horrible sound and a worse sight. The circle of open floor got smaller in a hurry, me at the center.

There was always a point—about halfway to me—where the pig-spiders went from dander up to the awareness that I was better grub than they were used to getting in the canyons where they hunted. Oh yeah, I'd seen them up there, usually when the moon was down. It's why I'd camp on a canyon rim, never on its floor, no matter how good the source of water was.

I dropped two more afore Charley lifted me off my feet. I

had the rope looped around me in a harness so I could use my hands. Big Charley had hoisted and carried heavy loads all his life, and he was a consistent champion at the tug-o'-war, which was another reason I liked to have him along.

I was clear, higher than the porkers could jump. I could have picked off a bunch more on the way up, just for practice, but I saved my bullets. Might need more shots afore I got to the top—lots of echoey holes twixt the bottom and the surface above.

First thing I did when I scrambled up beside Charley was thank him. Second thing was I got him to help me with the kegs we'd dragged down there.

Charley asked me whether or not this cave was worth our while. Oh yeah, I told him, it's worth our while.

There was a shrieking from the pit below us, but the noise was nowhere near as loud as it was about to be. Charley and I dumped out two kegs, watching the streams of oil sluice down into the dark. Charley said he pissed about that much after that night in Cayuse, and I said, Yeah, you saw two streams then, too, and you were the only one pissing.

Then I got my torch, which I'd wedged in a crack well away from us, and I dropped it down the shaft. Everything lit up down below, and I saw the reflected glow on Charley's face as he tried to glimpse the craithers. But I wasn't watching. I was busy using our little crowbar to pry the reinforcing hoops from the third keg.

When I'd pulled them off over the ends, I unscrewed the stopper, turned the keg over so it was starting to dump, and then tossed the whole thing into the pit. I stepped back, and there was a tremendous *WHOOOMMF* as that keg hit bottom and split like a pumpkin. That threw fire pretty far. The squealing rose something awful, and it was hard not to feel a mite sorry for doing that to anything alive. But those things did prey on men. I knew it for a fact.

The fire wouldn't hurt the gold any, and I was glad we'd just used oil this time. As far as I could recollect, the dumbest thing I ever did was when I lost a motherlode about half as big as this one by chucking a stick of dynamite down the shaft. You'd think I'd have learned something from Crazy Billy Dance, at that cave near Woolpit, Missouri. Granted, what was chasing me when I did it was a damn sight worse than pig-spiders. But that dynamite brought down the whole cavern roof and buried everything under about four vertical acres of the Arizona Territory. Charley wasn't with me then, so he didn't know about that, and I was keeping it that way.

Third thing I did was reload the Schofield.

Toting the two empty kegs, Charley and I worked our way up out of the canyon to the place we had the horses tethered, a basin among the rocks screened by mesquite and saltbush. The moon was just past full, like a big dollar coin. The breeze smelled of the silver sage along the trail, those fragrant leaves with their fine hairs like on a woman's forearm. Off in the brush to the east, I heard a pack of coyotes yipping in their mournful way, and I silently told them we'd just dispossessed them of a few natural enemies, so maybe their coyote pups could grow up to carry on the yipping.

Afore we settled down for a few hours' rest, waiting for
the cave to cool off and the smoke to filter out, I stood at the
canyon rim and looked down. I could see the last red firelight
dancing over the rock walls. I got some water from the draw
and brewed coffee. Charley heated up the last of the beans, we
munched on hardtack, and we sat there listening to our fire
crackle the dry sticks. I was glad Charley hadn't brought any of
the rattlers up here to finish cooking. Charley was frugal that
way, and I wasn't one to waste food, either, but I've never had
a hankering to eat the cursed of all cattle, and especially not
when it spent its life crawling around a pit of the Old Things.

I tried not to let Charley see the toll exacted on me by the
Craither, though sometimes he looked at me with worry in his
eyes, and sometimes he asked me if I was feeling all right. I
hadn't told him about the otherworldly thing that dogged my
steps. There was nothing he could have done about it, and it
only would have worried him more.

Charley asked me about the cave, and I told him about
the mounds of gold. That cheered him up. We'd come a long
way this time, and Charley was surpassingly patient with the
vagueness of my head-pictures and the tattered old map. He
knew it was no good asking many questions, on account I
usually don't know any answers. Charley was patient overall:
he was saving every spare nickel with the dream of buying a
ranch. I reckoned someday he'd get it done.

We didn't know this particular country well; hadn't been
out this way. A man feels even smaller under the stars when he
doesn't know what's over the next ridge. Of course, that's the

way life is: you never know what's coming. I reckon that's for the best, but not for the first time, I wished my visions were a little better at keeping us out of trouble. They've always been symbolic most times—I'll see three ships at sea, and it turns out in real life to mean three wagons in a sea of grass. Even back then, I usually had to do some guessing, and sometimes I didn't get there till after the fact, and I was looking back, and it would all come clear.

Another reason Charley was good to have along is on account he knew how to use his Remington pistol and his eight-gauge, a gun that truly wasn't pussyfooting. There's quite a lot, both above and below the ground, that an eight-gauge will put down. He kept it right beside him as we stretched out.

Charley grew up in Rochester, New York—a booming town even then—in a family of free Negro folks. He was a Navy man in the War. He'd told me stories of a childhood that was pretty miserable, on account his father never showed him any warmth or love. Charley figured he would finally get the old man's respect when he joined up and fought the Rebs, but it didn't pan out. His own brother had kicked him out besides.

I never slept too deep in those days; it was like a part of me had stopped being able to sleep, and I kept opening and closing my eyes all night beside that canyon. It wasn't all caused by the Craither, though I remembered that titanic longing I'd felt when I grabbed its hand beside the Grand Canyon. I knew it hadn't stopped wanting whatever it was it wanted.

At one point I saw a shooting star. It flashed long and bright, like a fiery liquid. I always took that to be a good sign.

After a rain, the Almighty's bow of colors in the sky is one kind of promise; a shooting star has to be another, though it isn't spelled out.

I dreamed about the woman I could not actually see in the cool, green garden. Her presence was there, the powerful sense of a woman watching me—but like the Craither, I couldn't see any details of her face. It was the first time I'd had a woman other than Nancy in my head, and I didn't much like it. She was in a fragrant garden among colorful and aromatic blossoms, but I couldn't even make them out—unsettling. It felt like she was calling me, telling me to come there. Somewhere among the stone ruins was something new, and she wanted me to see it—that's what the dream felt like. But I have been known to misinterpret women's messages.

I woke up with a hollow ache, part of me now wishing I could be inside that dream with the woman and find out who she was.

You got to move on when you can, Chervil had told me. Nancy ain't coming back.

I told Chervil he had no grounds to talk, on account he had a daughter he couldn't make peace with who lived far away from him. Fact is, most of us have trouble moving forward and doing the best thing. We keep on chewing on the bitter cud that's ours—it's no one else's, and belongs to us.

Things seemed peaceful and uncomplicated where the woman was, in her garden, though I reckon that's the thing about visions: they aren't real life, they're messages of a sort, so of course things are simpler inside them. Her almost-face lingered, that face I couldn't get to come clear in my head. We were rich now, Charley and me, but it didn't fill me with any joy or contentment. I was still searching for something beyond my reach, something I couldn't name.

I wished Nancy Mavornen were there with me. I wished things had gone differently in Lennox.

Charley was scouting on the ridge, and the sun wasn't up over the hills yet. Everything to the east looked pink and golden, with the rocks and yuccas and sumacs etched in blue. There was a clean appearance to it all, as if the dust that would show up later wasn't there in the early morning.

I watched an owl glide up from the canyon and along the cliff. He was late getting home. Slim pickings on his hunt, maybe. One by one, I thumped out my boots to be sure nothing had crawled inside them. I breathed the scent of charcoal from our burned-out fire . . . the perfume of the sage . . . and I wondered what the woman in my dream smelled like. Her essence would be nothing out of a fancy bottle.

Stop thinking about it, I told myself.

Me, I was quite rank right then. I guessed that woman was lucky she was in a dream and didn't have to smell me.

Charley came back and we drank up what was left in the coffeepot. Charley had set it back on the coals afore he went scouting.

There's a town, Charley said, through that gap past the canyon. About three miles, he reckoned, and added that we were out of food. Just figuring I could use a bath, I said. Yeah, he said, I figure you could. As if Charley weren't rank himself.

We got moving and threw the empty saddlebags over our shoulders. Twixt them, torches, guns, and rope, it was a hazardous climb down the arroyo, but pretty soon we were looking into the pit, its walls all sooty. It reeked of charred meat, and not Texas beef. Whatever pig-spiders were made of, I hoped the fumes weren't poisonous to breathe. The canyon floor was still in deep blue shadow.

You know, I said, I don't always have to be the one who goes down. You could do it just fine.

How you going to pull me out of there? asked Big Charley, and he had a point.

I told him I could get Jack down here. Hitch around the pommel, I allowed a horse could do it handily. But we both knew I was the one who went down, always; that's just the way it worked. I wouldn't let Charley even if he wanted to—I just had to say he could.

We slid down into the first, bigger hole—like a funnel in the canyon's bottom—to where the shaft proper began. All the dead rattlers were gone, snatched up by buzzards or maybe the coyotes. I struck a sulfur match and held it under my torch, which was cloth-wrapped and treated with resin. One thing I'd gotten good at was making torches that burned bright and lasted Charley kept the long guns up top—his eight-gauge and my Winchester lever-action. I had my two pistols. After tying up my harness again, I hefted both sets of saddlebags. With a last look around at the morning glowing on the rocks all murky and blue, I backed over the edge, and Charley fed out rope.

My boots scraped along the charred wall. The clammy

chill had already returned to the cave, and the stench was worse than when the fire had been raging. I could hardly move with all that leather hanging from my neck and arms, so I hoped I wouldn't have to.

At the bottom, there was a carnage of seared meat, black and raw red, and twisted legs sticking up. Big as they were, those unholy swine curled up just like regular spiders when they died. The stench made my eyes water fierce, and I wondered how I was going to breathe long enough to do what I had to do. Burning juice came up the back of my throat. I gagged, but I kept it down.

The light showed me only black carcasses, jointed legs like field stubble, and nothing moving. The gold was still there, glinting in cascades. It would need the smoke wiped off, but there was every bit as much as I thought—probably more—and no need for refining; it was like finding a hoard of Spanish doubloons.

To my dismay, I saw there wasn't a clear path to the bottom of the rubble mound: I either had to step on dead porkers or get them out of the way.

I eased down the side of the boulder. Charley felt the tug and gave me more slack. The Schofield aimed, I prodded the first carcass with my toe. The obscene thing stayed stiff and dead. I stepped right across it, having nightmare visions of it coming to life and chomping on my crotch.

Next there were two pressed together, in a place where all the rocks wanted to slide toward a crack in the floor. I checked my footing and gave the pigs boot shoves until they came loose and rolled with a shower of gravel. They flopped over the edge and vanished.

That was about the time I heard the hissy-oinking.

I'd figured we hadn't cleared the place. I blew away two of the varmints that were rushing me from a hole in the wall. Then it was quiet again, and I stood there with my heart walloping.

Finally I moved forward, and Charley paid out rope. I sidled around three more dead ones and nearly lost my balance on a teetering rock. Red light flickered on the stone needles above me, and I hoped my shooting hadn't loosened any of them.

I made it to a drift of shiny gold coin-plates. Propping my torch where it threw plenty of light, I shrugged off the saddle-bags. I'd just holstered the Schofield when coins flew up like a sandstorm. A pig-spider lunged at me from under the gold. It must have burrowed there—either to get away from the fire or maybe it knew how to ambush.

I'd never had to quick draw on a pig afore, but I just barely managed it, spraying his brains over the coins. Turning to a clean patch of them, I filled two saddlebags, cramming that gold into every inch of space. When I was done, the saddlebags weighed like a pair of boulders.

Leaving the torch burning where it was, I lugged the load up to the boulder's top, threading around and over the dead craithers, trying not to tumble into some bottomless pit. As I set the bags down, Charley yelled, How you doing? I hollered back, All right.

I duckwalked my way back down and filled up the second

set of packs. Two more pigs showed themselves, but they were at a distance and didn't even seem interested in me. I think the fire had messed them up; maybe they were blinded. I couldn't work with them lurking behind me, though, so I plugged them. The last one took two shots—now the Schofield was empty. I still had the LeMat, but why take chances?

Everything was quiet, so I reloaded.

My back was aching by the time I got all four saddlebags up the rock. I made one last trip for the torch. Next came the tensest part: I knew Charley wasn't fixing to leave me down there, even when he had all that gold up there with him. We'd been through some Hell and high water together out here. Still, watching the packs trundle upward, hitch by hitch, and me with no rope tied round me anymore—that wasn't easy. I imagined the torch guttering out, and me down there with the dead pigs as day passed into night, but it would be all the same to me on account the cave was always pitch black . . . and worse than what was lying all around me were those impossible and maddening designs engraved in the rock, the stink of the rotting meat and the cold behind it—that lingering breath of Things that were here once, and maybe still were, sleeping like that Dragon under the hills in Kansas.

The tiniest worm of doubt began to twist and gnaw. Was Charley up there thinking of how much richer he'd be on his own?

It was a Heaven-sent relief when the rope flopped down again for me. I blessed Charley and all his progeny, feeling ashamed of that little worm of doubt.

Then Charley and I poked around till we found a shallower arroyo, and we brought the horses down into the canyon. Jack didn't much like the heavy weights I set across him, but I told him the stuff in the bags would buy him lots of gourmet hay and princely boarding. Charley's roan took his share of the load in stride; after all, he was used to carrying Big Charley. We figured toting that gold was plenty to ask of our horses, so we stayed out of the saddles and led them out of the canyon for the last time. I wasn't a bit sorry to be leaving.

The day got hotter as the sun climbed. We went through scrub country with some pink-blooming chitalpas and stands of pinyons and desert spoons standing up like ships' oars. We kept to the shade when we could. A desert willow leaned right over us, its flowers giving way to long, thin pods like it was offering Charley and me a cigar. Past the gap and out of the rocks, we saw a road we could follow, but we chose to stay in the trees. I've always liked to look a place over afore I commit myself.

A stand of bigtooth maples had been ravaged by moths. The white moths fluttered around, looking for more leaves to devour, I guessed, but they hadn't left much—just the raggedy rims of the maple leaves. So far, they'd left the other trees alone. I wondered if it was a matter of time afore they gobbled up the whole woods along that stretch.

Swinging a little east at the sound of water, we came into a gulley full of deep, delicious shade. The mimosas were crowned with spiky blossoms, and the weeping mulberries put me in mind of the ones I shinnied up when I was a kid. We unloaded the horses, and they drank their fill from a sparkling stream.

On foot, I climbed a rise and studied the town away through more trees and across the plain.

It was a small town—one main street, a handful of businesses, a scattering of houses. Looked tranquil enough, but I knew from bitter experience that no good comes from riding into town with saddlebags full of gold. That's the way Charley and I lost our only other big find: robbed at gunpoint by the Noonan gang when we should have been rich enough for Charley to buy his ranch. Two weeks later, on a Sunday morning, the Noonans all got gunned down by a posse in front of the Salt Fork courthouse; but they'd hid that gold somewhere, and we never did find out where, though we spent considerable effort looking.

Charley was despondent for a long spell, on account that ranch had slipped right through his fingers. I didn't get any visions of where to hunt for that gold, which probably should have taught me something. I was letting gold distract me, when that wasn't what I was seeking for at all. That wasn't why my visions were dragging me all around Robin Hood's barn.

I'd met Charley Rim some years previous, when he was a wandering soul like me, but a lot angrier. We'd ridden together a while, gone our separate ways, and now we were riding together again. Gentlehearted and soft-spoken, Charley was still harboring his anger. I couldn't blame him.

Big Charley's father and his uncle had started up a business afore the War, at a time when, even in the North, it was a considerable feat for two Negro men—Rim Brothers Moving and Storage. By the time of the War, the uncle had died, and both of his sons—Charley's cousins—fought for the Union and perished of smallpox. Charley himself served on an ironclad and blockaded Charleston. He was a kid when he went to war.

Now, Charley's father was convinced that Charley was no businessman, and he'd always favored Charley's younger brother, Reeney, whom the old man carefully taught all the ways of his trade. The old man got it into his head to make Reeney the boss of the company, though he was just barely coming to the age of majority by the time the War ended. A few weeks afore Charley, weary and scarred, came home, the father died. Reeney said Charley could work for him at the same wage he paid the hired labor, though Charley would be working like a mule on account of his size. There was lots of heavy lifting to do in moving and storage. Reeney wouldn't make Charley a partner, just an employee, which of course stuck in Charley's craw. The company was still called Rim Brothers, but Reeney wanted to run it by himself, nothing brotherly about it.

Charley told Reeney where he could shove his crowbar, and he got himself in with the merchant marine and looked for his way forward on the sea. That worked for a while, I guess, but eventually Charley wound up on dry land, wandering, getting employment when he could, looking for where he belonged.

I first saw him in Lincoln, New Mexico Territory, beaten half to death, lying in an alley.

In the green haven of shade and singing water, I found us a big rock I liked that was mighty distinctive. Charley and I hid the saddlebags in a hollow behind that rock and buried them under loose stones and dirt, sweeping and rearranging until we were satisfied it looked like nature undisturbed. Up the stream a ways, we left the empty kegs, torches, grub sack, skillet, and coffeepot; they weren't worth stealing, and they'd point us right if we happened to forget where the rock was. We mounted up and circled way back, coming out of the trees down by the road.

The sun was just past overhead as we crossed the dry plain. We were getting into the hottest part of the day. The buildings shimmered in heat waves. Charley's gray Stetson was soaked with a dark band of sweat. My hair was all matted and sweaty under my hat, and I was thinking of that garden I'd seen behind my eyelids, where it was cool and dim and the woman was waiting.

Charley was a steady presence. I always felt a little better with Charley riding alongside me. He hadn't left me in the cave. And I hadn't left him on that night I first saw him, lying there in the dusty alley, face covered with blood.

I reckon it was just unlucky that Charley had gotten himself into town for the thick of the Lincoln County War. He took his pounding just about three days afore the Regulators killed Sheriff Brady. Charley was minding his business, drinking and playing cards peaceably enough, when some liquored-up pokes on Murphy and Dolan's side had supposedly got wind that Charley worked for John Chisum. It wasn't technically true at that point; Charley had left Chisum's employ some weeks previous. It didn't matter to those boys. I wouldn't be surprised if they hadn't even heard that—if they were just looking for an excuse to thrash a Negro man for enjoying himself like everyone else.

Charley didn't have his gun with him that night, which probably saved his life. Those boys of Dolan's dragged him outside, gave him a hellacious pummeling, and left him in a heap. No one watching could be bothered to see if Charley was dead or alive. When I came across him, I got him to the doctor. Then I got us both out of Lincoln County, and not a day too soon. It was no place to be then, with ranchers and gangs throwing in, killing each other over dry goods and the cattle interest. It came down to that weary old war, Catholics against Protestants, which my mama used to call Catlickers and Potlickers, though she was a Potlicker herself.

I do recall, about a week afore I met Charley, passing by a lone poke leaning against the corral fence behind Dolan's place, The Store—a scrawny kid barely old enough to grow the fuzz of a mustache. I remember his eyes—never forgot them, the way they assayed me and that town like he owned it all from horizon to horizon, and he was defying me to say that he didn't. And later, of course, I saw his picture, those same eyes looking out from under that lopsided hat. That day at Dolan's, I was face-to-face with Henry McCarty, aka William H. Bonney and a few other names, though he's remembered now as Billy the Kid.

As we drew closer, Charley said, Look, and I saw a building that had burned recently. Only a charred black skeleton of beams and rafters stood, and at one end, the ruins of a tower.

Not a tower—a steeple. Up at the top, I made out a scorched cross.

Church burned down, Charley said.

That didn't sit too well with us, and we wondered what it could mean. I saw people moving about. Boy carried a saddle around the corner of the livery stable. Laundry billowed on a clothesline. The blacksmith was hammering, and every so often he'd make his water hiss with something red-hot.

Straight out of the blue, Charley asked me: You ever hear what happened to Cincinnati?

I thought he meant the city. Something happen to it? I asked, wondering what calamity I'd missed hearing of.

But Charley was talking about General Grant's horse named Cincinnati.

I shook my head and told him I never did hear.

Lived in peace to the end of his days, Charley said: I read

about it. Lived with Grant a long time, and he finally went out to pasture at Admiral Daniel Ammen's place in Maryland. Died of old age. Charley got a faraway look and added, I like to think he was watching clouds when he died—maybe in a big patch of clover.

That's a real fine way for a good horse to go, I said.

I tried to think why Charley had Cincinnati in his head as we rode into that town. Maybe he had a sense of trouble coming and was looking for comfort.

A faded signboard on my side of the road said the town's name was Discovery. That's ironic, said Charley. I guessed he was thinking of all that gold we found.

Sure is, I said.

We came in closer, and out in the fields, I saw a barn that was burned down just like the church; enough was left for me to tell it had been a barn, brittle sticks against the horizon. I wiped the sweat out of my eyes. Up in the sky, the white cloud puffs looked so hot they were almost pink. I wished I were watching them from a bed of clover, like Cincinnati.

But there was new construction, too. End of the street, four men were building something with new lumber. Where the clothes bellied on the line, a woman was doing the wash in a tub, scrubbing away on the washboard—a bony woman, looking tough as soapweed. She glared at us, and when Charley and I tipped our hats, she went right on glaring.

As we were about to turn the corner onto the main street, we came up on an old-timer sitting in the doorway of a feed shed. He was chewing a plug, his white whiskers yellow with tobacco juice. We greeted him cordially, and he appraised us. Then he held up his left hand with the fingers spread, and I figured he was waving to us. But then he held up two fingers on the other hand, making the number seven.

Charley and I pulled up our horses and stopped cold.

That could only mean one thing.

We sat there real quiet, looking around and listening. Food or no food, bath or no bath, I was thinking the smart thing to do would be to turn and ride straight back out of town.

But it was too late for that.

A gunslinger sidled out of a doorway behind us, hands on his hips within easy reach of two pearl-handled six-shooters. He was narrow-eyed, with a shaggy brown moustache and a little ribbon of beard in the middle of his chin.

Don't matter what your business is, he said. You're in town, you gotta talk to the boss. Go on up around the corner now, nice and slow.

I glanced at Big Charley. Out in front of us appeared another man with a rifle and bandoliers. Looked like we had no choice.

We coaxed the horses, and they ambled forward. We turned right and followed the main street, an avenue of well-trampled dirt. What few folks were about suddenly remembered things they had to do indoors. I counted eight horses tied at the hitching post in front of the saloon. The faded sign out front called it the Ruby Diamond, like the proprietor couldn't settle on one gemstone. The rifleman and the gun-slinger walked along behind us. The latter said, Keep a-going, down to the hotel.

A man with a slick new haircut came out of the barber-shop, took one look at us, and scooted back inside.

I saw the hotel now: it was straight across from the saloon, which wasn't where I would build a hotel. No name—just HOTEL in fancy gold letters.

As we advanced, faces watched us from windows. Hands parted curtains. What I saw were fearful, hard-ridden people caught like a mouse with a boot on its tail. I'd seen this sight afore, more than once. The sheriff was either dead or useless. In that hotel, I assayed, there was some bully who called the shots, and for reasons unfathomable to me, he'd claimed this little nowhere place for his own. With a name like Discovery, maybe there was a mine nearby—or had been once—though the town didn't seem to be booming.

Stop right there, the gunslinger ordered, and we reined in. Jack snorted and twitched, and I gave him a pat. Keep your hands in the clear, the man said. Don't do nothing stupid.

We didn't wait long. Out onto the hotel porch stepped some kind of a dude. He was in the upper end of his forties, dressed in black with a purple velvet waistcoat and shiny la-pels. The derby on his head had a tiny little brim that wouldn't do him a lick of good in the sun. He was packing a pistol, too, and kept his jacket pushed back behind the holster. It was too hot for that heavy black jacket.

Gentlemen, welcome, he said.

He talked sort of like an Englishman, but not quite. Maybe an Englishman who'd grown up somewhere else.

Hot day to be riding, he said.

Yes, Sir, I said, thinking what he sounded like was an actor, like he'd practiced filling up a room with his voice and making love to the words.

Xavier Conroy's the name, he announced. To whom do I have the pleasure of speaking?

Thomas Keyes, I told him without missing a beat. This here's Will Broaddus. We're just passing through, Mister Conroy—not looking for trouble.

Looking for trouble here would not be wise, he said with a smile.

No, Sir, I said.

Where are you boys headed?

Up Saro way, I told him. Will's cousin's got a job for us helping his boss with his cattle.

He swatted away a fly and said, Do you know what the penalty for lying was in ancient Assyria?

I told him, No, Sir, I don't, but I'm not lying to you, if that's your impression. We just came for supplies, and we'll be on our way.

He scratched his ear and took a few thoughtful steps, his fancy boots clunking the pine porch boards, and he leaned against a post. Now I've got a theory, gentlemen, he said.

Charley and I waited, the sweat dripping off us. That fly buzzed around my neck, too, but I let it buzz. The gunslinger behind me looked like he might enjoy any excuse to use his guns.

My theory, said Conroy, is that I might just be talking to
Ovid Vesper, whose reputation precedes him: the man who
finds things . . . the man who crawls into caves and comes
back with the Crazy Gold. I've seen it, hammered out long
and flat, with the curious designs. Conroy watched me closely.
Why waste time with shiny dust in a pan, he asked, when you
could find gold like that?

That Noonan crew had kept busy talking in their two
weeks of life after they'd robbed us. Unflaggingly stupid to
the last. Didn't take much for rumors of gold to catch on.

Crazy Gold, I silently repeated. I'd never heard it called
that, but the name fit. You'd have to be crazy to go after it
in those dark places, and it certainly made people crazy. All
the while he was talking, Conroy watched me for a reaction. I
gave him the blankest look I knew how, trying to figure what
options we'd got.

Would you like to hear the support for my theory? Conroy
asked. When we didn't answer, he told us anyway: Two days
ago, my scout observed two men entering the canyon south of
here, up in the hills. His description of them is hard to mistake:
a white man and a Negro man, riding a pale horse and a roan.
Do you follow me so far? I was most curious, said Conroy,
why two travelers might be poking around in a canyon with
their horses left up top. But I predicted you'd stop here when
you were finished, and you could enlighten me. If that was
indeed you, Mister Keyes and Mister Broaddus, you're not in
any hurry to get up to Saro.

We got a few extra days, I said with a shrug. Probably won't see this piece of country more than once.

Furthermore, he said, it's a long way to any other town. You boys are traveling awfully light.

Seemed we were damned if we brought the saddlebags, and damned if we didn't. All we had was our guns, water jugs, tool kit, rope, and bedrolls tied up behind the saddles.

The gunslinger grinned and looked like he was getting itchy, opening and closing his hands. The rifleman with the bandoliers held his weapon loose and ready.

Conroy strolled over to another post, *clunk, clunk, clunk,* and leaned against it with his other shoulder. He pushed his derby back a little on his head. Now, I don't believe you came all the way without packs, he told us. I suggest that your packs are hidden somewhere in the brush an easy ride out of town. I'll wager they're stuffed with Crazy Gold. Am I right?

He should've been a Pinkerton. I said: You burn down that church and the barn?

I did, Mister Vesper. You see, I have to make my point sometimes. I am all the religion these people need. The barn? That belonged to a man who took exception with me regarding the church.

Conroy straightened up and rolled his head around, stretching his neck. Now here's what we'll do, he said. You gentlemen will drop your guns, very slowly, right there in the street—starting with you, Mister Vesper.

I heard two hammers cocking, and I saw the gunslinger had his six-shooters pointed at me.

I knew what was coming next. We would drop our guns, lead Conroy's men to the saddlebags, and then—no matter what promises Conroy would have made—we'd be dead. We might have prolonged things by telling him there was still a mountain of gold in the cave, but once we'd led him there . . . no further need for us.

Doing as told, I lowered my right hand to my side and eased the Schofield out of its holster.

That's it, said Conroy soothingly. He didn't bother drawing his piece; he had every confidence in his men.

I watched the gunslinger. He and the rifleman had about a dozen feet of space between them, which was smart. The rifleman hadn't raised his gun, but I figured he could do it fast. A breeze blew his thick hair, making it flutter around his neck. The gunslinger's pistols were trained right on me. There was no way I wouldn't get both bullets. No chance even for a blaze of glory.

I moved my arm out a way, getting ready to drop the Schofield.

Just then came a loud squeak of boards, and a wheezy old voice hollered, It's a mighty hot one, ain't it, fellers? The gunslinger's gaze flicked toward the voice.

Mine didn't.

I put a bullet in his chest, and another in his gut as he lurched backward. A shot of his went wild.

Despite his size, Big Charley wasn't slow. He whipped out the Remington and shot the rifleman.

Conroy finally had his gun out, and we went at each other. He was in a panic and Jack was bucking, so we both missed spectacularly, him putting slugs into the saloon front, me blasting chunks out of the porch rails.

Then he flung himself back inside through the open door and was gone from sight.

Charley leveled a shot from the eight-gauge in through the doorway, which wasn't the most sensible thing to do, considering all the innocent folks in there. But it made his point. Conroy didn't stick his head back out.

The rifleman was face down in the street, not getting up. On the end of the porch, the old-timer gave us a salute, followed by his hand opening and closing, flashing five fingers. I was mighty grateful to him, but there was no time for feeling good.

Jack and I were off at a charge down the street. Charley and Hugh came right behind. There was lots of clamor, and about the time we turned a corner, lead was screaming past us, hammering the storefronts.

We raced along a lane and turned left again, past where the carpenters were building. They'd stopped work and were gawking down from high beams like a cage full of scared birds. I tried to figure what to do. Charley's roan Hugh was as reliable as you could ask, but he hadn't been too fast since he tore up his leg on bob wire. If we rode out into the flat, Conroy's men would pursue and could close enough distance to shoot us afore we got to the trees.

I reined Jack in, although he felt like running.

Charley pulled Hugh up, too, and dismounted when I did. That was another point in Charley's favor: he never needed to hear an explanation in the moment. I got the Winchester out of its sleeve, and Charley still had hold of the eight-gauge. We had to finish this business, and I had rather do it on foot so our horses would be away from it. I patted Jack's neck and said into his ear, I'll see you later, Jack. I hoped they wouldn't shoot the horses out of spite. I didn't think so—they were good horses.

There's five more, I said. I guess that's counting Conroy.

We holed up against the side of a house long enough to fill our guns. Charley, I said, and just gave him a look.

He nodded. We weren't giving speeches, but if either of us or both were about to leave this life, we'd said enough.

Hooves came pounding up the cross-lane. Afore we could run for cover, the rider cut loose on us with a pistol. I felt a searing pain under my left arm, along the side of my chest, like I'd been run through with a branding iron. I'd been bitten and clawed and stabbed afore, and lead had passed close enough to leave powder burns, but getting properly shot was a first. You can feel the bullet tearing through you, and it's hot as a sonofabitch.

Charley fired the shotgun, but the man's horse was still running. The rider took a little of the shot but not enough to knock him down. Then he was gone past the corner.

You hit? Charley asked. Yeah, I told him, I'm all right.

I didn't know that for a fact, but I could still run, so we headed back the way we'd come and took a new lane past a row of barrels. There was dust hanging in the air, and more hoofbeats walloped. Conroy's men had expected us to light out on horseback. Now they knew we were on the ground, and they were hollering to one another about where we were.

More hooves came near, and Charley and me threw down on where the rider would be, but there wasn't a rider. Just a black horse, saddled up and running free.

We started to turn a corner but were cut off that way. Gunfire also came from above us, and I saw a man on the roof of the stable. We dashed straight for the stable to get below his line of fire; it was the only place we had a chance to run to afore he picked us off. To keep him ducking, I squeezed off two shots at him, but I couldn't aim on the run. I saw three stable hands clearing out.

Just afore we scuttled in through a side door, we got a glimpse onto the main street out front. Another gunslinger stood there, all dressed in black, with a cape down to his elbows like he was going to the opera and a wide-brimmed hat with a low crown—like some sort of priest.

Aw, shit, said Charley when we were inside a stall.

What? I asked, leading the way along the side of a chestnut mare who was giving us the eye. I opened a timber-bar door with Charley a step behind.

That's Ring Linder out there, he said. What the Hell is he doing with Conroy?

Who's he? I asked.

He's a hired killer out of Nevada, Charley said. They call him Ring on account he always rings the church bell when he leaves a town where he's killed a man. He rings it with a shot from his Peacemaker as he rides out. It's like a dirge for the deceased, but also his signature: Ring's been here. Some towns have got bells all full of his holes and dents.

Well, I said, Conroy hasn't left him a church steeple in this town.

Lead came flying through the stable.

We kept our heads down and reloaded. I used the Winchester, crouching in the aisle between stalls, chambering rounds and firing over horses' backs when shooters sprang up in the windows. Blood ran down my side, soaking my shirt. I could feel the injury; there was pain sort of like I had a bad cramp, but I was breathing all right—I had both lungs. The blood was seeping, not spurting. I reckoned I could go on for a while, though I was thinking of Hat Toynbee on that mountaintop in Montana in the golden hour of sunset, and what she'd said about the Tree of Life, and the river.

Conroy was out there now; he must have felt safer with his hired gun present, and I saw that Conroy had two revolvers now.

I caught a flash of red bandana as the man from the roof jumped down out of the hayloft. He was inside with us. I rolled across the aisle to give him something to shoot at. Bullets struck the stall door. One ricocheted with a long, loud whine.

From a stall right beside that bandana man, Charley let him have it with the eight-gauge. The man flew across the aisle and landed in a hay trough, tearing it loose from the wall. Charley took a careful look, but he was done moving.

I kept firing the Winchester, and I think one shot winged Conroy, on account I heard him yip. The men outside were filling that stable full of lead, and I was most afraid for the horses, who were rearing and screaming. I wished we hadn't led Conroy's men there.

When the rifle was empty, I set it down—we had to get out of there.

The stable wasn't very defensible, with all the open windows and doors. It was hard to get completely out of sight and under cover, and the idea of letting horses shield us was abhorrent. Conroy was covering the front entrance and the aisle inside it. His men worked the sides, pushing us back. They had us in a crossfire. There wasn't any barn left behind us. All that was saving us so far was the rickety, wide-gapped stall fencing and the tumbledown walls themselves, boards swinging loose, sun-bleached.

Ovid, said Charley, sticking bullets into his Remington, we gotta go. He was out of shotgun shells. I figured it was no good running out the back, but we had to do something. They knew where we were and where to shoot. I spilled out my empties and filled up the Schofield.

Charley made a dash for the back door, but just afore he crossed the threshold into the light, I caught sight of a shape through the cracks in the boards to the door's left. A man was out there, up against the stable's back wall, just waiting for one of us to run out. There was no time to stop Charley.

I drew the LeMat, remembering the firepower of its grape-shot barrel in the middle of that cylinder. Just as Charley crossed the doorstep, I blasted the wall where that shape was blocking the light. Enough of the grapeshot got through. I followed the initial shot with several from the LeMat's revolver barrel, pouring hot lead through those splintering boards. When I hit the threshold just behind Charley, I saw a man wriggling on the ground there, trying to raise his gun, and I put one more bullet in him so he stopped trying to kill us.

Another hot poker slammed through my left arm above the elbow. The LeMat fell out of my left hand. I saw Ring Linder over to that side. He winked at me.

Then I was running after Charley, and I could move and breathe all right, though my shirt was soaked with blood. We zigzagged like jackrabbits. There was nothing to get behind— we were in a big empty corral with a fence around it.

Conroy and his men were laughing at us. I reckon we looked mighty pathetic.

Charley took a shot to the knee and went down, rolling over in the dust. I swung around, crouched down with him behind me, and raised the Schofield.

Who shot him was the one we'd seen on the horse earlier, a skinny little cuss dressed in blue. He kicked open a gate and came into the corral, gun blazing. His bullets tore up dirt, not missing by much. He had fancy guns but wasn't very good with them. Trying not to pass out, I kept my arm steady and sighted down the barrel, not believing I hadn't been finished off yet—maybe I'd gone right into the dream men have when they're gunned down, the dream that they're still fighting, that they can still do something. The Schofield was feeling heavy.

It took me two shots, but I dropped the blueboy. He staggered backward and his clothes or belt caught on the gate he'd kicked open, so he didn't fall all the way down; he hung there like a half-toppled scarecrow.

Charley writhed and cussed behind me, but he got the Remington up, and Ring Linder played with us from the other corner of the stable. He shot from cover, and we had none.

Charley said to me, Get out of my way, you ornery shit.

He said it quiet and kind, and I knew what he meant. But I kept myself planted there like a tree stump, betwixt him and Ring.

And then I clicked on empties, Charley was empty, and we were bleeding into the ground.

A breeze swirled the dust clouds, but it was a hot breeze and didn't cool things off. My left arm hung useless, throbbing in a way that made me sick. Conroy came out the back door of the stable; he'd walked straight through it. From the stable's corner, Ring followed the fence and let himself into the corral by the gate on that side. Conroy said to Ring, Easy now, hold your fire. They each had two pistols trained on us. Conroy in his shiny boots stepped carefully around the horse apples.

They were quite a pair: Ring in his opera cape, Conroy in his fancy vest and derby. Ring's whiskers made a neat little ring around his mouth.

I guessed the Craither wasn't about the business of saving me today. Maybe it had gotten what it wanted.

The two men stopped about ten steps away from us. A muscle ticked at the corner of Conroy's eye, and blood dripped out of his sleeve. Well, you boys have put on quite a show, he said in that smooth thespian voice. Lot of good men dead, Vesper. I want that gold.

I looked him in the eye and said nothing.

Good men dead. There sure were. Quite a show. I reckoned it was, and I'd seen it.

For no reason, I saw myself sitting on Jack beside Mister Bowdler sitting on Chapultepec, surveying that herd of three thousand longhorns ranging out over North Texas in the sun. Like leading the children of Israel, Mister Bowdler had said. And then I saw my mama and my dad. They were no particular age, not old, but happy and laughing with their voices and their eyes.

And then I saw Nancy, filling my mind's eye, her pretty face and gray eyes and shy little smile. She was wearing that lilac-colored dress with the print of flowers, like on that day I'd kissed her and we'd decided on the month for our wedding.

The vision shifted, Nancy's form becoming another, this one in the green light of trees . . . the garden again, cool and fragrant. It was the woman among the blossoms, with the chattering stream and the sleek wildcat. Now I saw her clearly for the first time: a strong, lovely face . . . intense eyes that shone with a purpose.

Conroy didn't like whatever he saw in my face then. He twitched, and a shudder ran through him.

I was waiting to be shot for the third and final time in my life when I heard two shotgun blasts. First Ring Linder pitched over, looking surprised. Then Conroy sprawled in front of me, right afore my knees. He was missing the derby and most of his head.

To my right, holding a double-barreled shotgun across the fence rail, was the very woman I'd been seeing in my visions. I knew it was her—same stance. Same piercing eyes. She wore a long skirt, blue as the twilight, and a gray blouse.

We could only watch to see what she'd do next; it was like watching a lightning bolt in human form. She strode over, prodded Conroy with the toe of her boot, and spit on him. She muttered something in Spanish I didn't catch.

Finally looking us over, she said, It's nice to meet a pair of men who don't just bend over and take it. You gonna make it?

With some effort, I put Charley on my good side and got him to his feet, and we hobbled over to the gate. Charley couldn't set any weight on his busted knee.

The woman's black hair floated on the wind, and her throat was all shiny with sweat. She was packing a pistol on her hip, which I guessed she'd have used if the shotgun hadn't got the job done. Charley and I thanked her humbly and well, fully cognizant of the fact that we'd have been dead by then if she hadn't come along.

By that time we had a lot of help: people came out of doorways, pointing and chattering and breathing in the way plants breathe in the spring. Someone ran ahead to let the doctor know we were heading his way.

When I told her my name, the lady said folks called her Ruby Diamond. Turned out she was the proprietor of the saloon.

Someone had rounded up Jack and Hugh for us, and they were tied at the hitching post. While two men helped Charley along, I stopped to check on Jack; we were mighty glad to see each other still breathing. Neither he nor Hugh had any injuries. And when I inquired later, I learned that for all the lead that poured into the stable, none of the horses there were killed or had to be put down; there were some grazes, and one lost most of an ear, but that was the worst of it. I suppose the Catlickers might say that St. Francis was interceding for those good horses. Anyway, I was grateful.

The old-timer sat in the shade of the saloon's porch, grinning and spitting tobacco juice. I shook his hand and thanked him, and with a chuckle he curled his fingertips to his thumb and held up his hand, showing me a new number—zero.

It was better than I'd expected with my left arm. The shot had missed the bone but gone through the muscle and come out clean. Same with my chest: the bullet had cracked a rib but passed on through and wasn't inside me. The doctor, one Elias Bradshaw, was a fair sight more trained and skilled than I'd expected in a Territory town of this size. He'd learned new techniques from a colleague of his named Goodfellow, who washed his hands, instruments, and gunshot wounds with lye soap or whiskey and would get better results. Our doc didn't dig around in us with his fingers like the docs did in the War. He said that Charley would keep his leg and I was going to keep the arm, and that my chest and rib would mend. It took me a good while to get back the full use of the arm, and I've never stopped feeling both those shots when the weather's wrong. The doc bound and splinted Charley's knee; Charley was able to gimp around with a crutch as it took its sweet time healing. When it comes down to it, it's quite miraculous how our bodies are built to recover if they can.

What's Ruby Diamond's real name? I asked Doc Bradshaw.

Ruby Diamond, he said.

That sounds like a name that came along later, I said. Where's she from?

The doc eyed me over his spectacle rims, smiling faintly. No name but that, he said. No past.

After the order of Melchizedek, said Charley, quoting Scripture.

So Ruby Diamond really had come here to start over.

When the doc had finished, Charley and I made our way to the saloon, where Ruby Diamond and her patrons made sure we got all the free drinks we could hold. I saw that she commanded respect—not a man in the place treated her like a saloon girl.

Some gents found us the most comfortable seats. It struck me how pleasant it was indoors—I'd have gone so far as to say blissful, after all that sun and anxiety. The place was dark as a deep grove and cool as a cave. It was the garden in my visions; I could recognize the feel of it. And there at the end of the bar, curled up and blinking languid green eyes, was her black cat— significantly smaller than what I'd seen in my head.

Once my eyes adjusted, I noticed where the cool was coming from, and at first I thought I was dreaming again. All around the edges of the room, leaned up against the walls, were big stone slabs like doors and half doors. There were broken posts, too—pillars. They were all carved with strange writing and pictures the like of which I'd never seen. It didn't look like the work of the Old Things that punched the dots in gold; this didn't feel wrong like their caves do, though I reckoned this was some other kind of Old.

The wonder was that the slabs and pillars gave off a blessed chill like sheets of ice up in the mountains. Ruby said she found them in a cave in the hills and sweet-talked some of the boys into hauling them here. So Ruby was a cave-crawler like me. Said the cool made her place the most popular in town, and we laughed, on account it was the only place in town with whiskey—she might have burned offal and brought in rattlesnakes, and these pokes would come in. Running my hand over those stone relics, I allowed they were the ruins in my vision of the garden.

We stayed around, mostly to be sure Charley really was on the mend. The stories we heard about Xavier Conroy ran pretty typical: he'd blown into town with his gang and figured he'd make his fortune being the king of these parts, even though he called himself the Mayor. In Discovery, he'd encountered just the proper lack of local backbone so that he'd succeeded for a short span. Out there in those days, it was a story one heard a lot.

Some evenings later, when I asked, Ruby Diamond came with me to dinner at the hotel. She wasn't afraid to be seen with me, didn't give a good day what the town might say about it. I also knew it meant only that she was having dinner with me, for now.

She stayed mostly quiet, sizing me up, though she did not seem ill at ease. Ruby asked more than she told. She heard about Illinois, the War, and some of my perambulations, and she smiled at the right things. But always I had that sense of a cyclone in a box, that force of nature in her eyes. She had a big story to live, and I couldn't begin to fathom what it was.

You are a good man, Ovid Vesper, she pronounced once.

You don't talk about what's behind you, I said casually but carefully.

She held my gaze and then shook her head. Mi pasado es el desierto, she said.

I watched her carefully, understanding why she had lapsed into Spanish. It was her way of letting me in, a step closer to her. She was showing me that she knew she didn't have to work extra hard for me—she could use the words that were most comfortable. There's a lot of desierto in my past, too, I told her.

She laid a hand on my wrist and stared very intently into my eyes. He visto al diablo, she said.

I thought of thunder and smoke in the East, and of certain men I'd met in the West, many of whom I haven't even told you about, like Doc Nightingale. Yeah, I said: I reckon I've seen him, too.

Nuevas raices aqui, she said.

I nodded slowly. This wasn't much of a place, but roots could get down through most any soil, if they were determined. New roots. One way or the other, I needed them, too.

One hot night, Charley and I sat out for some air under a dusty
old ash tree by a corral. We had a jug of whiskey, courtesy
of Ruby Diamond, and passed it back and forth. Some coyotes were yipping out past the canyon. We admired the round
moon, gleaming like a polished plate. Both of us were thankful for hotel beds to sleep in and regular baths. It was good to
be settled, even for a few days.

We got to talking about how close we'd come to meeting
death in this town.

It ain't ever easy, Charley said, taking a man's life. It
adds to the faces, he said.

I knew what he meant: those faces you see behind your
eyelids. Ovid, he said, do you remember the first time you
killed a man?

I do, I said.

For me, Charley said, it was in the Gulf off Mobile.

In the blockade, I said quietly.

He said, We were part of that long line, the Big Snake.
It was always the blockade runners, attacks when we'd least
expect it. That time a Reb submarine came up—a boat for
underwater, you know? I didn't know what I was seeing—like
some giant turtle had come up out of the waves. First time I'd
seen one. Then the Rebs were shooting and shelling, lots of
boats in the dark. Our cannons opened up, but some of us were
just on the deck, trying to keep our heads down and shooting
with rifles. I'd done some shooting afore that, Charley went on,
though I don't know if I hit anyone.

He got more serious then.

That night, under a bright moon like this one, I was killing for certain—one man, then another and another. First was a kid with yellow hair. Next I got an officer, figuring that would do more good. I didn't feel too much about it then, just that we had to get this thing done.

Charley seemed to be finished talking, so we sat and listened to the breeze in the ash leaves. The coyotes had gone quiet, but I could hear an owl somewhere. The ground was still warm from being baked all day, like the top of an oven underneath us. After a while, Charley said, That kid, and took a pull from the jug.

After a space, I told him how it was for me. I'd practiced hard at aiming true. I could plug a bottle off a fence, or hit dead center in a circle I scratched on a stump. But when it came to shooting men . . . the enemy . . . I couldn't do it at first. I'd sight up on a Reb, and I couldn't pull the trigger, even when men around me were going down—my comrades in arms, and I couldn't do it. Until I did.

Where was it? Charley asked.

Bull Run, I said. The first one.

I told Charley: There were hundreds of folks in bonnets and top hats and straw hats—civilians, I mean, from Washington. Whole crowds of them. They'd come to watch the battle. Had blankets spread on the grass, and picnic baskets. Thought they'd come to see a rousing spectacle that would be over in a couple hours. Well, the Rebs had us in a rout, a full save-your-hide retreat, and we ran headlong into the spectators, and they were all screaming and trying to run, too.

The memories were coming back clearly. Now Charley and I were both done speaking, but I was remembering: It was my captain that got me to fight—John Clement, who was later to bury two of his children and raise his daughter called Grace Given who stayed alive. Right in the fury of it, I still wasn't shooting at the Rebs, and Captain Clement came up behind me and shot off his pistol right beside my head. That was as effective as if he'd knocked me to the ground. He didn't say much, just cussed me, and I knew what he meant. I had to kill. Then I had to again, and like Charley'd said, it finally got to where I didn't think or feel too much about it—at least not in the moment when it needed doing. It was always afterward that I thought about it.

But I couldn't recall the individuality of those first men I killed. They were faceless men on a battlefield, running at me through the smoke, yelling and shooting. No names. Boys in a field.

Charley crossed his ankles. When he ignored his turn to swig on the jug, I knew he was thinking hard about something, so I watched the night and enjoyed leaning against that tree.

He cleared his throat after a while and said, Ovid, I figure I better go talk to my brother. I better go see Reeney.

You figure it's time? I asked.

Yeah, he said.

You ready to put this Territory behind you? I asked.

I reckon so, he said.

That's good, I said.

Charley grinned and said, It don't hurt none that I could buy Reeney right out of that business if I had a mind to. That was right—Charley and I were about half as rich as Croesus now, if we could keep from getting bushwhacked again. But I ain't going to do that, Charley said. I'm going to buy myself a ranch. You ought to go in with me, Ovid. You're the one who can talk to horses.

I laughed at that and thanked him for the offer, but I didn't think my visions had quite played themselves out yet. I said I still had a thing or two to do out there.

With a sly glance, he said, You got to see about Ruby, don't you?

I hadn't thought too much about it, but I reckoned that had something to do with it, although I didn't want to admit it to myself. It felt disloyal. I could hear Chervil's voice: You got to move on. But that wasn't the entirety of it.

All that—notions of the future—felt like a pantomime, not real. I was pretty sure it was almost over with the Craither, which probably meant I was about to die. More and more lately, I'd wake up in the small hours, forced awake by pain, and I knew the Craither was nearby. I almost told that to Charley, but I didn't want to interfere with his course, now that he'd resolved to do the good thing.

Couple days later, Charley rode east. I made sure he knew what to do with his share of the gold: not to sell it hastily or all at once, but little by little, to different gold buyers of good reputation. That way he could get the best prices. It was hard to part ways, but I'd hoped we might cross paths again. He had the general idea that he wanted to wind up in the Wyoming Territory, which was pretty country. That's where I could start looking for him, anyway. It eased the sting of parting to know that he was bound first for home, to do right by his kin.

In fact I did not see the man again, but I got a letter through to him later, by good luck and with the help of a good-hearted postmaster. We wrote back and forth several times over the years. Charley did well. He married a big, Charley Rim–sized woman of Norwegian descent, and they started having babies who grew up and helped their folks ranch. One of his boys became a lawyer and one of his girls opened a school—a legacy to be proud of.

When I was fairly sure I could ride without making my injuries worse, I asked Ruby if she'd show me the cave where she'd found the cold slabs and pillars. She didn't take much persuading—I guess she was seeing about me, too.

Out on the range, she watched me and said little, riding easily—she was no stranger to the saddle.

Ruby had a handsome pinto named Saxon. That was his name when she bought him as a yearling, and she hadn't seen a need to change it. She brought along her twenty-gauge and pistol, and with a gray Stetson shading her face, she led Jack and me up into the brown hills to the west of Discovery.

It was dry out that way, like everywhere else. The feathery sand sage looked like the ghosts of plants that used to grow there, and leadplant with its silver-gray leaves stuck up its long, pale purple brush-blooms. It took Ruby some wandering around, but she relocated the cave. Down in a rocky bottom, it had a good-sized mouth that you couldn't see till you came round the boulders up close. From up the slope, you wouldn't know there was a cave at all.

I asked Ruby how she ever found it.

Chasing a coyote, she said.

I couldn't help smiling at that. Why? I asked.

She said, Looked like he wanted to show me something.

I studied the cave mouth. What made you want to go in? I asked her.

The coyote wanted to show me, she said with a smirk.

I couldn't help thinking of Richard Decalne's green children. They'd followed a goat into a cave and ended up in Blow Land.

We had a pair of lanterns from the saloon. Ruby said it was better for the horses to come with us, out of the sun. So we lit the wicks and poked our way down among the stones and into the maw of darkness. The chill wafted out to meet us. I saw old tracks in the silt there at the threshold—prints of hooves and boots, probably from when the men had hauled the cold rocks out for Ruby. Coyote tracks, too.

At the bottom of a slope inside, the cave opened out into a giant room, elliptical, with a high-domed ceiling. This was where Ruby had found her slabs and columns. There were still some of them here, radiating cold and covered with the same ancient writing. It was mostly dry now, not growing dripstones or curtains—just a huge cellar of the earth, old beyond count.

The horses were calm enough, though I felt uneasy. I'd been dreaming about caves and black pits since the run-in with Conroy, and I often felt the Craither right behind me, like it was looking over my shoulder. When I turned around to holler at it, it was never there. I knew this place had something more to it, something I was meant to see.

Ruby waited with her hands on her hips, watching to find out why we'd come here, not afraid to be with me in this dark, lonely place. When I'd made a careful circumnavigation of the chamber, studying the artifacts that remained, I eased on back through a farther arch, where the floor dipped down again. The cavern ran deeper. Still, the space was wide and high—I didn't see any danger of getting lost.

We left Jack and Saxon in that first big room, and Ruby came along behind me. The second chamber was even larger, an echoing vault so wide that our light just barely reached to the far wall. The floor tumbled sharply down at our feet, like a steep ramp. We had entered high up, a hundred feet or more beneath the ceiling, but a lot farther than that from the distant floor. Back in the shadows on all sides were structures—some kind of pueblo city—open doorways, empty windows, row on row of dwellings, all stacked up. It was silent now, but someone had lived here once.

Ruby peered around, wide-eyed.

You know this part was here? I asked her.

She shook her head and asked, Indians?

I reckon so, I said, or maybe people who came afore the Indians. Or maybe, I thought, something that came afore people. It was hard to tell, though I was remembering that time I'd camped with Joseph and Tallman, the pair of Hopi brothers, and they'd pointed out the mesas where the Katsinas lived. Looking at these pueblos now, I felt like I'd felt looking up at the bright cloud on the sacred mesa's rim. I wondered if these dark dwellings really were empty.

I felt another presence, very strong—and then the all-too-familiar draining, as if my insides were being sucked right out of me. This time, the pain was so intense that I lurched against the cavern wall and nearly collapsed.

Ruby rushed closer to steady me, staring in alarm.

What is it? she asked, but I only shook my head.

What are you after? I said in my mind to the Craither—as if it were going to tell me now.

An energy mounted behind the pain, growing intense; I could feel that tremendous longing, even though I didn't have hold of the Craither. I thought I could hear a sound it was making, a series of soft, groaning whimpers.

I don't know if Ruby heard anything. I must have been a terrible sight. It felt like the Craither's presence might just pull me inside out this time, and that would be the end of me, but then I heard something. It was not quite a voice . . . but something clear. An idea . . .

A request.

At the edge of my last strength, right on the brink of dropping where I stood, I had a flash of understanding. The Craither had gotten through to me at last—it had reached my mind with an effective translation from a consciousness as far from human thought as the stars are far away.

The Craither needed my help. It was going somewhere, and it was utterly lost in this world of mine; I gathered in that instant that I was just about the only thing here that it could see with any recognition. Nor was I any clearer to it than it was to me. It needed to go on just a few more steps, and it needed me to guide it.

It was trying to get home.

My head was singing now, surging with the crucial comprehension.

The Craither had clung to my image, following me through my travels since the War, growing weaker and more desperate even as its nearness drained me. I saw a rush of images from my own past—faces and objects—but I saw them in that moment as the Craither had, vague shapes of terror. A simple yellow flower in a field was to the Craither something monstrous . . . a cannon was a nightmare . . . the rising sun like an open portal into Hell. Being here was steadily killing the Craither, just like its presence was killing me. It wasn't trying to hurt me, nor had it intended to incinerate those homesteaders who were too close when it made its own attempt to get from this world back into its own, using Earth's energy lines. It probably hadn't even known the settlers were there.

I wanted to tell Ruby that she didn't have to come any

farther. This was something I had to do, and I didn't suppose I would survive it. But I had no voice for speaking. The Craither's mind, or some part of it no bigger than a dust mote, was all I knew then. She came with me, though; I could feel her hand on my arm, helping me as I lurched forward, one foot after another.

We ventured down that slope. Rocks slid underfoot, but Ruby kept me upright. After a long descent, we reached the flat floor where the pueblos rose up in cliffs around us. Ruby had the shotgun tucked into the crook of her arm—I saw its barrel and recognized what I saw, though its shape was unspeakably horrific to the Craither's awareness in me. I had set down my lantern, or else Ruby had set it down for me. I hardly needed light anymore; it did little for me in my state.

There was a darkness ahead that I walked straight into, on account I knew we were headed there—the Ovid Vesper part of me knew it was where the Craither belonged.

It wasn't just a chamber in a cave. It was like we stood at the very farthest place that was still part of the Earth, which ended here. We were looking ahead into nothing: that's how it appeared to me. I never asked Ruby exactly what she saw. I think she tried hard to forget it afterward.

Near as I can explain it, what opened there was the ultimate shadow, the darkness beyond everything. I glimpsed figures that moved, unnumbered millions of them, nothing very clear.

Space itself was different there. It bent back on itself; I felt it more than saw it. Nothing could be counted on. Solids flowed, emptiness was hard as adamant, things that seemed alive flew and crawled at the same time. I couldn't look for long, so I threw an arm across my face and tried to tell Ruby to do the same, but my voice was the wordless roar of thunder. Or music. Or something like the cry of a bird.

Then I felt the Craither right beside me, and it seemed no bigger than me; I saw it without looking. Now it had arms, legs, and its still-gleaming eyes. I laughed at how delightfully clear it was, and how wondrous, a being like nothing I might have imagined.

I felt its sudden recognition of the place. And in the next moment, I heard what could only have been: Thank you.

I didn't know how to answer it. I couldn't bridge the gulf as it had managed to do. But I guess that was all right. What I might have said to the Craither didn't matter. It was home.

Its shining arms spread out, maybe wings, maybe clouds, maybe beautiful words. The Craither tumbled away in the vastness, rising or descending.

For one instant I saw the Craither's world. I saw it in a way that my mind almost grasped, though even that, I am sure, was not how the Craither saw it, not even close. No words of mine could describe it. It felt like those aching memories that you wish more than anything you could recall, but you never can, and then you're not sure if they're really memories at all, or if they're a longing for something that you can never have in this life.

In the Craither's world, I almost saw one of those memories with clarity.

When I knew that wonder, that ache, something went out of me, something I'd carried for a long time. Another darkness I'd gotten in the War recognized its own essence in that cavern, in that enormity of shadow, and was gone from me, like a glob of quicksilver rejoining the mass it had come out of. I didn't cast it away. It went. And as we stumbled away from the Edge of that other world, I felt lighter.

That's enough to boggle your mind, if you think much about it: what I'd carried was from the horror and pain of the War, but that burden was attuned to the Craither's unspeakably lovely world. How could those things be of the same resonance and substance? I can only conclude that what comes to us as burden and blight is something that just doesn't translate here, so it can only hurt us. We are not built for it, and we do not receive it in its true shape. There is so much we don't yet understand.

I let Ruby guide me then. We headed back toward the sunlight, just as when Richard Decalne and I had come back from the border of St. Martin's Land.

I understood that the Craither hadn't stolen into this world of ours at Antietam. It hadn't wanted in at all. It had been sucked in, caught in an inrushing stream like a pollywog in a drain. If it had seemed angry at me, it was because I'd brought it here; *I'd* made the vortex that sucked the Craither in. All it had wanted was its home, just like all the rest of us at Antietam, the living and the dead.

I'm pretty sure my visions weren't all about helping the Craither, or caused by it; I think they were for a larger purpose, on account they had other good results. But who is to say what leads to what? Maybe there was no separating the Craither's journey from mine, or from anything else. Maybe it's all part of one thing, from the cannons to Francis Eames to Hat Toynbee . . . to Nancy Mavornen. To the smallest wisp of cloud, here and then gone.

So was I helping the Craither get home, or was it helping me, on account it knew, with its unknowable alien perception, that the cave where it was headed was also the one place that could draw the War's specter out of me?

I don't much remember leaving that cave. If Ruby hadn't been there, I might not have returned to the sunlight.

Ruby and I saw about each other, and we both saw at about the same time what we needed to know. For a moment, buoyant with relief out there in the sun, the blowing dust, the heat waves, and the velvet nights, I almost felt something—I almost imagined, in her darkly blazing, beautiful intensity, a refuge. But that moment passed. Ruby's saloon was her dream; she'd put her money into it and given it her own name, which she'd also given to herself when she settled in this wilderness town to start new. If she wanted a man on a permanent basis, which I think she was questioning, it was one who would tend the bar, bounce out the troublemakers, maybe become the leader Discovery needed. I wasn't that man. Maybe *Ruby* was that man. She'd settled the score with Conroy handily enough.

As for my perspective . . . I remembered how I'd felt when I promised to marry Nancy. I didn't feel that way about Ruby, lovely though she was. She wasn't Nancy.

The visions weren't pulling me forward anymore. I was done with going in circles, but this wasn't my place to land—I could go home now, like Charley could. Like the Craither had. I hankered for oak trees around me and familiar, flat fields of rich, dark earth. That brick farmhouse on the Illinois prairie was calling me. Whether I'd really live there wasn't yet clear, but it was time to start from it again like I'd started in life.

All the yanking and crushing on me was gone. I'd for sure die of something when the time came, but I was pretty sure now that it wouldn't be from the sickness the Craither had caused me.

I gave Ruby an abundant measure of the Crazy Gold to set her up nice and keep her secure. I still had more than I'd ever need, and without her, Charley and I never would have lived beyond that day in Discovery, New Mexico.

And now I've got just a little more of the story to tell you.

INTERLUDE

I didn't puzzle long about why the Craither hadn't saved Charley and me from Conroy and his men the way it had saved me from Bellamy's bunch in Flagstaff. Chances are it had no idea of the effects it had—did I really know anything about the effects *I* had? Do any of us, ever?

As Jack and I headed on eastward, I was thinking more and more of Illinois and the years I'd spent there, and my old folks.

I've told you a horse story about my mama, how she stopped that wild one that bolted. There's one about my dad, too, and it involved another of Judge Broaddus's horses.

Once when I was about six, a kid named Wirt was plowing for the judge. My dad called Wirt a kid, though he looked like a fully grown man to me. He was plowing a little too soon after a drenching rain, and too close to the ravine at the back of the field, thinking he could get one more row in. The plow horse slipped in the mud, tumbled down the steep bank by the creek, and took the plow down, too, right on top of it. That poor animal broke two of its legs. There was nothing for it but to put it down.

Judge Broaddus came and asked my dad if he could do it. I can shoot a rabid cat, even a dog, the judge said, but I can't shoot a horse.

My dad got his gun. He didn't like doing it, either, and

I'd overheard and started crying. Huddled under the bushes, I wanted to cover my ears, but I couldn't somehow, and pretty soon I heard the shot. Just one shot, and then silence, and a horse that had stopped moving. When he got back, Dad called me, and I came out to sit with him on the porch. He wasn't one to show much physical affection, but he put an arm around my shoulders and pulled me close against his side.

Ovid, you know why I had to do that? he said. You can't set a horse's leg. That horse was in awful pain. That was the only thing to do—the merciful thing.

Why? I asked.

Why what? he said.

Why did it break its legs?

On account the world is broken, my dad said. It's why we get old, why we get sick, why we die. Why things go wrong. Why we get our hearts broke.

We watched the clouds moving and the low sun setting the clouds on fire. Birds were heading home for the night.

But you know, my dad went on, it's also why I fixed that leak in the barn roof—it needed fixing. It's why your mama took that pie to Missus Hoffner. It's also why I did that for Judge Broaddus. He couldn't shoot that horse himself. He needed me to do him a kindness.

I wasn't sure I understood that very well.

Someday, my dad said, things won't be broken any more. Till then, we've got to fix what broken things we can.

A lot of things my dad said have made more sense to me as time goes on.

CHAPTER SEVEN:
THE OLIVE TREE

ILLINOIS, 1891

The visions had decreased, both in how often they came to me and certainly in kind. Jack and I headed steadily eastward; we hadn't gone so far in one direction for a good number of years. Images in my head came mostly in dreams now, two different ones. I saw a low, twisty tree with smooth green fruits on it about the size of grapes. It was an olive tree, like on that mount where the Lord went to sweat blood and pray. I'd eaten olives; at first I thought they tasted like feet, but they grew on me. I'd seen the trees out in California. Still, I was pretty sure I was right to be going east. The other vision was of a rider, far off against the horizon but coming closer. I couldn't even see the color of the horse—just a black, moving silhouette where the land met the sky.

Homeward.

In Missouri, I went to see John Clement again. His family was doing well. Grace Given had grown up, pretty like her mama but with John's pale, piercing eyes. She'd also started to talk—just a few words now and then, in a musical, soft voice

like a dove. Margaret told me there was suddenly no shortage
of local boys wanting to come and work on the Clement farm.
Didn't know we had so many boys around here, she said. John
growled something about keeping his shotgun close to hand.

After many miles, we came to the mighty Mississippi River
and crossed on the chugging steam ferry at Alton. The pilot
looked as sunbaked as his boat, with a straw hat and a glistening white beard. He patted Jack and said that was a fine horse,
and I allowed that he was; I told him how Jack and I had been
all over, and now we were bound for Christian County, where
we'd both been raised.

Besides seeing the Clements, it felt right to cross the river
at Alton, which seemed to me a kind of gateway betwixt where
I'd started out and where I'd gone. My dad had brought me
down here to the river when I was no more than seven or eight.
He'd had some reason to go to St. Louis—I'd long since forgotten what it was. But he also figured I ought to see the Piasas.

On the bluffs there, the Indians of ancient times had
painted two monstrous craithers to look down over the river.
My dad talked about how those paintings of that thing called
the Piasa had given bejeebers to Father Marquette when he
and Joliet had first come down this way, following the river to
see where it went.

As a boy, I couldn't even fathom how artists long ago could
have reached a place so high on the rock. The Piasas were
badly faded, but I could still see the traces of green, red, and
black—two monsters with deer horns, red eyes, beards, and
faces like those of men. Each Piasa had scales and a long tail

winding all around the body, ending like the tail of a fish. In that moment of childhood, eye to eye with the Piasas, I think I knew that monsters were real, and that I was going to meet plenty of them.

It was good I'd seen them when I did. The paintings are gone now. Not long after the War, the Mississippi Lime Company quarried away that part of the bluffs. They hadn't ought to have done that, though it wasn't the first time mortals had wrecked something that was better left alone. Sketches of the Piasas still exist, of course, like in Father Marquette's book and in good libraries.

On the north side of Alton, Jack and I rested under the oaks at the sprawling cemetery where all the Confederate boys were buried, those who'd died when smallpox raged through the Reb prison—over two thousand prisoners dead. This was the town where the Reverend Elijah P. Lovejoy had become the first martyr of the Abolition movement, gunned down in front of his print shop while he was trying to keep the rabble from destroying his presses for the third time. Alton may have lost its Piasas, but I reckoned it still had plenty of ghosts.

As the days went by, Jack and I headed up through the timbers of hickory and hackberry, sycamore and elm and black walnut, and always the oaks, pillars of the world. I'd missed the oaks out in the desert, where there's nothing to hold the sky off your head. The woods were alive with squirrels and birds, a grand fair unfurling above us, the leaves rioting into crimson, gold, russet, orange. Jack was excited. I think he knew that our traveling days were almost behind us.

Illinois is a numinous land: well-lit fields out in the sun, edged by the dark, quiet timbers and creek bottoms. There are secrets in the ground, flint arrowheads shaped and shot by hunters long afore ever a squirrel or a deer was brought down by lead. There are dangers, such as the wells dug by pioneers, covered with boards and dirt when the frontier moved on westward. Those wells can whisper open when the boards rot away, and a throat of the Earth can gape right under your feet, or out in a moonlit cornfield with no one to see it happen.

We passed through the country of the mound builders, those hills that house the dust of folks who were Illinoisans long afore they'd be called that.

So we crossed the Flatbranch a little prior to its freeze-up and came into the familiar fields and past Judge Broaddus's old place and along the road where my mama had stopped that Hell-horse Acheron in his tracks.

I spent the winter cleaning and shoring up the house and barn, making it all livable, and I got familiar again with my neighbors and other folks from town, some who remembered me, others who were new. Most older ones had kind words about my parents.

Something about the way Jack settled in was the last confirmation I needed that this was where we ought to be. Jack and I both felt a particular contentment in the barn, with its vine-clad north wall and its mismatched stalls that had been built and rebuilt by a long line of farmers. There were gnawed crescents in some of the boards where horses had honed their teeth. Even when I first lived here, the stalls had been carpeted with moldering straw and hard, dry manure. I shoveled it out, making Jack a clean barn. In a dark trough at the back, there was still a salt block, licked and rounded off but gleaming like a part of winter that never melted. Mama cats had used that trough to birth their litters—we'd often find them there, usually long about Easter—little mewing craithers with eyes not yet open to the world. That barn was a marvel even in winter, and it would only grow more redolent and sacred when the spring lit it up with emerald light through the creeper leaves.

I found a secure hiding place to store the Crazy Gold. I won't say where, in case I might need the hiding place again. Little by little, I began the task of selling those coins and transferring the money into several banks here and there. I could retire on all that, but I started planning ways to keep myself productively occupied.

My good neighbor, the grandson of old Judge Broaddus, was happy to keep farming the field along with his own. I would take a small share of the profit each year, but I arranged for him to have most of it. The land ought to be put to use.

I took up life there again. I attended my mama's Lutheran church. The congregation had built themselves a new building, but they'd kept the stained glass from the old.

Late on a January afternoon, Jack and I were out along the Flatbranch, looking for tracks in the new snow on account one of my neighbors thought he'd spied a wolf prowling at the timber's edge behind his pasture. I wasn't seeing anything out of the ordinary—snowy hares and deer, lots of bird prints, and coyotes. Nothing with a big track like a wolf. The air hung quiet among the stark trunks. Sounds seemed to travel forever.

There was snow coming. We were just turning for home when I saw a saddled horse wandering in a field, nosing at the stobs and brown tufts that stuck up through the snow. No rider. I made a wide circle, searching and listening.

Sure enough, down by the creek, someone moaned. As we got closer, I could hear a man's voice calling out to the Lord. Then there was the man, writhing in obvious pain, leaning up against the trunk of a mulberry. He only had one leg, which gave me momentary pause. But then I saw that his leg hadn't been lost recently; he had a wooden peg leg below his right knee, and the peg leg had come off. It was lying in a patch of bloodied snow. The man had a gash on his head, with blood and leaves clumped in his gray whiskers. At the sight of me, he beseeched me for assistance.

I got down beside him and checked him over. Save for the gash, which appeared to be a surface wound, he seemed in one piece—nothing broken that I could tell. He'd looked the wrong way and gotten dragged out of the saddle by a tree limb. He seemed most in danger from the cold.

I made ready to get him to the doctor, but he insisted that he was sound, that he needed to get home afore the snow. It wasn't far, he said. I still thought the doc ought to look at him. Clinging to me, the man was able to strap his leg back on; when I brought him his horse, he mounted up and rode for home.

At the least, I wanted to see that he made it. He was advanced in years and had suffered a tumble and a knock on his skull, so I rode along with him. He crossed a field, followed the Allenton Road, and headed for the Box place, a towering relic up on a rise, set against a row of cottonwoods. I remembered that imposing house, probably a century old at least, one of the oldest in the county; and I vaguely remembered Sam Box and his brother John, both of them coal miners. It was John who'd lived in this house with his wife when I was a boy. In fact, this man was John Box. I hadn't seen him since afore the War, and hardly knew him back then.

I told him who I was. I remembered that my dad and granddad used to bring his people sassafras, dug up and bundled for brewing tea, although that would have been to old Beulah and Abel Box, parents of these boys. Sam had died in a mine collapse back in the mid-fifties. By the look and silence of the house, I guessed John's wife was gone, too.

While John cleaned himself up, I took his horse out to the barn and got her unsaddled, brushed down, and fed. I took the liberty of doing the same for Jack, on account the wind kicked up fierce, driving the snow, and we had a blizzard. We couldn't make for home until at least the wind died down.

In the whirl of whiteness, it was all I could do to find my way from the barn to John's house. He had a fire going and made coffee, and we sat there in his kitchen, listening to the house twist and pop.

John looked all right. He was going to have some bruises, but he'd pasted brown paper on his gash and gotten it to stop bleeding. He brought out brandy and poured splashes into the coffee. It was pitch dark outside. The wind made no sign of abating, so John said I might as well just bunk down for the night. He had plenty of room.

I allowed that probably was for the best. We stoked up the fire and talked about people, folks we remembered, and what all had happened to whom. We were neighbors in the general sense; his place couldn't have been more than six or seven miles from mine, as the crow flew.

We talked about the War. He hadn't been a young man then, but he'd gone to fight. John wanted to know where I'd been. He offered that he'd lost his leg at Shiloh—Army of the Tennessee, under Ulysses S. Grant, set upon by Johnston and Beauregard. Pyrrhic victory, John said: We won, but we lost more than they did. Ain't that how it all goes? He said: We keep winning until life kills us entire. That was the end of the War for John; they'd sawed off his leg and let him come home. John's wife, Maisey, had nursed him as he convalesced and eventually learned to get around with the peg leg and a crutch. But afore the War ended, Maisey took sick and died. It saddened me to hear it. Like so many others, John had gone into the War with everything a man could want and come out of it with nothing.

We let the fire burn down, the storm still rampaging like it wanted to take off the roof. That's about the time things got passing strange.

Once or twice while John was talking, I thought I could hear something, off in the dark depths of the house. Everything was creaking as the house wrestled with the wind, so I figured it was that. But John looked up, too, and narrowed his eyes.

When I heard the distinct wail of a woman's voice, my scalp went icy. John looked at me apologetically. I should have warned you sooner, he said: Maisey's been in her grave these twenty-three years, but she ain't ever really gone to rest. She didn't want to go, so she didn't go. That's true love, Ovid; that's the one thing I ain't lost. She's still taking care of me, in her way.

I didn't know what to say to that. Hinges squeaked, and a door closed somewhere over our heads.

It ain't a hainted house, John said. So you don't need to be afeared. I reckon she's telling me it's bedtime.

I nodded like this was perfectly normal, wondering how, precisely, it wasn't a hainted house if there was a ghost in it. My mind worked on it quickly. Could John be lying or confused? Was Maisey really still alive, not a ghost at all? But no, I remembered: I had heard from another Christian County soldier that Maisey Box had died. It hadn't registered much with me at the time, on account we had a lot to occupy our thoughts, and I didn't know the family well. Maisey Box was most definitely dead and buried in the churchyard on—most coincidentally—Shiloh Hill. Shiloh, the Giver of Rest, Place of Peace.

Maisey won't hurt you none, John assured me. You won't even see her. The dear woman is here for me; she don't care about anyone else among the living, unless maybe you're fixing to rob me. Then she'd probably take exception.

John chuckled and slugged down what was in his cup. We hadn't poured in any coffee the last time around—just brandy.

I generally make my bed down here, he explained, pointing off toward what I assumed might be the parlor. He said, Don't have much use for those stairs, if I can avoid them. But you go on up, Ovid. Guest bedroom's right at the top of the stairs. Plenty of blankets and quilts. You'll be warm enough, though I'm afraid you'll have to make up the bed yourself.

I gazed at the dark staircase but made no move to stir from my chair.

John grinned, his shoulders shaking with quiet laughter. Now, don't be timid, he said. After what you been through, ain't nothing to be afeared of here. It's just Maisey, and we're just your old neighbors. She'll keep out of sight.

I found little comfort in the fact of what I wouldn't see. I was sure that whatever walked in that house could see me plainly enough. Still, he had a point: there was no reason to think that Maisey's spirit, if it truly was earthbound, bore any ill will toward me. Wasn't I here on account I'd picked John up off the frozen ground and got him indoors?—not that I wanted Maisey to thank me.

I was remembering what I'd seen that night with Captain Clement, when we'd shot his daughter's murderer in the witch-hazel grove, and what we'd found around his neck, dug into the skin.

If you're down here, I asked John, why's your wife up there?

She likes the quiet, he said. And the dark. Besides, she's

shy around company. She'll be down when all the lights are
out and we're settled. It's all right, Ovid. Go on up.

I didn't want to be rude, and I certainly was ready to be
under a pile of quilts. With the kitchen fire down to coals, the
temperature was dropping fast. Outside the windows, the
snow flew past horizontally, sometimes even being swept back
up toward the sky. It was snowing in every direction out there.

I hoped Jack wasn't shut up in a hainted barn for the night.
If any other horses of John's had preceded his current one in
death, I hoped they'd just gone on and not stayed to help look
after him. I lit a lamp and bade John good night. Then I made
the long, squeaky climb to the upper story. Every protest of
the house against the wind took on new overtones now. I fancied I could hear a snatch of sniffling and weeping—or was it
the wind in the eaves? I could have sworn footsteps crossed a
room somewhere—or was it the rafters, fighting to keep their
burden out of the wind's arms?

When I reached the door atop the stairs, I peered into the
dancing shadows of the corridor. No cave I'd ever crawled into
had been more ominous than this space—dark-paneled walls,
cobwebs drooping in the corners. Other doors, closed against
the night. Had the brass knob on one of them turned by a few
degrees? Or was it a trick of the lamplight?

My breath came out in visible puffs. I hoped there were a
lot of quilts.

I grasped the frigid knob afore me. This must be the room
John had meant, the first one. I turned the knob . . . and found
the door to be locked.

After twisting the knob back and forth, assuring myself
that it really was locked, I pondered what to do. Should I try
another door? Had John meant the first *unlocked* room? No—
opening doors up here was most certainly not the thing to do. I
would have to go back downstairs and ask John about it.

I had a nearly overwhelming impulse to back down the
stairs, to avoid turning my back on the black corridor. But of
course that was ridiculous. Nagged by the question of why
John would lock the door of his guest room on a floor of the
house where no one came—no one living, anyway—I eased
down the endless, unquiet stairway. At the landing, my light
fell upon a portrait that I'd somehow missed seeing on my way
up. It was a painting of a small girl in antique dress, her round
face like a cherub's, her wide blue eyes fixed on me.

There was still the faintest glow from the kitchen, but I
saw no other lamplight. I was sure John could hear me coming from a long way off, boards creaking under my feet. As I
passed through the kitchen, I noted that my Winchester lever-
action rifle was leaning against the wall inside the door, right
where I'd left it. I had the Schofield on my belt, though the
LeMat was unloaded and packed away. Maybe I'd just take the
Winchester with me, too, when I went back up.

I called out John's name, keeping my voice low. Getting no
answer, I called again, a little louder, and made my way in the
direction he'd pointed.

The wind shrieked. Something thumped against the outside of the house. It was probably some barrel or bucket from
the yard, at the mercy of the wind.

Raising my voice a little more, I called for John. This time I heard a muffled reply, and my light shone into a large, wine-colored parlor.

It was fancier than anything I would have expected in this county, and I couldn't help wondering how the Boxes had come to dwell in a house like this. I couldn't recall ever hearing old folks talk about this house, and it was decidedly a residence that would have been talked about. No one had built or paid for such a place by mining coal. Thick drapes were drawn over most of the windows, though one had been left uncovered. I saw snow piled up in the corners of the panes. The light glinted on glass baubles and gilt frames. Stuffed chairs hunkered around like craithers ready to pounce. What my first wild impression took to be a coffin on trestles was actually an elegant piano.

I didn't see a bed.

When I called John's name again, he stuck his head out from under an ornate table.

What is it that you need, Ovid? he asked me while I stood there blinking.

I stammered that my room was locked, whereupon he apologized and crept on all fours from a nest of blankets. Apparently his bed was under the table, which stood on massive legs carved with elaborate curlicues, leafing vines, and lion's paws at the bottoms.

It was a process for John to hoist himself onto a chair and scoop up his crutch. I said that I was sorry to disturb him.

He waved away my apology and said, What kind of host

am I?—leaving my guest locked out! He didn't bother cinching on his peg leg. With the crutch, he hobbled closer, borrowed the lamp from my hand, and searched along the mantel of a gaping fireplace. Here we are, he said, taking a brass key from a box surfaced in red satin. He handed it and the lamp to me.

As he sank back onto the floor again, he took pity on my bewilderment. I find it peaceful to sleep down here, he said, because of the singing.

Singing? I asked.

This table, he said, is from a monastery—that's what they always told me. Brought over from Europe. When you lie beneath it and are very still, you can hear the monks singing. Faint and far off, he said, like voices from Heaven. It helps me sleep. Do you care to listen?

I didn't care to crawl with John Box into his nest of blankets, so I thanked him politely and retreated, leaving him to his singing table, the creaking darkness, and the snow piling against the glass.

I took along my rifle.

The cherubic girl gazed at me from the painting. The upstairs corridor, of course, was still empty. I stuck the key into the lock and carefully turned it. After the click of the tumbler, I removed the key, pushed open the door, and looked into a modestly comfortable bedroom.

As I crossed the threshold, though, I heard a woman's voice whimper once, and sob. The sound came from directly ahead, in my room.

Then there was silence. I stood in the doorway for a long

time, holding the lamp, tracing every detail of the place with my gaze. It was an empty room. I pulled open the door of the closet, which was full of old coats and a wooden trunk, shoes, a hat on a hook.

The wind moaned. I wished I could believe I'd only heard the wind.

More cobwebs festooned the eggshell lamp. I looked beneath the bed and saw only dust on the floor's planks. Having locked myself in, I leaned the Winchester where I could reach it, put the Schofield on the bedside table, and made the bed with the sheets and blankets folded on a cedar chest. Then I shucked off my boots and trousers. I decided not to undress beyond that. The bedding seemed laundered—or rather, it had been, long ago. The headboard and table were free of dust.

Shivering, I unfolded two more quilts from the pile and spread them on the bed. Then I climbed under all the covers, took a last look around, and blew out the lamp.

Lying there, listening to the wind and the house, I couldn't decide if it was more unnerving or more comical that John Box was down there under the fancy table that sang to him. The brandy had helped with warmth, and the thick quilts helped more. I was tired from the day. Here I was, going to sleep in a weird place, but I allowed I'd slept in weirder ones. Nothing here, I reminded myself, had anything against me.

Even afore I drifted off, I was seeing that olive tree, which brought me a sense of peace. That olive tree wasn't in this sad, dark house. It was someplace beyond fear, in full sunlight. I saw the rider far off in the field, too, and I wasn't sure how to feel about that . . . a rider coming steadily closer.

I reckoned later that I dreamed about a voice singing, a woman's voice, low and gentle and a little husky. I guessed it was an old hymn I'd heard afore:

> LORD, YOU KNOW I LOVE EVERYBODY,
> DEEP DOWN IN MY HEART.
> LORD, YOU KNOW I LOVE EVERYBODY,
> DEEP DOWN IN MY HEART.
> LORD, YOU KNOW I LOVE EVERYBODY,
> DEEP DOWN IN MY HEART.
> AMEN, AMEN, AMEN.

Once that night, I sprang wide awake.

A hand was grasping mine, the fingers wrapped around it, holding firm. It wasn't a cold hand, all bones. Instead, it was solid and warm. After the initial stopping of my breath, the first wild hammering of my heart, I figured that the solidity made sense: Why should a ghost's hand be bony and cold? That wasn't the way a ghost remembered its hand from when it was alive. It remembered warmth, and breath, and touch.

It was utterly dark in the room. I couldn't even tell there was a window. I just kept completely still. The wind had gone quiet. When the hand didn't move for a long time, I opened my mouth, and finally, I found enough voice to murmur: Ma'am, your husband's downstairs, under the table.

There was no answer. That hand kept hold of mine, but that was all. After what seemed a very long while—though maybe it was only a few minutes; time does odd things when a ghost is holding your hand—the fingers let go. I sensed no other movement. I couldn't tell if a presence moved away from me or kept sitting there, still as the winter night.

Then I was asleep again, or dreamed I was asleep again, or maybe I'd been sleeping the whole time. All I know is, eventually morning light filtered in through the curtains, and I was alone in the dim room.

I got up, dressed again, and looked all around for any sign that someone else had been there. I found none. The door was still locked, and nothing had moved from where I'd put it. I padded over to the window, slid the curtains back, and looked out on a thick, deep blanket of snow, a few flakes still floating down in an uncertain gray light.

John was cheery. He'd taken the paper poultice off his head and had an ugly scar, but it wasn't bleeding. He fried us eggs and some bacon he unwrapped from grease paper, and while he was cooking, I tromped out to check on Jack. The snow came up almost to my knees, heavy and wet and pristine as I made new tracks in it out to the barn. It felt like being the first living thing to make tracks on the Earth.

Jack was fine and happy to see me, and I was delighted to see him. He looked rested and calm. Maybe he'd had a lot to talk about with John's horse over in the next stall. I saw that he had feed and told him we'd be on our way soon.

The house looked like some huge animal buried under a great weight of snow, its windows peeking out eyelike beneath the white mounds on the gables. I stopped in the yard and looked up at those windows, wondering if something was looking back down at me.

John asked if Maisey had caused me any alarm in the night, and I truthfully told him she'd done no harm. I didn't go into detail beyond that. I figured that John might be cross with her or have his feelings hurt if he knew she'd come and held my hand. We had our coffee and finished breakfast. He was still set on not going to see the doctor, but he seemed to be all right. I thanked him for his hospitality, and he thanked me for the company and for not leaving him to freeze out there by the creek. I reckon these are the things neighbors do for each other.

I meant to go see John from time to time, but one thing and another kept me from following through—you know how the best of intentions can slide. I thought of him, and once I saw him at the store, and we jawed a while. He kept living his life out there in the old house up Allenton Road.

The days rolled on toward spring. I inquired of folks who would know about the old Box place. The postmaster, Hawk Geisel, who knew just about everything about everyone, told me that Abraham Box, the father of Abel, grandfather of Sam and John, had moved out here from somewhere East to take possession of the house from a distant cousin when the cousin died. This cousin was a man name of Enache—no one remembered if that had been a surname or a Christian name. Enache had come over from some Old Country; Hawk didn't know which one, but Enache had what folks thought was an ill-favored look, kept to himself, and had come out to the prairie to be left alone.

The building of the house was a big splash in local legend. I tried to remember if I'd heard any of the old folks in my family talk about it; I couldn't recall any mention, which was curious. Like the postmaster, they tended to know things, too. Maybe they thought such talk wasn't suitable for my tender ears, or maybe there were some things they didn't care to ask too much about. Anyway, when hardly any such houses were built out here, Enache had carted in materials and builders from far off, didn't employ any local help, and built himself a castle on the prairie. Of course there were the rumors you'd expect of Enache's having hidden a vast fortune in the house. But if that were true and the Boxes knew about it, it didn't seem likely that all the boys would have spent their lives mining coal. Well, Hawk said, it always tantalizes the imagination to think of folks hiding away a fortune—and the way he grinned made me suspect he already knew some things about me.

Then Hawk lowered his voice and, with no one else in the post office, told me that the Box place had gotten something of a sinister reputation in recent years, since the War. Not that folks went out there much, and not at night, but those who did talked about a candle behind the windows, going from room to room, like maybe John—if it was John—was searching for something.

Or maybe it wasn't John holding the candle. There were boys at the store who'd made the occasional delivery out to John, and long after his wife Maisey was dead and buried, they swore they'd heard a woman's voice in the house, weeping or laughing or singing.

In his dealings with people, John Box didn't hide the fact that Maisey was still with him, that she'd stayed out of the Great Beyond to look after him until he could go with her. That's what he said, humbly and plainly, to anyone who heard Maisey making moans. He'd even spoken of the ghost to Pastor Farlane, who looked in on John sometimes and tried to get him to join in some Christian fellowship.

That was all quite curious. I guessed I hadn't left weird behind me after all. But John Box was no trouble to anyone, so folks let him be. I reckoned most of us live with our own ghosts; John's was just a little more apparent.

So it went until one day in the early spring, when it seemed some wheel had come around, and the past and the present came down in a thunderbolt on John's head.

Pastor Daniel Farlane of the Lutheran church had become a fast friend when I came back to Christian County. Farlane was an unlikely name for a Lutheran. His people had come over on the boat as Fohrleinn—he'd also seen it written Furleine and Worleinn—but his grandparents had thought Farlane looked more American. Pastor Farlane liked it; he told me his name helped point to that far country, the Beulah Land, and on to where the streets are paved with gold. He liked to drop far lanes into his sermons, the high lane that leads to the narrow gate.

Pastor came to see me one morning. As we drank our coffee on the porch, admiring the spring beauties that had cropped up across my yard, under the oaks, he asked if I could go with him out to John Box's place.

Sure, I told him. It's been too long since I talked to John, I said.

It became clear that Pastor was concerned about John. He related to me an incident that had occurred two days previous. Two of the Keller boys and Ed Jeisey had been out to John's to dig him a new well. During a rest break, they fell to a loud, fairly heated discussion. They were right in the middle of it when John Box accosted them with a pitchfork. Seems John commenced swinging it and saying he'd run it through them if they didn't get the Hell off of his property and not come back.

I could only stare. That wasn't like John Box—not at all, and I told Pastor Farlane so.

He agreed. Pastor knew John a lot better than I did. He said, I'm afraid he might be going hard in the head, Ovid.

John certainly wasn't getting any younger, and he already had a ghost and a singing table—not that I believed either one of those things was a delusion; I'd encountered one, and the other was hardly a stretch. But maybe he had begun to slip into a reality that wasn't ours, and that would make it difficult for him to get by without some help.

What were those boys talking about, I asked, when John came down on them?

Pastor said he'd questioned them about that most carefully. Near as he could piece together, they'd been talking about how things were going in the South, with Reconstruction over and things restless. Either the economy was or wasn't picking up, depending on whose opinion you heard. Anyway, Ed Jeisey had brought up the Negro Congressmen who'd been elected in the South, and who were out of office now. Otto Keller said there was no such thing as a Negro Congressman in the South— never had been and never would be. Ed had told him there sure had been, former slaves who served in all kinds of political offices during the Reconstruction, though the Democrats had thrown them all out now. Black men had been making speeches and making laws right alongside white men, and they ought to go back to that, Ed said. Frank had taken his brother's side, of course, and both Kellers commenced to cuss and holler at Ed, and that's about the time they were all trying to keep from getting skewered on John's pitchfork. They'd all hightailed it out of there, and they said John could dig his own damn well.

I reckon I better pay him a visit, Pastor said, afore he gets himself in worse trouble. Better me than the sheriff. Pastor said he'd be much obliged if I came along. I knew John, too, and I could witness what was said—and be an extra presence in case John was still inclined to wave his pitchfork. I agreed that we ought to hear John's side of it. I couldn't fathom why an argument like that would set him off. What difference did it make to him?

We had us a mystery, and we were about to have us an apocalypse.

We rode out there. All the while, I was puzzling about John. Maybe sorrow and loneliness had finally gotten to him. Maybe that table had stopped singing.

There was toothwort along Allenton Road, and Dutchman's-breeches, bloodroot, and trillium back in the wet, low places. Spring was taking hold.

If I'd been up to see the sunrise, I might have noted how ominous and red it was. The day got swiftly darker as we went. Why was it, I wondered, that I always headed for John's place when a storm was rolling in? This one came up quick, thunderheads all across the northwest, wind whipping the branches. By the time we saw how bad it was, we were closer to John's house than to town, and Pastor said we'd better keep going.

The storm came on in a black wall, racing us to the Box place. Jack galloped now, as did Pastor's horse Teddy. But even the best horses can't outrun nature. We were still two miles out when the sky lit up in a tremendous tower of lightning with many forks, searing and blinding, with an immediate blast that made both horses stagger.

The rain didn't come yet. In another minute, we saw smoke pouring upward, straight ahead of us—where the only things it could be from were John's house and his barn.

Pastor hollered the Lord's name then, and unlike when my old friend Chervil Dray said it, I believed it was a prayer. Our horses ran like they had the wings of Pegasus. When we came up through the hickories, we saw that the Box house was an inferno, blazing from the foundation up, flames lolling a hundred feet into the sky.

Still there was no rain—not that a deluge could have put that fire out. We yelled for John, riding up as close as we could. I tried to see if there was any way to get inside, but fire was rolling out of every window I could see and curling from under the front door. While Pastor rode around the house, shouting John's name, I hastened into the barn and brought out John's horse, who was bucking and terrified.

As I'd expected, the wind lashed fire over, and the barn went up, too. We had to get back a way. I hoped by some miracle John was out somewhere, buying feed or looking for new well diggers.

Pastor came around from the back, shaking his head. I couldn't tell if it was sweat or tears on his face—probably both.

We got farther back, and I let John's horse just run. There was no calming him now. Jack was steady beneath me. The cottonwoods stood in a row of giant torches. Smoke flowed up into the black clouds. A midnight ceiling spread above us, spring's wrath gathered there.

Our mouths fell open when there was a crash, the last of the front door falling away, and out of the flames came a hunched figure, stumbling backward, hard to see against the glare.

Dragging something.

It was a woman, her back to us. She was wrapped in a burning blanket, which she shrugged off. She had John Box under the arms and tugged him across the scorched grass.

Pastor and I dismounted and dashed toward the pair. It was so hot I couldn't really see. The heat felt like bees stinging me, and I couldn't tell whether my clothes were on fire or just felt like it. But I got hold of John, Pastor assisted the woman, and we got ourselves away to where we could breathe.

There wasn't any helping John. It was hard to tell even that it was John, though the woman had done everything she could to save him.

The woman wasn't Maisey, and she wasn't a ghost. She had dark skin and wore a plain, simple dress, and there was a deep furrow along the side of her head, from her brow and through the hair above her ear—not a new one, an old one that had healed long ago.

An African woman. She looked at us with wide, anguished, liquid eyes and then fell across John, crying like her heart would break.

John looked up at me and at Pastor, and he smiled with what was left of his lips. I am much obliged to you, he said. Those were his last words.

Pastor gathered his wife, some other ladies, and the doctor to look after the woman, who was able, eventually, to tell us who she was. Her speech was strange, and she often lost the thread of what she was saying and broke into a song, or started laughing. It was the dent in her head that had addled her. Her name was Hannah. She had run away from a plantation in Georgia, and once, some slave hunters had gotten close enough to shoot her in the head, but they hadn't caught her.

It seemed impossible that she'd found her way from Georgia to Illinois, but she'd kept to the woods as much as she could, and every night, she picked a star to follow. It wasn't always the North Star. Who knew how long or far she'd wandered afore she got up North?

John Box had come across her, sleeping, in the thicket down along the Flatbranch. Hannah didn't know how long ago that was, but it must have been after the War. She had no memory of Maisey Box, who was already gone when John brought Hannah home. At first, John told Hannah that his house was a safe house on the Railroad, that he would hide her there and then she could go on.

But then he told her that there was no place else to go; he told Hannah that the War was over, that the Rebs had won, that everyone owned slaves now, even up in Chicago, even in Canada, and that he was the only one who could keep her safe, here in the castle on the prairie. It was all right, John said. No one would hurt her. I gathered that Hannah and John lived together as more or less husband and wife for at least twenty years.

There'd been secret spaces behind the attic and between the walls of adjacent rooms where Hannah spent most of her time, especially when anyone came near the house. John would tell her that men disguised themselves as teamsters or delivery boys and were actually slave hunters, that they were always on the prowl, always asking if John had seen any runaway slaves. Hannah would peek out at these men and give thanks that she had John to keep her safe. Her room had a soft bed and a table, and all through the warm seasons, John would bring her flowers from the yard and field to put into a vase. Sometimes, when no one was anywhere near John's place, he would lead Hannah out into the yard, and they would sit together or walk among the trees, and she could feel the sun on her face and the breeze in her hair; but such times were brief and widely spaced, and only happened when John kept a careful eye on the road.

There was a passage that ran all around the attic, with secret ways into every room on the second floor. Enache had built the house that way for reasons of his own, reasons now unknown—I doubted his purpose was anything good.

Hannah stopped in the middle of a sentence to sing Lord, you know I love everybody . . . Amen, amen, amen. But I'd already figured out it was Hannah whom I'd heard weeping and singing that night, and Hannah who'd held my hand in the darkness. Hannah could never keep completely quiet or still for very long, so Maisey's ghost made a good story for John to tell people who overheard Hannah. Who, after all, is going to intrude on a man's ghosts?

Now I knew why John had run off the well diggers.

Hannah was always watching, always listening, and he couldn't have her overhearing about a South where there were Negro men in Congress. John Box had brought slavery right up into Christian County. I reckoned that, in the end, that cheery old man, my neighbor, was one of the worst monsters I'd run into in all my travels.

When Hannah understood that we weren't going to whip her and send her back to Georgia—when she understood that the Confederacy had lost the War, that slavery was abolished, she sang and danced and wept and looked at the world like the Lord was coming on the clouds, and all things were being made new.

Hannah stayed on in Christian County—we could tell that sometimes she forgot that there weren't slave hunters in the rest of the country outside of this fellowship. Folks found her a house, and she made herself a living by taking in mending and cooking for elderly folks. She found friends and became famous in town for the pies she baked.

I asked Hannah once if she ever heard John's table sing. She nodded happily, hummed a little, then sang something I wrote down. Later I figured out part of it was this: Dona nobis pacem. Give us peace.

You might think the story ends there, and that is the end of John's Box's part, but not quite the end of the tale I've been telling you. I did come to understand those last two persistent visions.

Later that same spring, I was out by the field, looking at the new-turned soil where Tom Broaddus was about to put in the corn. It was good and black and rich; the earth anywhere else just wasn't quite like it. The primroses were over, but along the woods' edge, there was celandine and sweet violet, and a profusion of daffodils. The trees were all coming into good foliage; soon, one wouldn't be able to see very far through the trunks. The secret curtains of summer were going up.

A movement caught my gaze, way out across the field at the west horizon, away toward town. It was the vision I'd had uncounted times. I stood quite still, thinking, Here we go.

It took a long time for that tiny, quivering figure to grow bigger and bigger. My heart started to race, and I had to remember to keep breathing.

A silhouette. A person on a horse. This is where I've been coming to, I thought. The wind kicked up, raising a whirlwind of dust. Sunlight sparkled on the turned earth, the remnants of old stalks and stobs, glimmering across the field like the ground had been sown with gold.

The horse and the rider got bigger, nearer, and then they were close enough.

My heart leapt. I knew the rider's face. I knew the gray eyes.

It was Nancy Mavornen.

She looked down at me from the saddle, and I stared back. Was I seeing a ghost? Then my knees gave way.

She was down on her feet now, taking my arms, looking me in the face. Ovid Vesper, she said. I've been looking for you.

I've been clear out in Montana, on account Chervil Dray told me that's where you'd gone. I've been all over the West.

So have I, I said woodenly.

She was crying now. You have any idea, she asked, how famous you are out there? I heard stories about you everywhere I went. I'd get someplace, and they'd tell me you just left.

I'm sorry, I told her. She'd been looking for me? *She was alive!*

Nancy leaned her head against me and squeezed. I'd do it again, she said. I'd have gone to the North Pole.

Had I died? Was this what it was like, no line to cross at all, a fluid continuing of life?

But Nancy was real. She was warm, and I had my arms around her. She held on to me. We were still breathing. She was a little older, but still lovely as a painting, her face only wiser and warmer and kinder, with a mouth I wanted to kiss.

Nancy had ridden the tornado, just like Windwagon Smith and I had done, and it had eventually put her down again, like it had laid me back down on the plain. It had carried her a lot farther away. When she woke up at the edge of a field, she couldn't remember anything—not what had happened, not where she had come from, not even her own name. Her memory returned to her in time, and she made it back to Lennox. But by then, I was gone from there. In desperate hope, I'd waited as long as I could bear to, but it hadn't been quite long enough.

Remembering the oak stump at Nancy's old place with Jubal's initial and her own carved into it, I carved ours, inside a heart shape, into the oak behind the house. Our tree wasn't a stump, cut off and dead, but a towering oak with a soaring crown that casts abundant shade to this day. We planted a garden together again, and this time, we prayed we'd be able to see it bloom. Our prayers have been answered. We've watched the garden grow new each spring for all these years. The flowers always sprout up from the soil. The rain comes, and clouds, and the sun.

We settled into this place of contentment that was home. We decided our farm needed a name. I wrote the words on a plank and hung it over our door: The Olive Tree. I know it's strange to call a farm a tree, but that's what it is to us, though olive trees can't actually grow here. We meant its name to recall that bright new day in the book of Genesis:

> Then the dove came to him in the evening, and behold,
> a freshly plucked olive leaf was in her mouth; and
> Noah knew that the waters had abated from the earth.

I sit with Nancy on the porch in the golden hour of sunset, when the world is bedding down and yet also coming alive in the gentle night ways. This enchanted hour has been sacred to us for a long time, Nancy and me. We watch the whole firefly show from beginning to end, on account nothing seems more important in a summer dusk. The fireflies rise up from the grass, from beneath the wild rose hedge, out in the purple gloaming under the oaks. Each one carries its small golden

lamp upward in a brief, glowing path, flashing and then darkening again, one of the many thousands within our sight. The
whippoorwill calls, and the owl. A bat swoops above our
heads, swimming through the air with its leathern whisper.
Tree frogs sing, and crickets fiddle their endless song. We listen
to the corn rustle when a breeze passes. There is the scent of
alfalfa.

When I sickle the grass, I leave borders, wild edges, al-
lowing a place for the little scurrying craithers of the woods
and fields to harbor. Harbors to drop anchor in . . . trees to
sit down under at last . . . they're what we look for. We're all
trying to find our way home.

I take Nancy's hand, or she takes mine, here in the peace
of it, this wild in the dusk. Out beyond the bushes, across the
road, the sun is still gleaming across the open fields, golden
and deep crimson on the grain, on the grasses and long trails,
lighting up all the country under Heaven.

ACKNOWLEDGMENTS

Many thanks are due to my agents, Eddie Schneider and Valentina Sainato, and to Carl Bromley for championing this book. I am deeply grateful also to Matt Rusin for his excellent suggestions, to Jason Waltz for running the contest that led me to write the first adventure of Ovid Vesper; to Shelley, Ariana, Susannah, Steven, Mark S., and Mark L. for reading drafts and encouraging me; and to my fellow Inkjetlings for spurring me on. Much gratitude goes especially to Gabriel Dybing for his unflagging (and sometimes emergency) assistance; to John O'Neill and Patty Templeton for being ardent fans of pigspiders; and to Julie for so much love and support.

FREDERIC S. DURBIN is the author of three novels and short story collections for adults and children. His novel *A Green and Ancient Light* was named a *Publishers Weekly* Best Fantasy/Sci-Fi/Horror book of the year; an ALA Reading List Honor Book; and won a Realm Award. Durbin taught English and creative writing at Niigata University in Japan for over twenty years before relocating back to the States.